Published by Stormy Night Publications and Design, LLC.
Blake, Zoe
Hensley, Alta
Brutally His

Digital Cover Graphics: Korey Mae Johnson
Photographer: Emma Jane
Model: Jeff V.
Original Custom Paperback Illustration: Yozart
Paperback Graphics: Deranged Doctor

INTRODUCING

**The sinfully decadent dream project
of best friends and USA TODAY Bestselling authors,
Zoe Blake and Alta Hensley.**

Alta Hensley, renowned for her hot, dark, and dirty romances, showcases her distinctive blend of alpha heroes, captivating love stories, and scorching eroticism.

Meanwhile, Zoe Blake brings a touch of darkness and glamour to the series, featuring her signature style of possessive billionaires, taboo scenes, and unexpected twists.

Together they combine their storytelling prowess to deliver "Twice the Darkness," promising sordid scandals, hidden secrets, and forbidden desires of New York's jaded high society in their new series,
Gilded Decadence.

BRUTALLY HIS

A DARK BILLIONAIRE ROMANCE

GILDED DECADENCE SERIES
BOOK THREE

ZOE BLAKE
ALTA HENSLEY

THE GILDED DECADENCE SERIES

A seductively dark tale of privilege and passion.

Ripping off the gilded veneer of elite privilege exposes the sordid scandals, dark secrets, and taboo desires of New York's jaded high society. Where the corrupt game is a seductive power struggle of old money, social prestige, and fragile fortunes... only the most ruthless survive.

Ruthlessly His
Book One
#arrangedmarriage

Savagely His
Book Two
#kidnapped/capture

Brutally His
Book Three
#officeromance

Reluctantly His
Book Four
#bodyguard

Unwillingly His
Book Five
#agegap

CONTENTS

CHAPTER 1

EDWINA

I glanced around the empty office. Did I dare?

No. I couldn't.

I hesitated, shivering slightly from the cool draft of the large office building caressing my face. The shadows cast by the dim overhead lights seemed to buzz and nervously twitch, urging me to retreat.

Taking a few tentative steps back, I peered down the entranceway. It resembled a void, its depths holding secrets I wasn't sure I wanted to uncover. It was eerily quiet, a stark contrast to the usual hum of activity when everyone was around.

I stepped forward and stretched my arm out toward the doorknob, then pulled back.

No. This was insane.

What if I got caught?

A sudden, familiar vibration in my pocket made me jump. My phone illuminated my surroundings momentarily, casting a pale blue glow. The message was simple, yet it bore the weight of a thousand implications.

Where R U?

The urgency of the situation pressed on me, but I knew I had to respond.

Held up at work. On my way.

I cursed under my breath.

Why had I chosen today to stay late?

Dammit.

Knowing it was useless, I trudged down the hallway and tugged on the restroom door handle again.

Locked.

I stomped back to my new desk, my eyes irresistibly drawn to the imposing door of my new boss's office.

Even though I'd not formally met him, the reputation of Harrison Astrid, the district attorney, was legendary in the city.

Everyone seemed to have a story or an impression of him. Not all of them good.

I was only assigned as his new paralegal this morning, and he had been away from the office all day at meetings. And I knew from his calendar that he was attending a social function this evening, so he wasn't expected back in the office until tomorrow morning.

I bit my lip and once more peeped down the deserted hallway.

My phone buzzed again.

Hurry up. The club is filling up and they won't let you in soon!

I had stayed late to prepare some files to make a good impression.

Too late.

Stupid security had locked the restrooms, and now I had no place to change out of my boring, conservative blazer and skirt and into the black cocktail dress I had brought with me to work. I so rarely allowed myself the luxury of a night out with my friends, I really didn't want to miss this one.

With one more nervous glance around the empty office floor, I let out a resigned sigh.

Feeling the pressure of the night ahead, and the urgency from my friends, I hesitated for just another beat.

Screw it. I'd be really fast. No one would ever know!

With shaking hands, I opened Mr. Astrid's office door.

The creak of its hinges made me wince. The opulence of the room was overwhelming as I crept across the thick Persian carpet to his private executive bathroom. Gingerly turning the crystal and brass doorknob, I swung open the heavy oak door and flipped on the light.

My mouth dropped open as I stepped inside. Quickly closing the door behind me, I just stood there for the longest moment, taking in the large, elegant space with the gorgeous green marble, gilt-framed mirror, and textured cream wallpaper. Were those real linen hand towels? I couldn't resist running my hand over them.

What the hell?

The ladies' room had dreary, putty-colored, painted cinder blocks with cracked linoleum floors.

Shaking my head at how lucky the "other half" was, I thumped my pink gym bag on the counter and unzipped it, pulling out my carefully folded cocktail dress.

"Dammit." My makeup pouch came out with the dress, thudding to the floor. I swept it up, banging my elbow in the process, and tossed it back into the gym bag. "Ouch." Kicking off my ballet flats, I grimaced as they each hit the wall, then shrugged out of my blazer and untucked my simple, white cotton blouse.

Not wanting to waste time with the buttons, I tried to just wrench it over my head, but those same buttons got caught in my long ponytail.

With my arms stretched high and the blouse pulled over my

3

face, I awkwardly leaned my hips against the bathroom door as I tried to untangle my curls from around the small pearl buttons.

Just then, the door swung open.

Pulled off-balance, I tipped backward into the office.

A pair of warm, strong hands wrapped around my exposed middle.

With a shriek, I ripped the blouse off my head, wincing as it tore several strands of hair out of my scalp.

In horror, I found myself in the arms of my new boss, Harrison Astrid.

My cheeks heated when I realized he was glaring down at my half-naked body.

CHAPTER 2

HARRISON

There were only so many hours in a day, and on this particular one, Mary Quinn Astrid had wasted far too many of them tonight with her mindless chatter and schemes.

In public, to avoid arguments she was *mother*, but privately, I hadn't thought of her as such since I was a naive little boy still hopelessly craving her love and affection. Neither of which she had ever shown so much as a drop of to me or to any of her other children.

So in my mind, she was always Mary Quinn Astrid.

It was fitting to use all three names when thinking of her, like how society referred to any sociopathic killer.

Under usual circumstances, when her meddling pissed me off this much, I would head to the gym and work out my frustrations on a punching bag.

Unfortunately, with the situation such as it was, that was a luxury I didn't have tonight.

Mary Quinn Astrid's antics had reached the toxic point of actually impacting my career, so much so that I had to work even harder to keep my upward mobility and reputation intact.

Not that I didn't already put in more hours than everyone else in my entire office. But as pompous as it sounded, my privilege required me to work constantly. If I didn't show up and prove myself to be the better man each day, then people would say I hadn't earned my job and that my daddy bought it like he bought my brother's cushy military officer position.

Not that my brother didn't work hard, he did. But strings were pulled, and because of that, he lost a fair bit of respect, and it had taken far more time and effort to regain it than if he had just earned the position outright.

He had people who were paid to respect him, a clear-cut chain of command that rendered his subordinates' smack talk mostly unimportant. It didn't matter if a soldier didn't respect the man giving the orders. Those orders still had to be followed.

The way I viewed it, for better or worse, the armed forces required people to be sheep. You did what you were told when you were told, and unless your parents paid for a position, you worked your way up, or didn't, in a logical manner. Independent thought and initiative were generally not rewarded.

Lawyers, even ones who worked in public office, were not sheep. They were sharks.

Every last one of them would make it their mission to take me out if they smelled blood in the water.

If they didn't respect me, my days as an effective district attorney would be numbered, and I would be replaced at the next election.

Like Machiavelli's prince, I had to be respected and feared at all times.

This was why, after dealing with the walking headache that was my mother, I was back in the office instead of at home or at the club enjoying a drink and maybe a waitress.

The office was dark and quiet. Peaceful. And although I didn't like it when I had to come in this late, I preferred it like this. There were no office politics to navigate, polite small talk to engage in, or other social niceties to observe, wasting my time. I didn't even have to lose work time wondering who was gunning for my job or, worse, who was actually good enough to do it.

This time was perfectly productive.

Occasionally, when it was like this, I would sit back and wonder what it would have been like if I hadn't insisted on proving myself in the public sector. What if, by now, I was a named partner at some large corporate law firm, and I could work from home most days? Where my office would always be completely devoid of the mindless chatter of office gossip and drama.

Not that I hadn't run into the occasional intern or first year ADA burning the midnight oil trying to make a name for themselves. A trait I admired, and I always made sure to note the names of the people I saw here often. I kept track of which assistant DAs and staff were dedicated to their jobs, who had a well-formed work ethic, who was ambitious, who was too ambitious...and who was lazy and lacked any ambition at all.

At least I hadn't seen any evidence of anyone using the quiet of the office to sneak a little extra-marital affair or rendezvous with a prostitute, a trait I admired less and which I knew happened in some of the private firms around town. Many of the higher-end escorts in the city slept with a lawyer or a judge to keep their records clean. They called it "community service," which would have been amusing if it weren't so accurate. Or perhaps that was what made it funny?

I wasn't sure. My sense of humor had been crushed under my workload in law school and never recovered once I entered the public sphere.

Those men all joked that a bit of stress relief in the office made them more productive or made it easier to deal with the pressure of their jobs. I had always thought they were making excuses, but after the day I'd had, part of me wondered if I shouldn't follow their lead. Not for stress relief but to work out some of the tension and frustration running through my muscles.

Maybe taking my frustration out on a woman's pussy...

Feeling her under my control.

Forced to take every inch of me inside of whatever hole I demanded.

Forced to obey me.

Forced to do as she was fucking told.

All with no ulterior motive. Just a clean exchange, a simple quid pro quo that didn't demand more of my time than I was willing to give, ending in the dopamine rush of an orgasm. Couldn't hurt, right? At the very least, it would clear my head.

There was a madam who was very respected in the area. She kept her girls clean and honest. A number of the men who went that route used her if they weren't blackmailing some other poor girl into it. I could get her number and see if she had anyone available this week.

With all the focus I'd been putting on my career, it had been too long since I'd been between a woman's thighs.

I turned the corner into the bullpen and saw the light on in my office. I frowned. Something wasn't right. My office was supposed to be locked with the lights off, precisely how I left it.

There were spare keys in the desks next to my door, one for my secretary and one for my paralegal. It stood to reason whoever was in my private office had gotten one of those keys. The only question left was who was going to be fired for doing so.

Of course, it could be someone other than an employee.

Although I had been keeping a tight lid on it, it was possible my secret investigation into the Irish mob's business affairs in New York had been leaked. With the right bribe, all information was for sale. Even sensitive files from the district attorney's office.

Not knowing who I would be facing, I stormed into my office with the idea of taking whoever was inside by surprise since I did not have the benefit of my gun, which was in my center desk drawer.

The office was empty.

My narrowed gaze scanned the file cabinets lining one far wall. None of the drawers were opened or seemed to be disturbed. The same could be said for my desk. If someone was in here attempting to steal files, they were either the neatest criminal I had ever come across in my career or I had interrupted them before they'd had a chance to ransack the place.

My head then jerked to the side at a dull thud coming from across the room. There was a sliver of light under the bathroom door. Setting my leather briefcase on the desk, I stretched my arm over its expanse, pulled open the center drawer, and withdrew my Smith and Wesson .38 revolver.

The average citizen assumed a semiautomatic pistol, like a Glock, was superior to the old-fashioned revolver. They were wrong. A macabre perk of being an attorney was access to gun data.

The revolver had a sixty percent higher fatality rate than a Glock. It was a more efficient gun if your intent when shooting was to kill—as mine would be.

Adjusting the gun's grip in my hand, I moved to the closed bathroom door, being careful to approach it from the side and not straight on, in case the perpetrator should suddenly swing it open and emerge shooting.

There were more thuds and bumps, the scrape of a shoe against the tiles, then a couple of muted bangs as if something had been knocked over on the sink's marble countertop.

What the fuck?

Judging by the noise, there was a struggle on the other side of the door.

Had two people broken in?

If they were fighting one another, then their intent was not to conceal themselves from discovery.

Which meant it was not someone affiliated with the mafia.

I was back to my original hypothesis.

It was someone from my staff.

Was one of them testing the boundaries of their job by bringing a lover into the boss's office for an illicit thrill?

It would be a bold move but ultimately stupid and career-ending.

There had already been too much time wasted today.

They needed to get the fuck out and hope I didn't recognize them.

Lowering the gun, I threw open the door.

CHAPTER 3

HARRISON

A beautiful woman trying to wriggle into or maybe out of a shirt fell into my arms.

The first thing I noticed was her warm, tanned skin and how impossibly soft it was under my hands. Then how her hair smelled of strawberries and orchids.

She had to be a hooker who'd just wandered into the wrong office building before it closed. Maybe it was my lucky night, and hers, with how much I was willing to pay to steal her from her date tonight.

Realizing she would be no threat, with my free arm, I reached up and placed the gun on top of the nearest bookcase.

The woman yanked her top off, wincing as she pulled out several strands of her golden blonde hair that had wrapped around a cheap imitation white pearl button. She took a step back then looked at me with wide, pale green eyes rimmed with gorgeous, thick lashes.

Instantly I pictured what she would look like on her knees watching me through those lashes as she worked those plump, pink lips over my shaft.

My cock lengthened.

Whatever the cost, I would pay it and then some.

"I'm so sorry. I just needed to get changed, and they locked the public bathrooms, and…" Her eyes went to the floor, the tops of her cheeks turning a pretty, dark pink shade. The blush traveled down her neck to the tops of her breasts until it disappeared under the pale pink lace of the bra she was wearing.

I barely registered her rambling excuse for trespassing in my office.

My mind was elsewhere, completely distracted.

Would her breasts taste as sweet as her hair smelled?

Was she a natural blonde? I knew a very entertaining way to find out.

Using her crumpled shirt to block my view of her breasts, she said breathlessly, "I'll just get out of your office."

I slammed my hand against the doorframe, blocking her way. "Not so fast, sweetheart."

I leaned against the jamb, crowding her as I continued to look my fill.

She stepped back, and I followed.

Kicking the door closed, I caged her in, my hands flat on the wall on either side of her.

She averted her face. "I know I shouldn't have been in here. I know it was wrong."

"You're right. You shouldn't have." I pulled at the crumpled shirt blocking my view of her body. "You've been a very bad girl."

After a brief tug-of-war, which she lost, I tossed the shirt away and let my eyes wander over her luscious curves. Taking in every tempting inch, from her full breasts which almost spilled out of her bra, to her flat stomach, to the gentle swell of her hips hidden under her skirt.

She shifted to the left but was stopped by my forearm. "I'm sorry. I'll leave right now."

I leaned down, letting my warm breath ruffle the soft stray curls against her cheek. "Bad girls don't get to leave without punishment."

The muscles along her slim throat contracted as she swallowed. "Punishment?"

I ran my fingertips along her collarbone, then down the center of her chest to her breast, her skin above her bra even softer than what I had already held in my hands. Pressing her lace-enclosed nipple against the center of my palm, I cupped her breast, testing the weight as my fingers pressed into her flesh.

Lush, real breasts on an escort. I really had captured myself a hidden gem.

She pressed her body back, her palms flat against the wall. "Please, just let me leave. We can pretend this never happened."

Completely ignoring her plea, I whispered in her ear, "Maybe as punishment, I should bend you over that sink and show you what happens to bad little girls who go where they don't belong."

Her soft jade eyes shimmered with unshed tears. "Please, I'm sorry. I…"

I slipped my hand up to cup her jaw, rubbing my thumb over her full bottom lip. "A girl like you should know there is only one way to beg for forgiveness, and it's on your knees."

My other hand slid down her body and under the cute little black skirt she was wearing.

Her small hand covered mine, trying to prevent me from raising the hem.

Once again there was a brief tug-of-war.

Once again, she lost.

My fingers splayed open over the warm skin of her leg, her thigh muscles tightening beneath my hand as she smashed her legs together.

"*Tsk. Tsk. Tsk.* That is no way to behave toward your next VIP client." I admonished her, pressing my knee between her thighs, forcing her legs open.

The movement made her skirt rise even higher, reaching the tops of her legs as I slid my hand inside her panties. When I pushed just my middle finger between her pussy lips, her eyes slid shut, and she let out a breathy moan.

I smiled against the curve of her cheek. "Good girl. Keep giving me those sweet moans and I'll double your price."

I wasn't ignorant, I knew prostitutes were paid to act like they enjoyed their client's touch. Still, her wet arousal when there was clearly no bottle of lube within reach told me her reaction to my caress was genuine.

Her head rolled from side to side against the wall, her brow furrowed. "No. You don't understand. You have to stop. We can't do this."

Her hand wrapped around my wrist in a futile attempt to dislodge mine.

There was no fucking way I was leaving without feeling her pussy clutch at my cock. "You must be new to this game. Trust me, babygirl. I can do whatever I want to this tempting body of yours and there is nothing and no one to stop me."

I spread the slickness from her entrance around her clit.

She moaned again, rising on her toes in a half-hearted attempt to shift away from my hand. The reluctant, innocent act was almost convincing. She would be worth every penny.

My gaze zeroed in on her mouth, thoughts of all the filthy things I wanted to do to it crashing around my already fevered brain as I watched her sharp, white teeth sink into the fullness of her bottom lip.

I rarely took lovers, and this would be my first paid experience. That being said, I enjoyed the satisfaction of a job well done. I would be making her come on my fingers, at least once, before I bent her over the sink and fucked her hard and fast.

"Do you know who I am?" I rasped against the edge of her jaw.

She didn't open her eyes, but nodded and bit her lip a little harder.

I was going to taste that lip soon. The dim light shone off the gilded edges of the mirror and reflected on her clear porcelain skin and her golden hair, giving her an ethereal glow. The woman looked like an angel, a sweet fallen angel, one I had every intention of corrupting even further.

She sold her body like a commodity.

I would buy it all.

I rubbed tighter circles around her clit, her thighs trembling as they brushed my wrist. My cock strained against my trousers, needing a release. When I did finally bend her over the sink counter, I was going to pound into her so hard and fast there was little doubt I'd bruise her sweet pussy.

So before the pain, I'd give her a taste of pleasure.

"Good. Then I'll count on your discretion. Especially since you know the power I yield and what would happen to someone in your *vulnerable* line of work if you don't meet my demands or betray me."

Her eyes widened. "Are you threatening to fire me if I don't give in to you?"

Leaning down, I nipped at her earlobe. "You're not hired yet, sweetheart. Consider this an audition. If you take every inch of my cock nice and deep inside this cute little body of yours, then I'll hire you."

I gently pinched her clit. "I'll expect you to be a wet and willing, obedient, submissive fuck toy ready to meet my every demand. No matter how painful or depraved."

She shoved against my chest. "How dare you! You can't talk to me like this. I don't care if I borrowed your stupid bathroom!"

The effect was that of a little kitten batting at a lion with her paws.

My hand shifted from her jaw to wrap around her throat. The tips of my fingers pressed into her delicate flesh as I squeezed. At the same moment, I added a second finger and thrust deep into her pussy.

Her mouth opened on a whimper as she stilled.

A growl emanated from deep inside my chest. "You like that, babygirl? Like the idea of a firm hand wrapped around your throat? You'll like the feel of my hand spanking this misbehaving ass of yours even more."

Her breath hitched, and a tear escaped from the corner of her eye.

Damn, she was good. If she kept up this frightened ingenue act much longer, I would have no choice but to fuck her first and then see to her needs afterward, because my cock was already a hammer looking for a pretty little nail.

My finger slid along her pussy, teasing her further. "If you please me, I'll lock you into a two-million-a-year exclusive contract. Plus bonuses any time you let me push your pain limits with a new, pleasurable kink."

Her body stiffened under my touch.

Fuck yes. She was close to orgasm. It made sense that a lucrative contract would be enough to push a hooker over the edge.

Instead, she tried to shove me away again.

I squeezed her throat in warning as I pressed my hips into hers.

"If two million isn't enough, we can negotiate after your audition," I offered while pulling one of the straps of her bra down over her delicate shoulder, exposing her perfectly round, blush-pink nipple.

It was the same pale pink color as her lips—and hopefully her pussy lips as well.

My mouth watered.

Her eyes opened, their intense green filled with undisguised rage.

The emotion caught me so off guard that I didn't see her hand move in time.

She slapped my face hard enough I actually stumbled away from the wall.

Giving her a chance to shift away from me and grab her shoes and blouse from the floor, thrusting them into her bag.

"I am not a whore. I am your new paralegal."

Her words were short and clipped, squeezed through tight lips as she slung her bag over her shoulder while righting her bra then shoved past me toward my office door.

I stared after her, slack-jawed, wincing at the slam of the door behind her.

Fuck. What did I just do?

CHAPTER 4

EDDIE

"There has to be someone else I can work for," I pleaded again, wincing at the whining tone my voice had taken.

This was it. This was the most embarrassing thing I had ever had to do in my career thus far, even considering what came before this incident.

Demeaning jokes about women who practiced law.

Hours researching basic case law for idiots who didn't understand *stare decisis.*

Days spent preparing trial witnesses and exhibits only to be told the case had been dismissed a week earlier, based off a motion I drafted, and the lawyer *forgot* to tell me.

Taking the blame in court so the lawyer didn't look incompetent in front of a judge.

Always being mistaken for the secretary or assistant instead of a crucial member of the executive legal team and someone who had a bachelor's degree in both criminal justice and pre-law.

All paled in comparison to this moment right here and now.

This was my all-time low, and far more degrading.

"I don't understand you." Mrs. Lakeson peered at me over her black plastic-rimmed bifocals. Her lips pursed in disapproval, but her eyes told me this meeting wasn't entirely unexpected.

When I came in early this morning, I went straight to her office.

She was the direct supervisor of all the support staff. Some of the upper management referred to her as the schoolmarm, partly because she handled all the paralegals and first-year assistant DAs but mostly because she favored a 1950s-inspired aesthetic, often wearing her hair in victory curls paired with cat-eye glasses and suits that had a more retro feel.

I wished I could pull off her chic, vintage-inspired style as gracefully as she did. She looked like the office version of a pin-up or that chick from *Mad Men* that all the other characters lusted after but were still a little afraid of.

Her look was everything I wanted but could never quite replicate, especially with cheap, thrift store clothes.

"What's to understand?" I asked. "It's simple. I'm not sure I will be able to fulfill the tasks that Mr. Astrid will require of a paralegal, and I'm sure there is someone more suited to his... needs."

I left the "like a paralegal willing to fuck her way to the middle" part silent.

I wasn't about to get in trouble for slandering the district attorney.

Though technically, since it was true, it wasn't slander, but I wasn't going to show my evidence to prove my point.

What was I going to say? "I broke into his private office, got naked, and he almost made me come?"

I was smart enough to know that wouldn't play out well.

I would be fired and blackballed in legal circles all around the city.

My dream of going to law school and passing the bar with distinction would mean nothing if a prominent district attorney was trashing my reputation to anyone who would listen.

He could easily say he caught me rifling through his desk or computer, and I would do time. My entire career would be ruined in a moment. No, it was best to handle this discreetly and pray he forgot about it.

"Ms. Carmichael, there is no one else available. I have already reassigned another paralegal to your previous post. I know Mr. Astrid can be somewhat... difficult."

She rubbed her eyes.

With a narrowed gaze, I scrutinized her.

Perhaps last night wasn't just an embarrassing misunderstanding?

Perhaps this sort of thing had happened before with our *esteemed leader.*

Lord knew he wouldn't be the first politician or lawyer to abuse his position, and he definitely wouldn't be the first trust fund baby to take advantage of women, knowing his family's money would bail him out of trouble.

But how dumb did a man have to be to try those kinds of stunts in a post #MeToo world?

However, it wasn't like Mr. Astrid had the same issues as the criminal that sparked the #MeToo movement. He wouldn't have to harass the women in his office to get laid. He didn't have to threaten careers, or flash his money around, or commit other criminal acts. And although I hadn't seen it, from the bulge in his pants, I was certain that, unlike that other guy's allegedly shriveled dick, Mr. Astrid's was hard, firm, and *big.*

No, if Mr. Astrid wanted some female attention, all he would have to do was crook his finger, and women would come running for those dark blue eyes, broad shoulders, and the intense stare that made a girl want to fall to her knees before him.

And wasn't that exactly what had happened last night?

He'd crooked his finger, and I'd almost lost my mind.

The filthy way he talked and the domineering way he treated me when he thought I was a sex worker was an unexpected turn-on. Who knew humiliation kink from a Dom would be my thing? It wasn't like I had a lot of experience with men and certainly not with anyone of Mr. Astrid's power and wealth.

Still, it was technically harassment.

Then again, it wasn't like sexual harassment was about sex.

It was about power.

He had it—and I didn't.

"Mrs. Lakeson, it's not just that the work is difficult. It's that I do not believe we are able to work together."

"Ms. Carmichael, I am going to level with you. No one works well with Mr. Astrid. He is a workaholic pain in my ass who demands the people around him constantly produce at the same level he does. He once had an ADA let go for asking to be at his first son's birth. To be fair, Mr. Astrid was not the right person to ask, and his timing was unfortunate, but still." She shrugged.

"I understand that, but—"

"No, I don't think you do. Even if someone manages to hit the speed and intensity he works at and maintains the level of excellence he demands, it is impossible to maintain. Every paralegal I have sent him ends up leaving the field entirely."

The last few even left the city.

"I did not want to give you this assignment. Partly because, while you are good, you're still very green. But mostly because I like you and don't want to watch the will to live fade from your pretty green eyes."

"Then how did I end up on his desk?"

I was so confused. Mrs. Lakeson assigned all the paralegals. If she didn't want me working for Mr. Astrid, then I shouldn't have been assigned to him. I should have been on some mid-level lawyer's desk where I could learn, get my paycheck, and earn a stellar recommendation letter for law school.

"He requested you by name," she said.

I froze.

He requested me by name, which meant he knew who I was last night when he found me in his bathroom.

I moved my purse in front of my body, needing to put something between me and the world. "How does he know who I am?"

"Sorry, not by name." She waved her hand in the air as if to brush off her mistake while she took a sip of her coffee, leaving a bright red lip print on the white porcelain.

With the delicate teacup holding her coffee in one hand, she typed away with the other. I was always amazed by how fast she could type one-handed with her long red nails.

Not quite feeling relieved, I said again, "I don't understand."

"Okay, here is the e-mail he sent." She pushed her monitor around so I could read it.

The e-mail was quick and to the point. There was no time wasted on pleasantries.

Mrs. Lakeson,

The Manellie Brothers' RICO case last month was an utter shit show. There was no way they should have walked. I want the lawyer who handled it under review. He is either dirty or incompetent. Either way, he does not belong here. However, his information, the precedents cited, and the research done were immaculate. Had a lawyer with a spine had that information, the case would have had an entirely different outcome, and the city would have been a better place for it.

I want that paralegal assigned to my desk. Immediately. Make it happen.

-Astrid

I re-read the e-mail four times before Mrs. Lakeson turned her monitor back to face her.

"His words are so sweet, it almost makes you want to print the e-mail and frame it," Mrs. Lakeson said.

She was being sarcastic, but I kind of did want to frame it. The things he said had my mind spinning.

He hadn't requested me by name, nor because he liked the way my ass looked in a skirt, nor because he was hoping to use his position to get into my pants. He had requested me because he valued my work, even if it had been misused in the trial.

He didn't blame me for the verdict, like the prosecutor on the case had.

Mr. Astrid saw through the posturing and bullshit and knew the work I did was excellent and on point, just poorly executed by the attorney.

"Ms. Carmichael. Eddie. I don't need to explain that working for the DA is going to be a massive boon to your career. Not only will it look fantastic on your law school applications, but when you pass the bar, you will have your pick of the top law firms in the country. If you can manage to suffer through Astrid's impossible standards, it will make your career before it's really begun."

"I..."

What could I possibly say to that? She was dangling the brightest future possible in front of my face. It would make every sacrifice worth it.

"This job can be the lynchpin that gets you into Columbia or NYU Law, and it can lead to some scholarships and grants. I am assuming the reason you needed to defer was the cost of tuition?"

I nodded absentmindedly.

"So you will stay on his desk. Unless there is another reason I should look at transferring you?"

My cheeks burned as I took a deep breath. "No, of course not. I haven't even *officially* met him yet. I will suffer through and make this work."

Strictly speaking it wasn't a lie. There was nothing official about our meeting last night.

"I'm glad to hear it." She gave me a bright smile. "Look, his secretary is going on vacation, so you will probably be pulling double duty soon. I will make sure that is noted in your file."

I gave her a grateful smile. Mrs. Lakeson always knew how to make you feel like she was on your side, not out of pity or charity but because she knew that was how to get the best effort and work product from her staff.

"Any tips to make my life easier before I return to my desk?"

"Yes, don't ever be late. And if you quit, there is a support group for other people he drove off. It meets every Wednesday afternoon at East Twenty-Ninth and Lex."

I laughed, thinking she was making a joke.

The look she gave me told me she was dead serious.

"You're going to be late if you don't move now."

"Thank you for your guidance," I tossed over my shoulder as I raced to the elevator, needing to head two floors up.

After pressing the button several times, I gave up and shoved at the stairway door. Despite my heels, I hoofed it up the two flights to my new desk.

What I needed was a positive outlook.

He must not have known who I was last night.

The paralegals whispered all the time about gossip they'd heard from some of their friends about men in the firms they worked at having their girlfriends in their offices after hours. I never thought anything of it. It wasn't my business, and I was usually elbow-deep in old case files looking for precedents.

The personal lives of lawyers around town didn't concern me, but maybe I should have paid more attention.

As I struggled to catch my breath after the stairs, I raised my chin and marched to my desk. It was a legitimate mistake that got way out of hand. That was all. Best forgotten and never mentioned.

He thought I was someone else, I reasoned.

He only knew me by my work, not by name or appearance, which if you thought about it, was extremely flattering. Most women would kill for the validation of being judged only for the quality of their work and not their looks.

And as any opposing counsel would argue, I had been half naked in his bathroom when he found me. So there was that to contend with.

It wasn't right for him to jump to the conclusion that I was a freaking escort, but strictly speaking, that was more of a hop than a jump under the circumstances. Also, I really shouldn't have been in his bathroom. I should have found somewhere to change outside of the office.

Mistakes were made on both sides.

Mrs. Lakeson was right. If I could make this work, then it would do wonderful things for my future career. It wasn't like I would be working closely with Mr. Astrid. He would work in his office, I at my desk and the law library. If we were both working late, I would stay in the library.

I decided it was best to disregard everything that happened, never mention it, never think about it at work.

I would wait until I got home to fantasize about it.

To think about the way he made me feel dainty, trapped between his body and the wall. The way it made him seem even bigger, more imposing, and how part of me liked it. I could indulge in fantasies of him doing the things he threatened me with.

Then I could touch myself, trying to remember how it felt to have him touch me. Pretending I knew what it would feel like when he used more than just his fingers.

When I was home, safe in my bed, my secret cloaked in darkness under the covers, I could let my mind roam to those forbidden thoughts, but only then.

In the light of the nine-to-five workday, only the most professional thoughts about this man would be allowed to cross my mind. I would be the poster girl for professional conduct.

I finally made it to my desk. Shoving my purse in the bottom drawer, I opened my computer.

There was an e-mail from Mrs. Lakeson letting me know if something else happened and I couldn't deal with the assignment, she would do what she could to reassign me within the DA's office, but there were no promises.

I sent her an e-mail thanking her for her time and telling her I would do my best to make this post work for as long as I could.

If I couldn't make this work, then I had no business being in a law office.

I pulled up the case that had been assigned to me last night.

With steady determination, I dove into the file in front of me, intent on making a much better second impression.

From this point forward, our relationship would be *strictly professional*.

CHAPTER 5

HARRISON

I had planned to work late last night.

But after fucking assaulting my new paralegal, I ended up going home and spending a little too much time in the shower picturing the things I could have done to her. The entire time strategizing a way to convince her to be more than just my paralegal.

Men had affairs with their secretaries all the time. Surely a paralegal would benefit from a similar arrangement. Except unlike most secretaries, she would know how to press charges.

The idea of facing off against her in a courtroom made my cock throb.

Her work was impeccable. That was why I wanted her at my desk. I wondered how much of a worthy opponent she would be as a lawyer. I leaned against the cold tile of my shower and stroked my cock, picturing her in a tight little pencil skirt sitting as opposing counsel in a mock trial.

If she did well, I could reward her for her hard work.

If not, I could bend her over my desk and show her what

happened to bad girls who didn't perform in court. They were made to perform in *other* ways.

I would make her work hard for a reward but delight in her punishment.

I had to clear my head before going into the office. It had occurred to me to hire another woman who would want to take the job of servicing me in my office or even in my home, but the idea left me cold.

Instead, I sent a message to Marksen and Luc to meet me for breakfast at the club. Let their talks of marital woe distract me long enough to get my head back into my work.

I sat at our usual table. Leaning back in my chair in the much quieter room, I stared out the windows overlooking the Hudson and watched the world start to wake up. New York was supposed to be the city that never slept, and that may be true. It was never completely quiet, but that didn't mean it didn't have its own circadian rhythm.

This morning was cold, and the world was moving sluggishly. The leaves had all turned for autumn, and most had fallen, preparing for winter. The wind was bitter, and those who were awake were either heading to bed or just getting up.

The large wooden doors on the other side of the room opened, the movement catching my attention. Marksen and Luc walked in together, wearing similar suits and already discussing something.

"Did you two get ready together this morning? What do the kids call that nowadays? Enemies-to-lovers? How does my sister feel about your extramarital affair?"

Luc's smile dropped, and his brow lowered in an unamused expression. "I have no extramarital affairs. I can barely keep up with your sister. Would you like to know what she—"

"No, please, God, stop," I said and motioned for them to sit.

Marksen snickered as he took his seat and signaled for the

server to bring more coffee. "It's okay, Harrison. We can always talk about Olivia and what she likes to—"

"Stop right there," Luc interrupted, glaring daggers at Marksen before turning back to me. "So I hear your mother has plans for you to—"

"Nope. Not going there." I raised my cup to my lips, refusing to let the subject go anywhere near my mother and her plans before taking a sip of coffee. I let the dark roast roll over my tongue, enjoying the richness with its touch of acidity.

"Yes, let's not discuss Mary Quinn Astrid. The amount of time I have already spent thinking about that conniving, manipulative bitch would last a lifetime," Marksen grumbled, sitting back and then looking at me with wide eyes. "Sorry. It's easy to forget she's your mother."

I shrugged. I wasn't offended. Nothing he said about my mother was wrong. She was a conniving, manipulative bitch. She was also an adulteress, an abuser, a snob, a narcissist, and pretty much one of the worst people in this or any other city.

The more I dug into what she was doing, the longer the list of her nefarious deeds and vices became. At this point, a small part of me half expected to find the deed for an office built into the side of a volcano or some other comic book supervillain's lair.

She did seem the type to have pet sharks with lasers harnessed to their heads, but only if some amazing, well-known architect designed the tank. And if it was assembled by a work-force that exploited children, all the better. Of course, Balenciaga would have to make the harness, with Prada doing a collab on the laser.

"So seriously, why did you two arrive together, and what were you talking about?"

"Coincidence," Marksen said. "That and our buildings are rather close to each other. And the wives are working together on a gala at the art school. Olivia is excited to cover it and is talking about setting up investor meetings. She even wants Amelia to help add a modern art section to her website. She hasn't talked about anything else in days."

"Nothing else? Shouldn't she be focused on your wedding?"

"You would think, but she is leaving most of that up to the wedding planner."

"What do you mean? I thought women got a little crazy about those plans."

"So did I," Luc inserted. "Amelia, once she got full control, planned every detail from the ceremony to breakfast. Nothing happened that she hadn't planned except, of course, for your mother manipulating Marksen into kidnapping Olivia."

Marksen winked as he raised his own coffee cup in a mock toast to himself. "Yeah, I don't think Amelia planned for that." He sipped his coffee, apparently not taking the bait.

"You know, if you want, I can still bring him up on charges for it," I offered with a smirk.

It was a bluff. Olivia was an adult, and she would have to press charges or at least tell someone what really happened, and that would make marrying her abductor a little awkward.

"Fuck you both." Marksen crossed his arms, and Luc and I both started laughing.

Laughter had become an unfamiliar feeling. The last several years had been about building my career and attempting to get a handle on my mother's meddling.

How had I gotten to the point where I was actually taking her advice to do damage control? No doubt her schemes were going to destroy the little peace I had left in my life.

I was grateful the three of us had started hanging out at the club again. It used to be a tradition, then we all went our separate ways, to build our empires. It wasn't until a broken engagement, some blackmail, and a kidnapping that we were able to connect again.

Nothing like a few felonies to bring old friends together.

Luc cleared his throat, pulling me out of my thoughts. "I do need to give you both a heads-up since we are all technically related now."

"Is it about some hereditary defect that we will have to deal with?" Marksen asked. "Are our nieces and nephews going to be malformed?"

"A family history of mental illness we need to watch for?" I chimed in.

"A curse from a distant relative that will have you dead on your next birthday?" Marksen added.

"Your father lose your entire fortune in a drunken poker game, and you are broke as fuck?" I quipped, adding to the fun and provoking laughter from Marksen and myself as a pretty blonde server approached our table to take our orders.

I had noticed her before. She was a lovely girl, but now I thought she looked dull compared to my new paralegal. Her hair was not as bright a gold, her eyes a dull blue that had nothing on a pair of vivid, jade-green eyes that haunted my dreams last night. Even her skin seemed lackluster, lacking the silky warmth of my girl's beautiful porcelain complexion.

My girl?

Fuck, that's a dangerous way to start thinking about a subservient staff member.

I shifted in my seat.

Subservient. Submissive.

Her on her knees sucking my cock.

Fuck. Did it again.

"Bite your tongue," Luc said, laughing. "I'd have the old man taken out and shot before I ever agreed to sign over a single share."

We placed our orders for breakfast and more coffee and sat around just catching up and talking about what was and wasn't happening and what it meant that Olivia wasn't planning the wedding herself. Once Luc and I had Marksen so paranoid he was texting Olivia every few minutes to make sure she hadn't changed her mind, I refocused on Luc.

"What was it that you wanted to tell us?" I asked.

"I have officially, and very much against my father's wishes, severed my family's ties with the Irish mob," he said, laying his hands flat on the white linen tablecloth.

"Okay, congratulations?" Marksen said after a pause. "But I'm confused."

"About what?" Luc asked.

I sat back, listened, and watched, wanting to get the full story before jumping in.

"The words that are coming out of your mouth are good. It's good news, but your face looks like you have an incurable disease that you just passed to each of us the second we sat at this table." Marksen's words were a bit overstated and dramatic, but he wasn't wrong. I truly hated how infrequently he was wrong.

"Legally speaking, we are all family, or at least we will be if Olivia doesn't run away screaming before the wedding. My father's former associates are not going to be pleased with being pushed out of such a lucrative business. I am worried they may try to strike out at my family to get to me."

"Is Amelia safe?" I asked at the same time Marksen asked if Olivia would be a target.

"I don't know," he answered with a shrug of one shoulder as he rubbed his forehead. "I already have extra security on Amelia as well as a few hidden GPS tags that she knows about and one that she doesn't, just in case she is abducted. The same goes for Olivia and Charlotte. Every precaution is being taken, but that is for my wife and my sisters. I wanted to give you two a heads-up as well. Just in case they were stupid enough to make a move on either of you."

"Which family is this?" I asked.

"The O'Murphys," Luc answered before taking a sip of coffee.

I lowered my gaze. Both Luc and Marksen were keen board-room negotiators. They knew how to read people and I didn't want to give anything way. Certainly not the fact that I already was developing a highly confidential case against the O'Mur-phys. A case I could not tell either of them about, regardless of any potential threat to our family.

"They are dangerous, and I'm concerned they have grown accustomed to a certain lifestyle with the work my father sent their way. Losing that could make them unpredictable."

"Seems like you know exactly what they want to do. I wouldn't call that unpredictable." I sat back and wondered how much I should tell Luc.

"Well, the threats they made against me and everyone I love were pretty clear," Luc said.

"Wait, are you saying you love us? I think I'm going to cry." Marksen put his hand to his heart as if the sentiment had touched him.

I rolled my eyes while Luc let out an annoyed groan. "I love my sisters and my wife, and they are protected. They love you too, so I wanted to give you a heads-up."

"What were their threats exactly?" I asked.

"You know, the usual. You need us, if you stop paying us, we will kill everyone you have ever loved, and anyone they ever loved and blah blah blah. I wouldn't be concerned, except the way my father's face paled when I told him what I did makes me think there is more to them than just your common, everyday thugs."

He wasn't wrong.

The O'Murphy clan was into some heavy crime, not just

running errands for his father. My office was building a case for the kidnapping and trafficking of young women into and out of the States. They were running an old-school human trafficking scam, going to impoverished areas in Eastern Europe and promising the beautiful women there a new life—a life with purpose, the promise of a job, and the American dream.

Then they would steal their passports, tell them the horrors of what happened in the custody of the American immigration system. Once those women were truly terrified of American police officers or anyone in a uniform, the mob got them addicted to meth or whatever else they could get their grubby little hands on and turn them out as prostitutes.

Not the high-end prostitutes that worked the high rises of Wall Street, judges' chambers, or even politicians' second homes, but the poor souls who were used and abused over and over until they died, their bodies disposed of in the Hudson.

It was heartbreaking every single time we recovered their remains from the river. It had taken almost two years to put this case together, and we were getting close. So close, I was going to advise Luc to sever the ties before he was dragged down with them. Telling him would have been extremely illegal. I could have been disbarred and thrown out of my office, but there was no way I would have allowed this filth to taint Amelia's world.

It was better now that Luc had cut the ties on his own. Amelia would remain protected, and I wouldn't have to break my oath of office.

"Do you want anything legal done, restraining orders or anything like that? It won't stop them from getting close, but if they do, we can lock them up for it," I offered like the good brother-in-law I was.

"No, thank you. For now, I just want the added security, and I have it handled. But I will let you know if that changes," Luc said.

"I'm letting my own security know to be more vigilant."

Marksen typed on his phone. "I know you say you have it handled, but I also want my security and yours to communicate. I don't want there to be any gaps in their protection coverage, and I don't want them chasing each other, leaving Olivia unprotected."

"Anyone you need to protect?" Luc asked. "Rose has been spending time with Amelia, so both of your sisters are covered."

"If Rose and Amelia are safe, then I am content. The only other woman I would need to have protected would be my mother. But I don't think informing her of any of this would be wise."

"Dear God, no," Luc said, slumping back in his chair in a way that told me he was as exasperated with Mary Quinn Astrid's antics as I was. Marksen just gripped his mug tighter and clenched his jaw. He was still mad at the way she'd manipulated him.

Though I understood his frustration, it was still his fault for letting her goad him into kidnapping and blackmail. I meant, really, Olivia only needed a few hours with his bank statements to trace everything back to my mother.

It was good that he managed to convince such a brilliant woman to love him, or his life would be much harder than necessary.

"I agree," I said, turning my focus back to Luc. "Let's not give her anything to meddle in. My father has security on her at all times anyway. Besides, who is going to retaliate by kidnapping someone's mother-in-law? That sounds more like a favor, even if it wasn't Mary Quinn Astrid."

Luc and Marksen both laughed at my joke.

It may have had a ring of truth to it, but mostly, I just wanted her out of the way. I had already agreed to another one of her schemes. That should be enough to keep her occupied and away from my case.

Marksen and Luc changed the subject, but I just wasn't able to stay as tuned in as I should have been.

My mind raced with questions, mostly about Edwina, or Eddie as I'd learned she liked to be called.

What kind of woman went by the name Eddie?

Was her golden hair a natural blonde?

Would she have let me take her in that bathroom if I hadn't insinuated that she was a prostitute? What kinds of sounds did she make when she was being fucked?

When I got to my office, would she be there ready to work, or had she asked to be taken off my desk?

Not that it would work. I would simply refuse the transfer.

She was mine and I had already decided I was keeping her.

I preferred to think my decision was strictly professional and that I'd made it to obtain the benefit of her keen legal mind.

But that was bullshit.

She intrigued me and despite the danger to my reputation, I wasn't ready to release my professional claim on her.

Not, at the very least, until I'd claimed her in an *extremely unprofessional* way.

CHAPTER 6

EDDIE

"Fuck!" I whisper-shouted as a courier ran past me in the hallway, knocking me out of his way and spilling my fresh cup of scalding coffee all over my bright white blouse.

A few of the others in the bullpen looked up to see what the commotion was. Once they saw it was just a clumsy girl who couldn't figure out how to get out of the way of a bike messenger on a deadline, they went back to their work.

I dropped the heavy law books I had been holding in my other arm off at my desk and tried to figure out what to do. I couldn't believe I had ruined this shirt already. It was brand new, and an amazing find, a bright white, no-mystery-stain button-down I had found at a thrift store with the Saks tag still on it tucked in the back. Some careless sales associate had missed it and gave it a two-dollar price, and it was just my size.

So, what did I do with this once-in-a-lifetime score? I dumped a cup of Starbuck's over-priced dark roast, one of the few extravagances I allowed myself, all over it.

Fuck my life.

"Looking good, Ms. Carmichael." Detective Patrick D. winked at me as he sauntered by my desk.

I looked down to see the stain had not only ruined my top, but the dampness of the coffee had made it transparent.

That morning, I woke up feeling terrible. The embarrassment from the night before still stung. Every fiber of my being told me to stay in bed, but staying in bed wouldn't pay the bills, and my bed was damn cold anyway. So I got up and went to work. After being told no and dismissed by Mrs. Lakeson, I wanted to run away with my tail tucked between my legs.

Did I?

No.

Running away and missing a day of work was a privilege I could not afford, so I didn't. But I really wished I had.

"Oh, dear, that looks like it hurts," Mr. Astrid's secretary, Cynthia, said, coming up behind me and making me jump again.

"It doesn't feel good," I said, and she gave me a sympathetic look.

"I am going to head out for a bit. Would you like me to grab you another cup of coffee, deary?"

Cynthia was the sweetest woman on the planet and looked like she had a Werther's candy in her pocket at all times. The other paralegals warned me about her. She was nice until you messed something up for Mr. Astrid. Then she was a viper.

She may have looked like a sweet grandmother who should've been home knitting socks for her grandbabies, but she was ruthless when protecting Mr. Astrid and keeping his schedule set.

"Yes, please. When is Mr. Astrid expected in?" I asked, deflating a bit.

"Not for some time." She patted me on the shoulder. "He had a breakfast meeting," she said as she gathered her giant purse and headed out at a deliberately slow pace.

I took a moment to breathe.

Mr. Astrid wasn't here yet.

I had time. I could clean myself up. I kept an extra shirt here in the office for this exact reason. It wasn't my favorite and didn't fit like this one, but it was clean.

I grabbed it from its hiding place, under the desk hung up against the wall of my cubicle. I kept it in a plastic dry-cleaning bag that I had swiped when a lawyer confused me for his secretary or his mother. He got his coat back, and I got a clean place to keep my top.

With Mr. Astrid not in for a while, I could take my time, get cleaned up and settled in, maybe drink my next cup of coffee instead of wearing it, and start my day.

It wouldn't be all bad. Unlike my shirt, the day was salvageable.

A shrill laugh came from the other side of the bullpen, and I watched Ally, my arch-rival, head my way with the mayor.

Because, of course, she was.

She and I went to the same high school, constantly competing for the top spot, which she won. Not because her grades were better, but because she got extra credit when her daddy paid for a class trip to D.C. that she arranged.

She and I also went to the same college and took the same classes, but that was where the similarities ended. I served her lunch as part of my college work-study, and needed to work for a few years before continuing on, whereas she could afford to jump straight into law school and was currently interning at the mayor's office.

While I was just a paralegal doing grunt work for the actual important people.

I couldn't face her, not this morning, not like this.

Unfortunately, she was between the restrooms and me.

Cynthia was gone, Mr. Astrid wasn't here, and Ally was

getting closer. It only took me a second to calculate the pros and cons before I slipped into Mr. Astrid's empty office and into his bathroom, holding my clean top over my front to cover the stained blouse.

Mr. Astrid's office bath was even more ridiculous in the daylight—all gleaming, highly polished marble with gilded frames and hardware. If I hadn't known better, I would've said this level of tacky opulence was right out of some reality show. But it wasn't my place to comment, so I didn't. I was just going to hurry and change again, then find somewhere a little less dangerous to hide until Ally and the mayor were gone.

The moment I closed the door, I had my shirt off and was looking for a paper towel I could wet and use to clean the sticky residue from my chest. There was nothing on top of the counter, so I looked in the cabinet under the sink.

At the exact moment the door was pulled open.

CHAPTER 7

EDDIE

*a*nd there I was...

Half-naked. Bent over at the waist, with my ass high in the air. My dirty shirt crumpled in a ball on top of the sink counter... again.

I closed my eyes and swallowed a groan of mortification.

Why, God? Why me, God? FML.

"Are you fucking kidding me? Are you seriously in my office without permission again?" a deep voice demanded.

I stood up quickly, smacking my head on the counter. The pain was instantaneous but not nearly as agonizing as the embarrassment that heated my cheeks. I rubbed my head to check for bleeding, then turned.

"I..." My words trailed off in a sucked-in breath as my fingers grazed a tender part of my scalp. Fortunately, there was no blood. Bleeding all over this tacky, expensive-looking tile would make this all so much worse.

He stepped inside and slammed the door shut. "Let me answer that for you. The answer is yes."

Uh oh.

His words were gritted out between clenched teeth. "Same as your answer when I tell you to bend over, lift your skirt, and take the punishment you have now more than earned."

I raised my chin and held up a palm to ward him off. I couldn't let him intimidate me. "I just spilled coffee all over my shirt, and I came in here to change."

He placed a hand against the wall over my head as he moved closer. "Does this look like a fucking Nordstrom changing room, Ms. Carmichael?"

"I wouldn't know," I said with brutal honesty. Unless they filmed an episode of *Sex in the City* there, I would have no idea. I looked around at the needlessly luxurious bathroom. "But probably."

He towered over me. "I'm glad you find this amusing, Ms. Carmichael. Apparently you need an attitude adjustment along with a lesson on trespassing law."

Realizing my lame attempt at levity had only ignited rather than diffused the situation, I shifted along the wall a few inches, trying to put space between us. "I'm really sorry. My shirt turned transparent when it happened, and then I saw the mayor headed this way. I thought it wouldn't look professional if I walked past him in a see-through shirt with my bra on display, so I ducked in here."

Surely the DA would be a reasonable man and understand. He should be grateful I was trying to make a good impression. After all, I was assigned to his desk. How I looked reflected on him.

Once again, I only succeeded in adding gasoline to the flames. I watched in horror as his gaze moved from my face to my breasts, then to my mouth, then finally back to my eyes.

"No," he said, once more glaring down at me.

"No?" I asked, not sure what to say.

"No, I think you're here on purpose. Maybe last night was an accident, but then you liked how I treated you like a whore and you're here for another taste."

Before I could process what he'd said, my hand was flying through the air, ready to slap him.

He grabbed it and pulled me into his chest. "One slap is all you get, sweetheart."

My stomach flipped.

I knew he was only using the endearment sarcastically but still...Damn.

This close, he smelled like cologne, coffee, and maple syrup.

I swallowed. "That's not..."

"That's not what?" he taunted me, tilting his head to the side. "That's not what's happening here? Maybe you wanted to try and sue for sexual harassment. Maybe you have hidden cameras in here and are trying to use yourself as bait? That's entrapment, Ms. Carmichael."

His words dripped with resentment and anger, even as his tone was demanding in a way that made my knees a little weak.

My eyes went to the floor, and I ignored the spark of excitement that shot down my spine and settled deep within my core.

"No, really, I just came in to change because I dumped coffee all over myself. There are no cameras. No hidden agenda. I want to forget all about last night, just like you."

He grabbed my chin and pulled it up so my gaze met his. "Who said I was willing to forget?"

Dammit. He is firing me for sure.

And after this I would be lucky to get a job as a paralegal for a scummy, ambulance-chasing lawyer in the Bronx because I could certainly kiss my legal career in Manhattan goodbye.

His eyes were so full of fury and disappointment, I had the

urge to drop to my knees and beg for forgiveness. Beg him to not fire me or pursue charges for breaking into his office without permission. Maybe he wouldn't if I swore I wouldn't sue him for harassment.

I dug my nails into my palms, letting the pain focus me. There had to be a way to convince him. "Please, I can prove it. My shirt is right over there, and I am sure I smell like my favorite stupid overly sweet coffee."

His voice lowered to a dark purr as he contemplated me. "So you're pleading your case. And the taste of your skin is Exhibit A."

Oh no! What is more flammable than gasoline because I just fucking poured a gallon of it on this situation.

He braced his other forearm against the wall, trapping me as he leaned down and ran his tongue from my neck to my cleavage.

The small sparks that were in my core lit on fire as I gasped in shock.

"Mmm, Italian roast, that's my favorite too," he growled before licking my breast again, running his tongue along the seam of my bra.

My palms ached to pull my bra aside and offer him my breasts, then run my fingers through his soft-looking hair while he devoured me.

Everything about this was a career-ending train wreck, but I couldn't get my body to understand even while my brain screamed for me to run.

One of Mr. Astrid's hands went to my waist, holding me still before it ghosted up my side to my shoulder and pulled down my bra strap.

A low groan of approval came from somewhere deep in his chest when my breasts were both uncovered.

"I think you are doing this on purpose, Ms. Carmichael. I think deep down you are a brat who needs to be taught a lesson."

Yes. Spank me. No. Fuck. Holy hell.

My head swam as I pressed my nails deeper into my palms, struggling to gain the focus I needed to escape.

Mr. Astrid didn't wait for a response. He just wrapped his lips around my nipple and sucked, giving me an illicit, taboo rush of pleasure.

I licked my lips and pushed my hands behind my hips, crushing them between the wall and my body so I didn't give in to temptation and pull him closer. "I didn't, I swear."

"Why should I believe you?" He kissed his way back up my chest to my shoulder, alternating between sharp bites and soothing licks that had my head spinning and my pussy throbbing.

"Because I wouldn't lie to you." My words sounded breathy to my own ears.

"If I catch you in this bathroom in any state of undress without having told you to do so, I swear I will bend you over my knee and spank your ass until it's bright red. You won't sit for a week, do you understand me?"

It wasn't a threat.

It was a promise, and I wanted nothing more than to call his bluff, but I was too shocked to form the words.

"Then I will push my cock into your tight entrance and pound into you until you scream for mercy. Is that understood, Ms. Carmichael?"

"Yes, sir," I whispered, not sure where those words came from.

I had never called anyone "sir" in a heated moment before. I had never gotten turned on by being manhandled by my boss, either. I was also positive I had never been this close to coming just from someone giving my breasts attention.

"Good girl," he rasped in my ear before sliding his fingers in my hair tight enough to force my head back before he pulled my lips to his in a scorching kiss.

His kiss was like him: direct, challenging, and punishing all at the same time.

Parting my lips for him, I melted into his body.

I wanted to fight him.

I wanted to shove him off me and threaten him right back.

I wanted to tell him it would be a cold day in hell before I let him touch me again, and that I was a professional paralegal who expected to be treated with respect in his office.

I wanted all of this.

The problem was, in that moment, I wanted him more.

Wanted his kiss. Wanted his rough hands. Wanted his dirty words.

For the first time in my life, I didn't give a damn about my career or my reputation.

I just needed his touch, now. Nothing else mattered.

His hand crept down to my throat and held me against the wall as he ripped his lips from mine.

Mr. Astrid looked at me with narrowed eyes. His lips were stained with my lipstick, a shade of red appropriately called *Inappropriate*. Which couldn't have been more on the nose than if it had been called *Bad Life Choices.*

He bared his teeth as he wrapped his hands around my upper arms. "Dammit... we can't do this here. Not in the office during the day."

Startled by his abrupt change, my eyes went to the massive mirror to the side, and I looked at my reflection.

I looked like a call girl, and a cheap one at that.

It jarred me like nothing else.

Was I really about to throw away so much effort and investment in myself? The hours studying and working on getting here so I could afford to take the LSAT and get into law school?

If this got out, it would destroy my career before I even applied.

He would survive the scandal. For him, it would be chalked up to an ill-advised indiscretion and brushed under the rug as boys will be boys.

I would be ruined, though. Just another woman trying to sleep her way to the middle or, worse, a dumb, low-class slut who didn't belong in an office or a courtroom.

This could not happen.

A box of tissues sat on the corner of the counter. I grabbed a few, handed them to him, and motioned to his face.

He looked in the mirror and cleaned up the red smear.

Taking advantage of his momentary distraction, I slipped around him and snatched my replacement blouse from its hanger. With my back turned to him, I shoved my hands through the sleeves.

His arm wrapped around my middle to pull me close. There was no mistaking the press of his hard cock against my lower back.

His tongue flicked my earlobe. "We need to work late tonight. We'll finish this later, after hours."

With a twist of my hips, I loosened his grip enough to swing the door open and step into his office.

After buttoning my blouse, I tucked it in and straightened my skirt. Throwing my shoulders back, I turned and said, "The only thing I will be finishing off is your briefs."

The corner of his mouth lifting, he crossed his arms over his chest and leaned a shoulder against the door jamb.

The embarrassed blush on my cheeks moved down my neck as I momentarily closed my eyes. "I meant your *legal* briefs. Despite our unconventional start, I have every intention of keeping this professional from this moment forward. I trust you will do the same."

His gaze ran over me before he quoted Lord Byron in response. "'We are all selfish and I no more trust myself than others with a good motive.'"

Before I could respond, we were interrupted by the hard clack of a pair of office-inappropriate designer high heels.

CHAPTER 8

HARRISON

*S*he turned and literally ran for my office door.

I lunged for her, intent on pulling her back, but she was over the threshold too quickly.

Several heads popped up to stare as I ground out, "Eddie, get back here!"

A hush seemed to fall over the entire office.

Eddie slid behind her desk and stared primly back at me, lips thinned, practically daring me to come and get her. Her eyes narrowed. "Yes, sir? Was there something you needed?"

Fuck yes there was. I needed her bare-assed and bent over my desk.

I cleared my throat as I buttoned my suit jacket to help conceal my highly inappropriate erection. "Yes, I expect you to only leave my office when you are dismissed. Leave without permission again and there will be consequences, understood, Ms. Carmichael?"

With her head held straight and her gaze frozen on her computer screen, the only indication she caught my meaning was the deepened blush on her cheeks. "Yes, sir."

"Good."

Not wishing for any more of our exchange to be on display, I turned and stormed back into my office. Leaning back in my executive oxblood chair, I was contemplating returning to my private bathroom and rubbing one out, knowing it would be the only way I'd be able to concentrate, when a high-pitched, nasally voice came from my doorway.

"Oh, Harrison, there you are."

"Do I know you?" I asked, arching a brow at the brunette with bright pink lipstick in my doorway. Her matching pink skirt was inappropriately short for the office, and the thin, white silk shirt she wore showed far too much of her surgeon-assisted cleavage.

"Oh, you are so silly. Of course, we know each other. I'm Ally. Senator Blackwell's daughter."

"What are you doing in my office, Ms. Blackwell?" I did not have time for this shit today. Especially not when I could still taste my new paralegal's kiss and my cock was still rock hard.

"Well, I just wanted to stop in and say hi. I work for the mayor now, and I was hoping that meant I would be seeing more of you. Maybe we could go grab a bite sometime."

"Ashley—" I intentionally got her name wrong to impress on this girl that she was wasting my time.

"Ally." She stomped her foot like a child.

I needed to end this now.

"Whatever. You need to go. I have work to do. I am sure the mayor will be happy to take you to dinner. He usually does when he fucks his interns. He is a class act like that. I, however, am far too busy to entertain the fantasies of little girls who look like they would be a terrible lay. Please leave." I had moved to the door as I spoke.

Her face whitened as I approached, until I slammed the door in her face.

I had barely gotten back to my desk when the door slammed open again, and she barged in.

"You can't talk to me like that. Do you know who I am?"

"A spoiled bitch looking for a rich husband. Leave." I didn't bother looking at her as I started my computer.

A loud screeching sound grabbed my attention. My secretary had grabbed the girl by her high ponytail and pulled her away. There was a bit of a scuffle before Cynthia was at my door again.

"Sorry, Mr. Astrid. I stepped away only for a coffee run."

"It's fine, Cynthia. Thank you for handling that."

"Of course." She gave me her soft smile that always made me think of a grandmother from a nursery rhyme. "I have your coffee and one for your new paralegal."

I traded Cynthia a large stack of folders for my coffee. "Please ask Ms. Carmichael for her usual coffee order and pick it up with mine in the mornings."

I nodded in the direction of my open doorway. "And make sure that useless fluff of pink is banned from entering the building again."

"Already done. Anything else?"

I leaned back and rubbed my jaw. "Yes, send Ms. Carmichael in."

A moment later Ms. Carmichael stepped into my office but hovered near the threshold. While her clothes could use some work, her makeup was once again flawless. More importantly, she appeared calm and collected.

Professional.

My jaw tightened.

Of course, it was preferred that she was presentable, especially with Cynthia standing just outside my door. Yet a dangerous, testosterone-driven part of me wanted her to still look thoroughly kissed and almost fucked.

"We need to discuss your duties."

She nodded curtly. Her green eyes stared at a spot just over my shoulder, refusing to meet my gaze as she finished for me. "I've already started reviewing the files stacked on my desk. Did you need them checked or—"

"No, they are mostly police reports. I need you to comb through them and make sure there is nothing that would surprise us later in court. I need to make sure everything is admissible, and if anything isn't, then find precedents to make it admissible."

"Is there a reason we are doing this by hand and not on a computer?"

It was a fair question.

"Yes, there is, Ms. Carmichael. When I need you to know, I will tell you, but for now, do your work and ensure that Cynthia has your coffee order for your morning and afternoon cups. We will be working a lot of long nights during this case. I need you focused and alert."

I wanted to explain that I needed her to work late for professional purposes only, but I had no intention of making a dishonest statement.

"Yes, si—"

My sharp gaze narrowed.

She licked her lips. "Yes, Mr. Astrid," she said with another nod before returning to her desk.

Dammit. Again there was a stab of disappointment.

I hated how much I wanted to hear her call me sir again, preferably while on her knees waiting for my punishment or praise.

I watched her through the doorway for a moment, taking a sip of her coffee, then refocusing on her work and moving through it at lightning speed. Skimming pages, adhering sticky notes, and annotating on a legal pad.

It was impressive. I wasn't aware new paralegals knew how

to work old school without a computer to assist with legal research.

Old school slowed us down, but it also protected the files.

I didn't trust everyone in this office, so she would be the only paralegal on a case that called for at least five. Really, I should have had ten working around the clock to speed up the research, since we were tackling this case without the benefit of digital files and online search functions. I just didn't know who else I could trust with this case.

When I committed to it, I also committed to doing a lot of the grunt work myself, and that couldn't change just because I wanted to bend Ms. Carmichael over my desk.

"Harrison, your mother is on line one." I jumped at Cynthia's voice coming over the intercom system. "She says it will be quick, and if I didn't patch her through, she was just going to show up... again."

There was nothing more effective at killing my sex drive than hearing my banshee of a mother was on the line.

I answered the phone with one last look at Ms. Carmichael, her head down and pen going a million miles an hour over her yellow legal pad.

"You have three minutes then I have to go to a meeting," I lied.

"Harrison, darling, you should be kinder to your mother. I told you not to let the world know about the unfortunate circumstance of your birth—"

"You cheating on your husband with a man who didn't love you isn't an 'unfortunate circumstance,'" I said, annoyed.

"Yes, well, be that as it may, you should have never told anyone about it and let it damage your reputation. But it's okay. I am going to fix it. I have the perfect solution that will wipe the entire slate clean."

"Good, do it." I hung up the phone and then got on the

intercom with Cynthia, letting her know if my mother called back, I was in a meeting.

I then got to work myself. The stack I'd handed Ms. Carmichael was a little less than half of what needed to be done today.

I worked through lunch, as did Ms. Carmichael.

Cynthia put sandwiches on both of our desks, but neither of us touched them. At about five o'clock, Cynthia came in to tell me she was leaving and to remind me that starting Monday, she was off the next two weeks for appointments.

"Atlantic City with your sister is not a doctor's appointment," I pointed out, not looking up from the stack of folders.

"I didn't say it was a doctor's appointment." She scoffed. "Anyway, I have the coffee orders placed with the delivery service. They should be here each day at eight a.m. and again at three p.m."

"Perfect." I sat back in my leather chair. "How am I going to survive without you while you're gone?"

"Please." She rolled her eyes at me. "Your main phone line will be forwarded so calls will be handled. You have very few meetings for the next two weeks. Your calendar has essentially been cleared for this mystery case. I'm useless to you for a while."

"Never," I said, meaning it.

"Don't work the new girl too hard, Harrison. I like her, and I would like to keep one around for a bit."

Certain my devoted secretary and I had very different definitions of working the new girl too hard, I only nodded as I told her to enjoy her vacation.

At about seven, Ms. Carmichael knocked on my door.

"Yes?" I asked without looking up.

"I've finished all those files, and the cleaning crew is giving me dirty looks."

I nodded. They were used to me being here late but liked the bullpen empty so they could dust and vacuum all the cubicles at once.

"I have another stack for you. You can work in here or go home if you aren't able to keep working tonight."

"No, I can keep going." Her words were tense as her arms crossed over her chest.

"I wasn't trying to offend you, Ms. Carmichael. You can go home and pick this up tomorrow."

"If it's all the same to you, I'd rather get more done tonight."

I handed her another stack, careful to avoid touching her. Afraid the chemistry between us would catch fire if we did. After what happened both times we were alone in the bathroom, I wasn't convinced we wouldn't ignite just by being in each other's vicinity.

"I am making notes today. I want to take all of this to the law library tomorrow. So far, I have found a few instances of questionable searches, and the chain of custody is a travesty. I think I have a few cases you can cite to have the best chance of a judge allowing them. But without the computer, I will have to pull them by hand."

"Good work. We will hit the library together to pull those cases tomorrow afternoon. It's usually quiet in the afternoons," I said. "The mornings are—"

"Full of first years trying to prove a point then giving up by lunch," she finished, looking at the first page in the top file.

"Exactly," I said, trying not to show my approval, and motioned for her to work in the little sitting area that I rarely used.

When I got my first office, the couch and table set were gifts from my father. Not my biological father, my real father. They had come with me with every move up the ladder. The leather on the couch was worn from nights crashing on it when my career was just taking off, and the coffee table had plenty of white, ashy cup marks and a few dents.

Ms. Carmichael took a seat and went straight to work, while I returned to mine.

But only after I stole a glance at her gorgeous legs, revealed as her skirt rode up slightly the moment she sat. Giving myself a mental shake, I returned to my file notes.

We stopped only to order Chinese for dinner around nine.

It was well after midnight when I next looked over at her.

She was resting her chin on her left hand. Her right hand had gone slack, the pen in her grasp falling forward at an odd angle. While her eyes weren't closed, she kept blinking in a struggle to remain awake.

She looked so adorably sweet, almost childlike with her ruffled hair and sleepy, slightly dazed expression. I wanted to sweep her up into my arms and carry her to bed.

Clearing my throat, I rose and stretched. "It's late, we should call it a night."

She looked at her phone. "Oh wow, yes, it's going to take me at least an hour to get home." She covered a delicate yawn with her fingertips.

Tearing my gaze from her open mouth, I asked, "You live that far?"

"No, I ride the subway and it usually takes longer with all the stops." She lifted her shoulder in a casual shrug.

As if she hadn't just sent a spike of fury straight down my spine at the very idea of her getting on a fucking subway at this time of night looking as tantalizing as she did.

The crowd of riders was the only reason the subway was safe during the day. There was safety in numbers, sort of. This late, it would just be her, junkies, and thugs. I had prosecuted enough cases to know what could happen to a person, especially a young woman, on those trains alone.

"The hell you are." I grabbed my phone and texted my driver, gesturing with my chin. "Gather your things. I'm taking you home."

CHAPTER 9

HARRISON

*H*er back stiffened. "I don't recall asking for your permission."

I shrugged into my coat. "You're right. And I didn't ask your permission. Now do as you're told and get your things."

She stood and exited my office, crossing to her desk, where she grabbed her purse. "This is ridiculous. I take the subway late at night all the time. I'll be fine. I'll see you tomorrow."

I blocked her path and snatched her purse from her hands. "I see countless cases come through my office of women being attacked on the subway," I ground out. "Some survive, several don't. The ones who did often wish they hadn't. Do you want the statistics of how many never even get that far?"

Eddie looked me in the eye, a move I would have respected under other circumstances.

"Mr. Astrid, this is New York. If I were to let the statistics of women being abused or attacked scare me, I would never be able to leave my apartment. I can't stop living my life because something might happen." She crossed her arms, a move that only served to draw my attention to her breasts.

I tilted my head to the side. "Why do you think we are doing this work by hand instead of on the shared server?"

"I assumed it was because of the sensitive nature of the case. You are going after one of the largest crime families on the East Coast."

"Right, and—"

"And I don't appreciate being talked to like a child," she snapped.

I let it go; it was late, and we were both tired.

No, that wasn't true. I let it go because if I didn't, I would bend her over my lap and spank her like the brat she was being, which would lead to me fucking her.

After having a day of mind-numbing work to cool down, I knew that at the very least my pursuit of her should not happen in the office. There were too many eyes and ears just waiting for me to screw up. Even if I could make sure Eddie didn't talk, there was no guarantee an unwanted person wouldn't see something they shouldn't and try to blackmail me.

It was a risk I couldn't take. Especially not now, with the O'Murphys about to go nuclear on the city. The only thing stopping them was the case I was building to put the whole crew behind bars.

"Think, Eddie. I am not using the shared servers. I sent Cynthia on vacation, and I am using one paralegal when I could have twenty to make this case go so much faster."

Her green eyes widened with understanding, and I had to stop myself from thinking about how they would look when I slid my cock in her the first time, stretching her for me.

"You are worried this case is dangerous. That if the family finds out you are building a case, they will come after you, and they could use me to find out what you have."

"Exactly," I said.

"Fine, but what do you suggest I do? Walk to Hunts Point?"

Her hands went to her hips and she raised her chin like she'd made a valid point.

"I'd suggest you move, but in the meantime, I'm taking you home."

"Could I just use the car service?"

It was a valid question and a solid solution to our dilemma.

"No. Get your coat. We're leaving."

She wrapped her hands around herself and looked anywhere but at me. She seemed uncomfortable, and I wondered if she felt the same tension I had been ignoring all day. "Fine, then I'm ready to go."

I frowned. "Woman, must everything with you be an argument? I said to get your coat."

Eddie trained her eyes just above me as she had been doing all day. It annoyed the shit out of me. I wanted to grab her jaw and demand she look me in the eyes.

"I didn't bring one today. I said I'm fine."

She was lying. For what reason, I couldn't guess.

Without saying a word, I took off my coat and swept it over her shoulders.

Immediately she moved to shrug it off. "I don't need—"

I snatched at the lapels and pulled the coat more tightly closed. "We'll discuss what you *need* another time. For now, if you know what's good for you, you won't take this coat off."

She sighed like she knew she had lost, and gave in.

Fucking finally.

"My driver is outside. Let's go."

I led her down to the garage where I had my driver meet us.

She was silent as she slid into the back of the Town Car and sat as far from me as she possibly could, pressing her body against the door. Gritting my teeth against the irrational surge of anger at the sight of her physically trying to avoid even casually touching me, I gave my driver the address she had given me.

I loved the city this time of night. Not as much as in the morning, but at this hour there was no traffic, no horns blaring, or people yelling. It was almost peaceful. There were still people around, bodegas were still open, and the streets were not empty, but everything flowed like a city that wasn't stuffed full should flow.

Twenty minutes later, the car slowed in what was easily one of the seediest parts of the city.

In prep school, my schoolmates lied about coming here to buy drugs, as if it were a life-or-death quest. As if they would risk their lives and their new Cartier watches to obtain the mystical, low-quality herb. I was pretty sure the only reason they legalized marijuana in New York was so those same precious assholes didn't have to send their staff down here anymore and could buy their weed from the comfort of Fifth Avenue.

"Why are we stopping?" I asked.

Between the chipped paint and gang graffiti over the cement foundation, the building we'd pulled up in front of also had several boarded-up windows, and there was a general feeling of neglect about the place. Not to mention the three men sitting on the steps to the main entrance, eyeing my car.

"Because this is my building," Eddie said, unbuckling her seat belt as if she hadn't just admitted to risking her life and well-being day in and day out by living in this fucking crack den of a hellhole.

I undid mine as well as I gazed out the car window at the building. "You're not staying here. I'll escort you in to pack a few things. Then we're leaving."

She got out of the car on the driver's side, ignoring me as I held the door open for her on mine. "Even as my boss, you don't have the power to dictate where I live."

I stepped close. "I thought I'd already established the amount of power I have over you?"

It was a dangerous game I was playing.

I had already crossed the line with her, a subordinate member of my staff, twice.

To go any further would be risking my career, yet despite barely knowing her, there was something about Eddie that pushed my buttons. She had an intriguing mixture of vulnerability and strength about her. It was obvious she was intelligent and strong-willed, yet when I touched her, it was almost as if she were begging me to force her to her knees.

The whole package was intoxicating and a temptation I was finding hard to ignore.

She tried to back away a few steps, her eyes wide again. "You are not coming upstairs with me."

I wrapped my hand around her upper arm. "This is not up for debate."

The men behind her started catcalling but a quick look from me silenced them.

With a huff, she said, "We need to get inside."

The *because it's not safe on the sidewalk outside my building* remained unsaid.

She led me up the steps and then into the building.

Her apartment was a three story walk-up, reached via a stairwell that reeked of cigarette smoke and other things I did not want to think about.

I ignored the garbage on the landings—empty cigarette containers, beer bottles—and the roaches that crawled over them. I even ignored the dirty metal spoon that was bent at a ninety-degree angle and got her to her door, at the end of another long, filthy hallway with a torn-up rug. I didn't even want to think about what had caused the myriad stains on it.

"Fuck your things. I'll buy you new clothes. We're leaving."

CHAPTER 10

EDDIE

I swallowed my embarrassment and pushed back tears. "You can leave but I'm staying. This is my home."

I wrenched out of his grasp and marched down the hall to my door.

It was bad enough he had found out which neighborhood I lived in. It was worse when he saw my building. But to have him walk me to my door?

There was no way I could say it only looked run-down in the dark.

No, he had seen where I was living and now knew exactly the kind of person I was and the kind of life I came from. There was no pretending that I was from some stable, middle-class family in the suburbs somewhere or that I came from people having anything of value.

That was the problem with trying to pull yourself from the gutter.

It meant you started in the gutter, and most people would never see past that once they knew.

The funny part was that this place, this absolute shit hole, was so much better than where I grew up. At least here, I got to sleep in my own bed. Even if the mattress was on the floor, it was mine. I didn't have to share my shower. Sure, the water was usually cold, some of the tiles were broken, and the pipes made horrendous sounds, but it was my own place.

With as much formality as I could muster, I kept my back to him as I faced my apartment door. "Thank you for the escort, but I can handle it from here."

He grabbed my shoulders and spun me around, pinning me to the door. "I'm serious. This isn't the place for you. It's disgusting and beneath you. Five Points is safer."

His words cut me deep. He had no idea how bad this really was or how much worse off I could have been, how much worse off I had been.

When I moved here, I was proud of the find. No, it wasn't ideal, but it was mine.

He may have had a point about the supermax prison being safer, but this was still my home, and I had some pride left.

"Of course it is. Five Points has a full staff of guards and thicker walls." I smiled. "If you don't mind, it has been a long day."

I needed him to leave before I opened the door. I didn't want him to see my threadbare couch next to my old mattress on the floor in a corner. No TV, no lamp, just the couch, mattress, and the sad little kitchenette in my sad little studio that was barely three hundred square feet including the bathroom.

"Do you enjoy living here? Is that it? The drug paraphernalia on the ground, the dried blood splatter on the walls, half the roach population of the city living on the carpet and in the walls?"

He stepped closer, and the tension that had been practically crackling between us since he caught me in his private bathroom again seemed to heat the cold air around me.

My mouth went dry, my heart thundered in my ears.

He leaned a little closer, towering over me like he did when he intimidated suspects and even other attorneys.

Intimidation wasn't what I felt.

My breath caught in my throat, and my blood started to warm in the frigid air as I remembered the kiss he'd forced on me earlier.

To my shame, I wanted another taste.

But it didn't matter what I wanted. It could not happen again. Ever.

Not just because it was extremely unprofessional but because I wouldn't be able to survive his look of disgust turning into pity the more deeply he looked into my life.

Even if I offered myself to him right here, even if he wanted me, a man of his position would never be caught dead fucking a woman in this place, not on my old mattress that sagged in some places or on my sofa that had springs sticking out in one corner.

I couldn't stand it if his poorly hidden, heated looks of lust— or his professional look of impressed surprise and pride as he reviewed my work—changed to pity.

The shame would kill me.

"Well, Eddie?" I hadn't realized he was waiting for an answer.

"No, my fondness for the roaches is not why I stay."

"Then what is it?"

"I can afford it." I sighed, giving the only answer I could without having to explain more of my situation. "My apartment is my own. I don't share, and the roaches tend to eat the salesmen and religious missionaries trying to save people in the building."

His lips turned up a little at the corner, the only sign I would get that he found the humor in my joke.

"Is that so?" His eyes drifted from mine down to my lips, and for a moment, I thought he was going to kiss me again.

If he kissed me again, I would never be able to recover the little bit of my dignity that was still intact.

I shrugged out of his coat, folded it lengthwise, and held it out to him. "Yes. Now, if you will excuse me, Mr. Astrid, it's late, and I have a boss that is demanding and will require my best work in the morning."

Refusing to take the coat, he said, "Harrison."

"What?"

He lowered his face closer to mine, his gaze focused on my lips. "My name is Harrison. Use it."

As the weight of his intense scrutiny sent butterflies fluttering in my stomach, I licked my lips but remained silent.

He lifted a hand to my jaw and tilted my head back. "I said use it. Now."

My cheeks warmed. "You need to leave. Now."

His thumb rubbed over my bottom lip. "Not until I hear this pretty mouth say my name."

Thank God I was already leaning against my door. Holy hell, who talked like that? Forget his reputation as a ruthless and extremely intelligent attorney, the man had an absolutely dirty-as-fuck mouth.

And to my everlasting humiliation—it did it for me.

"If I say your name will you leave?"

He wrapped his hand around my throat just below my jaw before leaning in to whisper in my ear. "I'd rather hear you scream it the moment I thrust my cock inside of you."

A tremor ran down my spine. "You can't talk to me like that. Inside or outside of the office. It isn't right."

He chuckled. "Nothing about what I'm thinking at this moment is right. In fact it is all kinds of dirty, nasty wrong."

I grabbed the doorknob behind me to keep from dropping to my knees and reaching for his belt buckle in the hope of hearing him call me his *good girl* right before he shoved his cock down my throat.

This needed to stop.

"Good night, Harrison. I will see you tomorrow."

Bracing a forearm over my head, he leaned in and rasped, "Good girl."

I closed my eyes, forced to lock my knees and squeeze my thighs together.

My voice was strained and high-pitched, showing my panic. "Please. I'm trying to be professional. I need this job. Thank you for the ride but please, I need you to take your coat and go."

His fingers brushed back a curl from my forehead. "I will give you tonight, but this isn't over, Eddie."

I tried again to hand him his coat.

Ignoring the gesture he said, "You better be wearing either that coat or your own tomorrow morning when you walk into my office."

Before I could object, he leaned down and kissed me on the forehead. "I'm waiting here until you lock your door."

Knowing there was no point in arguing, I turned, opened the door as slightly as I could to slide inside without letting him see the interior.

Leaning against the closed door, I tried to decipher what had just happened.

"Lock the door, Eddie."

I jumped at the sound of his command. Then I jumped to obey it.

Twisting the deadbolt in place, then engaging the chain.

I pressed my ear to the door to listen for his steps as he hopefully walked away. Instead I heard him on the phone.

"Get me Captain Raydar. This is District Attorney Astrid, badge number 75324. I need two uniform cars at..."

His voice receded as he walked down the hall.

I collapsed against the door.

It had to be all in my head. There was no way a man like him, brilliant, handsome, driven, and rich beyond any reason, would want me. There was simply no way a man like that viewed me as anything more than someone to do his busy work.

Men like him required women who were more than just women. They were investments. A woman on his arm would need to be able to help his career. She would need to know the right people, how to make small talk, and make connections that would serve him. She would have to be stunning and properly dressed for all occasions and give him heirs as beautiful and brilliant as he was. She would have to come with her own trust fund and a name that would open doors.

I came with an inferiority complex and a garbage bag full of Goodwill clothes. The most I could offer Harrison Astrid was filing his paperwork. He didn't want me. He needed more than I could ever offer.

I closed my eyes and gave myself the reality check I needed.

He and I were not attracted to one another.

We weren't. We couldn't be, we were barely the same species.

This began as just a case of mistaken identity, when he thought I was a prostitute who'd visited the wrong offices late at night.

He hadn't known I was his paralegal the first time we met.

The second time we interacted... was just a fluke.

It had to be.

He thought I was offering, which I was not. My body only responded the way it did because it had been so long since I had been with someone that I was touch-starved.

That was it. It was all just a misunderstanding that was aided by the need for human contact. It was a product of inconvenient chemicals and bad timing. Hormones and circumstance were not something worth risking my career over.

A loud knock came from the door behind me. I prayed it wasn't him. It was so difficult to maintain my professionalism. I didn't know if I could do it again.

CHAPTER 11

EDDIE

I opened the door expecting to see the still impeccably pressed suit. Instead, there stood a short girl wearing pajama bottoms with pink cacti printed all over them and a large black hoodie with the word "beg" printed across the chest.

"Girl, why are you getting home so late, and who was the sex on a stick that just walked you to your door?"

"Get in here." I laughed, making room for Sabrina, my best friend who lived across the hallway. "That was my boss, the DA, and he is not sex on a stick."

"Oh my God, please tell me you are hitting that!" She walked into my studio with our girl dinner under her arm. Three packets of chicken-flavored ramen noodles, half a bag of a discount store brand frozen vegetable medley, and a bottle of two-buck chuck. "I need protein. Do you have any?"

"There are a few eggs in the fridge."

"You know you don't actually have to keep eggs in the fridge. They are fine on the counter. Eggs in the fridge is such an American thing."

Sabrina was a sous chef at some fancy French restaurant.

Which meant she prepared food all day she couldn't afford to eat and worshiped at the altar of the head chef, some asshole with a name I didn't bother remembering, who belittled her talent as "too Americanized to be anything of substance."

"It doesn't matter. The fridge stopped working, so now it's just an insulated pantry," I tossed over my shoulder.

"You should call the super about that." She followed me to the little kitchenette that barely had more than a hot plate on top of one cupboard, a sink, and a broken mini fridge.

I turned to look at her as I pulled out the only pot I owned, and we both started laughing.

"I'll get right on that," I said, wiping a tear from my eye. "Did you just get in, too?"

"I did. Chef Jean made us all stay a little late tonight for a VIP table. It was ridiculous. Don't those entitled, wealthy assholes know that when they keep a restaurant open just to finish a glass of wine, the entire kitchen is stuck there just in case they want something else? We didn't even get overtime, and they stiffed the waitress, saying her attitude wasn't worthy of any tip that didn't involve finishing school. The poor girl was in tears. She worked her ass off for them."

"If they did know, they wouldn't care. It's the way the world works." I took a seat on the one rickety stool I owned and watched her take about three dollars' worth of ingredients and turn them into a delicious meal. Would it earn a Michelin star? No. Would it fill my belly? Absolutely.

"Why are you getting back so late, and why was your boss dropping you off?"

I was distracted by the sound of a police siren.

Granted, it wasn't an unusual occurrence. Nor was it unusual to see police cars pull up to my building. But I recalled the phone call Harrison had made as he was walking away.

He didn't.

He couldn't have!

Oh my God!

Two police cars with flashing lights pulled up to my building. The men who usually loitered on the steps selling drugs instantly ran off. I waited to see if the cops were going to get out of their cars, but they stayed put.

He did.

I wouldn't leave with him, so the man called in police surveillance.

Not wanting Sabrina to come to the window and ask questions, I answered her while I continued to watch the cop cars, praying they would move along. "We were working late."

"Ohhh, working late, burning that midnight oil all alone with DA Dreamy in his office, well past midnight."

She was teasing me, but a warmth still bloomed over my chest from thoughts about the way he licked the coffee from my breasts and the way he kissed me.

"Nothing like that. We were actually working."

"I bet you were working. Working that thick cock." She swayed her hips from side to side and dumped the ramen noodles into the now boiling water with the frozen veggies, then took out a bowl to start scrambling the eggs.

Thankfully, when Sabrina was in front of a stove, even if it was just a sad single-burner hot plate, her eyes didn't leave it, so I didn't have to worry about her seeing the guilt or longing that was probably written all over my face.

"It's not like that. We are from two different worlds. As far as he is concerned, I am just a sexless android there to be used as a tool to help win the case he is building. I might as well be a printer or a copy machine. A random piece of office equipment that he uses, and only really thinks about if it stops working or malfunctions."

"That is horrible. Tell me he doesn't treat you like some inanimate thing."

"No, he doesn't, he is professional and kind. He even ordered Chinese for us for dinner, and…"

"Wait, are you not hungry?" she asked, turning to look at me.

"No, I am starving. He fed me like I was some society woman who could live off of twelve calories. Keep cooking."

I motioned for her to keep going as I stepped away from the window. "What I am trying to say is that he was professional and sees me as what I am. Someone who is there to help win this case. Which is fine. I see him as a great bullet point to add to my law school applications and a way to add experience to help me land some fabulous job afterward. Maybe working with him again in the DA's office in, or at least somewhat closer to, an equal capacity. Or maybe I won't ever see him again because I will be working in some fabulous high-rise in Manhattan that will pay me enough money to live the good life."

"You mean to live like someone who can afford a chicken and not just a few eggs." She pressed the back of her hand to her forehead and pretended to swoon. "Oh, the dreams that dreamers dream. Aren't they so lovely?"

"I mean, like someone who can afford to invest in your restaurant, even though restaurants are terrible investments."

I got up to get the chipped bowls while she drained the noodles.

She then added flavor packets to the eggs and dumped them into the steaming noodles, scrambling them to perfection.

I would never understand how that worked. I did try it once. I made an inedible mess and went hungry that night.

She dished the bowls and handed one to me, and we moved to the thrift store couch where we sat crossed-legged, our bowls in our laps while we ate and chatted.

We talked about her day and the normal bullshit, then I gave her a rundown of my day, starting with the dumping of the coffee and the changing in the private bathroom to avoid being seen by Ally. I skipped all the stuff about what happened in the bathroom, but I did tell her how Mr. Astrid ripped into Ally when she made a pass at him.

We both cackled, and I really wished I could have seen Ally's face.

It was about one in the morning when Sabrina headed to her own tiny apartment to crash, and I tried to spot-clean my shirt before giving up on it and tossing it.

I lay down on my thin mattress and stared at the ceiling as the blue-white-and-red flashes from the police cars below created a tie-dyed firework display in my apartment.

It was fine.

Tomorrow would be better.

Tomorrow, I wouldn't let my mind drift to how he tasted, how the deep rumble of his voice made my knees weak, or how my skin prickled from his eyes traveling down my body.

Tomorrow, I would be the image of professionalism, and my work would exceed his expectations.

Tomorrow would be better.

It had to be.

Otherwise, I didn't know how I would survive Mr. Harrison Astrid.

CHAPTER 12

EDDIE

"Incoming," one of the other paralegals whispered as she passed my desk, pulling me from my files.

I sat up straight, enjoying the sudden crack of my spine and the burn of my back stretching out. I had no idea how long I had been in that same position, totally immersed in my work, but I had to remember to move more.

This week had actually been pretty great so far. After initially fighting it the first two mornings, I finally gave in when Harrison sent the car to pick me up or drop me off.

It was hard to refuse when the driver said it was because Harrison felt that the time I would have spent on the subway would be better served at my desk working on the case instead of being leered at. Since Harrison was not in the back of the car, I decided not to fight it and just enjoy the rides out of the cold.

We had managed to keep a professional distance. Focusing on the work and keeping our interactions courteous and cordial. Extremely courteous and cordial. To the point where I occasionally looked down to see if there were frosty puffs of air coming from either of our mouths as we spoke.

It was fine.

This was what I wanted, after all.

A formal, professional, highly appropriate relationship with my boss.

Yup. Everything was fine.

The fact that I got a flutter in my stomach whenever I caught him staring at me with those intense sapphire eyes or felt a spark of electricity up my spine whenever we were careless enough to allow our hands to brush as we transferred a file or notepad were easily ignored. Sort of. Not really. But it didn't mean that I wasn't fine.

Especially if I ignored the plainclothes police officer who routinely lurked on my apartment floor or the cops positioned outside my building night and day, and if I didn't dwell on how incredibly thoughtful and insanely protective it was of him to arrange for that.

If I wasn't vigilant about reminding myself that he was my boss, I'd almost fall into the trap of thinking it was a very boyfriend-y thing to do.

Fortunately, I was vigilant.

Very vigilant.

Because I was fine, in my nice new position at my very professional job with my very professional and powerful new boss.

Yup. Just fine.

That was, until I met his mother... and his fiancée.

My coffee order had just been delivered, and there was a fresh stack of files waiting for me with a handwritten note from Harrison telling me what he needed done and not to disturb him unless I had a question that needed an immediate answer to complete my tasks.

It had been a perfect morning. It was quiet. I had been

productive and had only had a handful of wildly inappropriate thoughts about my boss that I had to push away.

Sadly, I had a feeling my day was about to take a nosedive.

Two women, both stark bottle blondes dressed in head-to-toe white Chanel and sky-high Louboutins, walked toward my desk. The older woman had a face that was flawless and looked like it had been frozen by Botox, the look made more intense by her strikingly chic platinum bob. The more demure, almost matronly cut of her dress and the confidence with which she wore it were really the only things that gave away her age.

The other woman was younger, maybe in her mid- to late-twenties, so a few years older than me. Her platinum blonde hair hung in soft waves halfway down her back. Her dress was younger in style, with more movement. Her bubblegum-pink lipstick also gave away her youth. She looked like a perfectly polished Barbie.

"Who is that?" I asked one of the paralegal interns walking past my desk. She was a college student who had said she was prelaw and taking night classes, but I was fairly certain she majored in gossip.

"The older one, with the severe bob, is Mrs. Mary Quinn Astrid—Mr. Astrid's mother. The only thing I know about her is Cynthia hates her. I have no idea why. Cynthia has always been tight-lipped about her boss. But I know he doesn't like it when she just shows up. Cynthia never lets her in and usually has to add a few shots of Baileys to her coffee when she finally gets her to leave."

She leaned in conspiratorially. "The other woman, I have no idea, but if she is with Mary Quinn Astrid, then it can't be good. Oh shit, here they come. Good luck." The intern gave me a sympathetic smile as she scurried away.

"Excuse me." The older woman snapped her spindly French-manicured fingers in my face when I tried to get back to work.

"Yes?" I asked.

"Who are you?" she demanded. "Where is my son's secretary, what's her name?"

Since there wasn't a doubt in my mind this woman knew Mr. Astrid's long-time secretary, I determined that all the gossip and my first impressions were definitely accurate.

"Cynthia is on vacation," I said. "I'm Eddie Carmichael, Mr. Astrid's paralegal. Can I help you?"

"You are Eddie?" The younger woman looked at me. "Shouldn't you be a man?"

"No?" I had no idea how to answer that.

"I thought his new assistant was a man. Why would you go by a man's name?"

"My name is Edwina. I go by Eddie or Ms. Carmichael," I clarified, but I wasn't sure what they wanted me to do. A part of me wouldn't have been surprised if she demanded I get a sex change operation at lunch.

"Any relation to the Newport Carmichaels?" the human doll asked.

"No, not that I am aware of. How can I help you?" I repeated.

"Then who are you? How did you get this job working for Harrison?" Mary Quinn Astrid demanded as she crossed her arms over her chest and tapped her golden-lined French manicure on her upper arm.

"Because Mr. Astrid demands the best, and he saw my work and believed that was me. So now I work for him. Is there anything I can do to help you?"

Why was I explaining myself to these women?

"Yes, inform my son that we are here, then get each of us a coffee, skim milk, and two stevia." The older woman snapped her fingers again.

I wanted to tell her exactly where she could shove her coffee, but considering everything, I thought it was best not to insult my boss's mother.

"I'm sorry, ma'am. Mr. Astrid asked not to be disturbed."

"Excuse me?" the younger blonde said while literally looking down her perfectly proportioned, probably the product of plastic surgery, nose at me. "She did not ask if Mr. Astrid asked to be disturbed. She told you to get off your lazy ass and do your job."

I wanted to tell her that she was not my boss, and I was not his secretary. But I had a feeling her entitlement wouldn't allow her to hear anything she didn't want to hear, and it would just be easier to let him know.

With a fake smile plastered on my face, I got up, walked to his door, and knocked.

"Enter." He sounded annoyed.

I could relate. I straightened my spine and walked into his office. "I thought that note was clear, Eddie."

"It was, sir. You asked that I not disturb you unless there was something impeding my work," I said, closing the door behind me.

He looked up, his lips pressed together in a thin line. "What do you need, Eddie?"

Shaking off my reaction to him saying the word *need* as he gazed at me with those intense, sapphire blue eyes that screamed *bend over and take it like a good girl,* I concentrated on keeping my voice calm and controlled.

We had gotten through the entire morning like two strangers. There had been nothing but curt nods in greeting and the barest of communication regarding the work that needed to be done that day.

Everything between us was formal, professional and... cold.

He was simply justifying my supposition that he hadn't truly been serious about wanting a girl like me. And while I justified his approach by affirming that to cross the line any further with him would be a disastrous career move, it still stung a bit to know that I was right.

Taking a deep breath, I said, "There are two women at my desk asking for you. They are rather insistent, making it impossible for me to work. I believe one of them is your mother." I kept my tone as even and pleasant as possible. Just because the office gossip said they had issues didn't mean I was going to get in the middle of anything.

"Tell them I will be out in a few moments. I have a call to make, and then I will handle them myself," he said, rolling his eyes. He muttered something under his breath about changing his office location, but I didn't stick around to listen. This was a classic definition of not my circus, not my monkeys.

"Yes, sir," I replied and left his office, going back to my desk where the two women were standing, tapping their overpriced thousand-dollar designer shoes.

"He has a call to make and will be right with you." I took my seat and went back to the files, trying to ignore the smell of Dior perfume and snobbery.

"Why aren't you getting the drinks we asked for," his mother said.

"Because I am a paralegal, not a secretary." I was very careful to be as polite as possible.

"What is the difference?" Designer Barbie asked, popping her hip to the side and staring daggers down at me, her lips pressed together in a thin line. I wondered for a moment whether, if she kept her lips like that long enough, would her thick lip gloss help them stick like that?

"Mr. Astrid's secretary is in charge of his meetings and organizing his day, making sure he has whatever he needs, from coffee to files. I am here to assist with his caseload, which means I work with him on the cases he is building, doing the research needed, providing and filing legal documents, and things of that nature. If you don't mind, he will be out shortly, and I do have a lot of work to do."

"I still don't see the difference. People like you should be grateful to work for my son. You should be tripping over your ugly little shoes to get us coffee or whatever else we need." Mrs. Astrid's face twisted into an ugly scowl.

Nothing good was going to come from responding, so I didn't.

"I'm sure Harrison will be out soon," the Barbie said, turning away from me and facing Mrs. Astrid.

"Do you think the Plaza is the right place for the reception? Or is it a little too done?"

"It is the only acceptable place for the reception," Mrs. Astrid responded. "I just hope my son understands the caliber of guests that we are expecting and doesn't invite just anyone."

I didn't have to look up to know she was staring at me. The weight of her gaze and her judgment made my skin crawl.

"Well, when I am his wife, I will make sure he has better people working for him."

Designer Barbie's words made me freeze. I didn't look up, not wanting to see the expression on her face. I didn't know which would be worse, a smug smile that said she was having me fired, or a look of rage and indignation that said she knew what had happened between Mr. Astrid and me.

This woman was his fiancée.

I had kissed another man's fiancée, and that made me worse than her.

I clenched my teeth and took long, slow breaths through my nose, trying to slow my heart rate.

It didn't matter.

He was never mine.

This would just make it easier to be completely professional.

I repeated that over and over in my head until those manicured nails were in my face again, snapping at me like a dog.

"I'm sorry, what?" I asked, looking up at Mrs. Astrid, who was glowering down at me.

"I asked when my son would be out."

"I'm sorry, I don't know. He has been made aware of your arrival."

The future Mrs. Astrid put her hands on the top of my cubicle and gave me a cruel smirk. "You are useless and terrible at your job. I suggest you pack your things because I am going to make sure Harrison fires you."

Mr. Astrid's mother laughed, a high-pitched, shrill sound that hurt my ears.

I stared up at this girl and wondered what had happened to her to make her so needlessly cruel. Or maybe she was just born like that. It didn't matter, not really.

"Mother, what are you doing here?" Mr. Astrid strode out of his office.

"We are here so that you can take us to lunch," she said, the cruel laughter and smile gone the second she heard her son.

"I don't have time today. I have work to do."

"I'm sure your secretary can cover for you," his fiancée said. "I promise it will be a short lunch. We just have some things to discuss. You have to eat, don't you?" Her smile was wide and bright, and if I hadn't heard the way she'd just talked to me, I would have thought she was the sweetest woman on the planet.

"We have come all the way down here," his mother said.

"Had you called..." He pinched the bridge of his nose, and I couldn't help but notice how his entire body was rigid.

I must have spent too long noticing Mr. Astrid's body language because his fiancée gave me a chilly look, then stepped in between us and took his arm.

I took the hint and redirected my attention back to my work.

"I did call," Mrs. Astrid said. "Your new secretary didn't answer. She must need some time to get the hang of being on your desk."

"Right." Mr. Astrid's voice seemed overly formal when dealing with his mother, but it wasn't any of my business.

I was staring at the pages of the file I was currently working on, pretending I was reading the words, but I couldn't help listening to the conversation that was rudely happening practically on top of my desk.

They talked for another moment, then Mr. Astrid told them he would meet them at the car, and they headed down. I didn't look up until the air cleared of heavy-handed perfumes.

Mr. Astrid was standing by Cynthia's desk, leaning down, one hand flat on the desktop while the other was hitting buttons on her desk phone.

"I am heading out to lunch. I will be gone for an hour, maybe two. Are you available to work late again tonight?"

"Yes, sir," I answered.

"Good. Take this." He handed me a black credit card. "This is the office card. I want you to order yourself lunch and take a break while you can. The next few days are going to be brutal."

"Okay..." I took the card, not liking the idea of a handout. Dinner while we were working late together was one thing, but using his black Amex when it wasn't a working lunch felt like charity.

No, worse. It felt like he was buying my silence for what happened in the bathroom.

I watched him walk away, and felt sick.

I was disappointed he was taken, insulted he'd tried to buy my silence so cheaply, and mad at myself for being so affected by the actions of a man so far out of my league that it was practically a different sport.

If I told Sabrina about this, which I never would, she would tell me the best way to get over a crush was to find a new one, but not before abusing the card by ordering a lunch of rich people's food.

Despite what he'd said, publicly funded law offices didn't have black Amex cards. I looked at it. This was his.

I considered buying lunch for the whole office but didn't think I could get away with it. It would have been fun, though.

I tucked the black card into the top drawer of the small filing cabinet under my desk. Then, I put the rest of the files in the larger bottom drawer, locking it.

There was no way I was using that card, but I could, at the very least, find someone else to occupy my thoughts and some of my free time.

I downloaded Tinder and headed to lunch. There were always a few food trucks parked outside the offices around this time, and a few greasy tacos sounded like the perfect lunch to have while swiping right.

CHAPTER 13

HARRISON

*D*ammit.

The last fucking thing I needed was a social call from Mary Quinn Astrid.

I had enough on my plate keeping my mind on work and not on the curve of my new paralegal's ass in the skirt she was wearing.

It had taken every measure of willpower I possessed to walk away from her last week when every bone in my body was raging to pick her up, toss her over my shoulder, and carry her back to my place where I knew she'd be safe.

Safe, at any rate, from New York's criminal element. Not safe from me.

At least by giving Captain Raydar those tips I'd been able to secure protection for her until I figured out how to move her into one of my investment properties in a way that no one from the office gossip pool would learn about.

But that was a problem for later. For now, I had to deal with my mother.

Cynthia had managed to block my mother's numbers, all of

them, from reaching my desk and my cell phone in her absence. It was brilliant, or it would have been if Mary hadn't just shown up with the woman she intended for me to marry.

Then insist I interrupt working on what would quite possibly be the most important case of my career to have lunch at Le Bernardin. The food was good, and I didn't give a fuck about the cost of the bill.

What I cared about was the cost of this distraction to the case and how it took me away from my new favorite form of torture —watching Eddie work.

Fuck, if that woman knew the things that went through my mind every time she placed the top end of a pen in her mouth while lost in thought, or ran her hand through her hair as she leaned over a book checking a source...

But no, I was here, meeting my supposed fiancée.

Catherine Montague, daughter of Alaster and Courtney. Her father worked in the Financial District, and her uncle was a lord or duke or something or other. This meant that Catherine had the right breeding to help me regain the votes I had lost in my family's social circles, and she was heavily involved in some phil-anthropic causes, which meant she would soften how I appeared to everyone else.

Standing next to this beautiful woman who projected an air of constant sunshine and graceful generosity would wipe away the scandal that was my parentage, making me more palatable to the voters to whom it mattered.

On paper, she was perfect. In person, she was mind-numb-ingly dull.

"I don't know, Mary, a spring wedding? It's so soon. People might think there is a reason for the wedding," Catherine whispered.

"Don't worry, dear. We will make sure there is a photo of you sipping Dom, and that will silence any rumors." My mother patted her hand. "We will spin this as the wedding of the century. A young love that is just too impatient to wait. We will sell the story of a whirlwind romance for the ages."

"When will we make the announcement?" Catherine folded her hands under her chin, leaning in like a child listening to her mother tell a fairy tale.

"I think we should schedule a photoshoot next weekend. That will give me time to arrange a plausible story of when you two met and all of that. I want the photos published in all the best magazines and, of course, the *Times* and the *Herald*."

"No," I interrupted.

"Oh." Catherine looked at me, her bright eyes wide. "Do you think the *Herald* is too conservative? I know you are a Democrat, though I can't for the life of me imagine why."

"I don't care where you publish it. What I'm saying no to is the photo shoot and any other interviews in the next few months. I have work to do."

"Harrison." My mother scolded me. That tone didn't work on me when I was a child. I had no idea what gave her the impression it would work now.

"No, Mary, that makes sense. I can do the interviews and photo shoots. We can spin it so I am the face of this union. The woman who handles everything so her man can get the 'real work' done."

I didn't think I had ever heard a woman other than my mother say something so sexist in my life. And even then, my mother only said things like that about my sisters.

I made a mental note to check up on Rose soon.

My mother was busy with this wedding, but once it was done, Rose would be in her crosshairs and she wouldn't have anyone to shield her. Being the youngest was both a blessing and a curse. She'd had buffers growing up, since my siblings and I could take the brunt of my mother's schemes. But once she was done with us, all her focus would go to little Rose. Though she was born with more fight in her than my mother knew.

"I really don't mind," Catherine said.

"Right, well, I am going to powder my nose. You two get to know each other." My mother stood and headed to the bathroom.

I looked around at the pristine dining room with its white tablecloths, waiters in suits, and over-the-top, ornate floral centerpieces on each table.

"So, did you want to know anything about me before we get married?" Catherine tilted her head to the side and bit her lip. I assumed it was her attempt to look seductive.

She was very attractive, but I felt nothing for her. No lust, no admiration, not even a speck of attraction. She was the type of woman who could have men ready to come in their pants with just a wink. Yet my dick lay flaccid in my pants, completely uninterested.

It was fine. That wasn't what this was about, anyway.

"Sure. My mother mentioned you are a philanthropist. What charities do you work for?" I asked.

"Oh, I don't work, silly." She reached over and touched my hand as she threw her head back like it was the funniest thing anyone had ever said.

"Then what do you do for those charities?"

"I attend their parties if the theme sounds like fun and there will be people I like there, and I allow myself to be photographed. Then, my assistant will approve any photos that are good enough, and she will put a few of those on my social media. I have a few million followers, so it gets the charities a lot of exposure."

"I see..." I didn't see.

"Oh, and if the party is really good, I will have my assistant tell people to donate to whatever their cause is, protecting whaling rights, or fixing ugly children, or protecting third-world children's rights to work, or whatever. I'm big on supporting kids."

"Okay, so you really don't care about the causes?" I chose to ignore the entire children comment. I was far too sober to unpack that.

"I mean, there are a few charities I will never donate to. Anything that supports PETA or goes against animal testing. I refuse to have anything to do with that. I mean, can you imagine the travesty of not testing products on living animals first? What if a brand decided to skip that crucial step, and someone bought a product and had a bad reaction to it?"

Jesus fuck, this woman is the worst.

"But, like, I don't tell anyone really what I do and don't support. I like to leave them guessing. It helps me cultivate a sense of mystery. And you never know what is going to be canceled next, so it's best just to stay quiet and let people guess what you are about."

"Right." Was it a bad sign that I was relieved she didn't want to talk to anyone about her seriously fucked up views? I supposed it didn't matter, not really. She wasn't going to be by my side to take interviews. And even if she did end up having to take a few, she could be coached on what to say.

"So, what else did you want to know about me?" She looked down at her now empty wineglass then grabbed the nearest waiter. Literally reached out and grabbed his arm, almost making him drop a plate of seafood pasta. His save was actually impressive.

"You refill this wineglass now and check to see how much longer our food will be. We have been waiting for five minutes. Do you know who this man is and how important he is? I will have you fired if you don't fix this now."

To the waiter's credit, he nodded sagely and poured the wine with one hand, while handing the pasta off to another server. He apologized to Catherine and me, then went to check on the order.

I made a mental note to add another zero to his tip.

"I cannot believe how incompetent people are today," she said, giving me a look like I was supposed to agree.

"Yes, some things certainly tell you a lot about a person's competence," I agreed.

"Do you want kids?" she asked. She answered before I had a chance to. "I want at least four. Two boys, an heir and a spare, of course, then two girls who will make important connections for their brothers. I'll get pregnant with the heir myself for appearances and then of course use a surrogate for the rest. I think we should start right away. In fact, since we are getting married so soon, I don't see why we have to wait for the wedding night. We can start practicing now. How about I come over when you are done with work and give you a preview?" She placed her hand on my thigh and tried to move it up.

I grabbed her fingers and returned them to her lap.

"That won't be necessary. I don't want children." I hadn't even realized the truth of that statement until I said it.

It hadn't been true until this moment. There was no way I was going to give this woman children. Two boys to preen over and coddle and then two girls to shame and suffocate the individuality out of. She would have been worse than my mother. It could not happen.

"Oh, but your mother said..."

"My mother says a lot of things. I want to make this perfectly clear. This is not a love match, and when we are in private, I have no interest in pretending it is anything other than what it is: a business arrangement. I get a pretty girl that will paint me to be a family man and not a bastard, and you get to be the DA's wife, and eventually, my political aspirations may elevate you further."

"Oh…" She sat back, folding her hands in her lap.

"There will be a generous prenup, and if I ever decide to leave office and no longer require the services of a pretend wife, then we will divorce, and you will have adequate money to live how you want and where you want."

"And if you decide to run for a higher office, requiring more of my time and effort?"

"Then we will negotiate terms before I run."

"No." She crossed her arms over her chest and sat back in her chair. "I am worth more. I am far too valuable an asset to be shelved, and if you do have the political aspirations that your mother seems to think you do, then you will need more. You want to project a family man aesthetic, something the middle-American voter will be able to identify with. The child-free life-style may be understandable to sophisticated New Yorkers, but if you are going to make me First Lady someday, then you need the potato eaters in Ohio to like you as well."

She may have been rude and tactlessly abrupt, but she wasn't wrong.

"So, I propose that we get married and then start trying for a child right away. Also, to really sell this, we will need to meet for lunches and dinners a few times publicly in the next few weeks, and then you will need to be seen at Tiffany's. My registry is already set up, with not only the ring but a matching necklace, earrings, and bracelet."

"Excuse me?" She could not be serious.

"We want to really show the world how you feel about me, and PDAs will seem unnatural for you at first, so jewelry is the way to go. We will also plan the engagement and let it slip to a few trusted sources where and when it will happen. Don't worry about the wedding itself. Your mother and I will handle that."

I pinched the bridge of my nose as the back of my skull tightened with a pending migraine. "Is that all?"

"No, but it's enough of a start for now." She took out her phone and started typing. Then, she smirked down at the screen and laid it on the table, sliding it toward me.

It was open to some social media app, and there was a photo of us sitting next to each other, her hand in mine as she looked up at me adoringly. You couldn't even tell she was propositioning me and I was removing her hand from my lap.

"How…"

"My assistant is always around." She smiled and posted the photo to one of her other social media accounts, with a caption that read, "Sometimes you just know."

The little heart under the caption had a number that was going up faster than I could read it.

"By tomorrow morning, we will be all over the social pages, and there will be at least two dozen interest pieces on us as a couple. There is no going back now."

My stomach twisted as bile rose in the back of my throat.

She was right.

There really was nothing else I could do. Without my consent, she had actually announced our relationship, and there was no turning back. I could break this entire thing off, but it would do even more damage to my already sullied reputation.

Elections were coming up soon, and I would rather focus on the work that I had to do getting criminals off the street than worry about campaigning. This woman may be an awful human being and an evil genius wrapped in the superficial packaging of a wannabe Barbie doll, but at least I could have her work for me and with me rather than against me.

What was worse was that my mother had already guessed my long-term career goals, and although I might find this woman personally repugnant, she could be an asset on the campaign trail. She had already managed to fool the entire world into believing that she was a philanthropic angel and not the spoiled brat she was showing herself to be.

If I was being honest with myself, I didn't want a wife.

I didn't have time for a wife.

That being said, my career dictated that having a wife would be advantageous.

Specifically, a society type that would understand how to act in certain situations, know what was required of her, and what her role actually would be. A society wife would not expect me home for dinner each night. She would know better.

A society wife would not expect me to be faithful, nor would she expect me to have an active role in the raising of our children until they became a certain age. She would understand that I had the final say in anything involving our business and investments, that it was my role to make sure she had everything she needed, while it was her role to actually handle the day-to-day running of the household and our social calendar.

Just because I didn't find her appealing didn't mean she wouldn't look good on the Christmas cards. Once we were wed, I also wouldn't have to worry about her acting out of turn, because her livelihood would depend solely on mine. This woman would understand that it would be in her best interest to act in my best interest.

A few well-placed clauses in the prenup would also further incentivize her to stay the course and do her job.

I just hated the idea that I'd actually have to spend time with this vapid woman who would probably be more plastic than flesh by the time she was fifty. This entire arrangement had me feeling sick to my stomach, but as my mother had pointed out, it was a means to an end. A means that was expected of me.

So, I kept trying to convince myself that it was the right course. Every time Catherine snapped at a waiter, or she and my mother leaned together and laughed like they were in cahoots—

which I guessed they were—I told myself another lie about how she would be good in this role and how, after our children were born, our contact could be limited.

The hour and a half I had allotted for my mother to steal from my day felt like forever. Seconds ticked by into what seemed like hours, and by the time I managed to get back to the office, I felt as though I'd lost half a day's worth of work and momentum that I couldn't regain.

For the first time the pressures of my job, career goals, and family name felt insurmountably suffocating.

For the first time since high school, I felt like the choices that dictated my life were out of my hands. It felt like things were being done to me, not by me, and I had lost my control.

When I got to the office, I took the elevator up, hitting the "emergency" button before reaching my floor and taking a moment of complete silence. My hands gripping the metal railing, I did a breathing exercise I hadn't had to do in years.

Eyes closed, I took a deep breath in and counted to ten. Then slowly let the breath out.

When I opened my eyes, I looked around the empty elevator car for five things that I could see. I saw the beige carpeting under my feet, the golden trim around the buttons, the water stain on the elevator's ceiling, the stainless-steel panel, and the digital number three above the elevator door.

I took another deep breath and then listed four things I could feel.

The touch of the cold metal from the Rolex Submariner on my wrist; it was not my taste, but my father had given it to me, so I wore it. The soft, warm wool of my Brooks Brothers suit jacket, the tight, noose-like sensation of the tie around my throat, and the cool, stainless-steel railing I was currently gripping that went around the interior of the elevator car.

I took another deep breath, slowly in and out, then concentrated on three things I could hear. I could hear soft music play-ing; it sounded like pop from the early '90s. The *whoosh* of the other elevator passing mine in the next shaft. And finally, the sudden, shrill ringing of the emergency phone.

Ignoring the phone, I took another deep breath. Two things I could smell. I could smell Catherine's suffocating perfume still on my jacket and the stale air of the elevator. Whoever had been in here before me had just brushed their teeth or was chewing a very strong mint gum.

I took another deep breath. Finally, one thing I could taste. I could still taste the herb-crusted salmon I'd had for lunch. I tried to focus on that taste, but it faded, and instead, I remembered what her lips tasted like.

Ms. Carmichael's lips tasted like rich, dark roast coffee and something sweet, like honey, maybe. Or some type of agave syrup, a delicate, natural sweetness that was addicting.

I shook the thought out of my head and answered the screeching phone. The voice on the other end was asking if there was a problem. I answered no, everything was fine, and restarted the elevator.

It had been so long since I'd had to use that anxiety tech-nique, I'd forgotten how effective it truly was. By the time I reached my floor, I felt like myself again. I was stable, steady, and ready to refocus on my work and regain control of my life.

When I turned the corner, that feeling evaporated at the sound of Ms. Carmichael's sweet giggle and the sight of her flirting with the cop I believed had been protecting the entire O'Murphy clan.

My girl's hand was being held by the man I was determined to see behind bars.

CHAPTER 14

EDDIE

*W*hen I downloaded the dating app, never in a million years would I have thought the first profile to pop up would be of the very attractive detective who had winked at me last week.

Immediately, I swiped right with a little flutter of my heart.

It wasn't love, but maybe interest.

He was quite handsome, tall with dark red hair, green eyes, a cute smattering of freckles, and an easy smile. He was nothing like Mr. Astrid, and that was exactly what I needed.

Only about two minutes went by before I was informed that it was a match.

"Fancy meeting you here," a deep voice said behind me in the food truck line. I jumped, my heart racing as I turned around and was face-to-face with the gorgeous redheaded detective, Patrick Doyle.

He wasn't as tall as Harrison, and his shoulders weren't quite as broad. But he had a charming smile and an easygoing demeanor that could only come from having a blue-collar life.

Not exactly the man I had been dreaming about, but this man was attractive enough, available from what I could tell, and much closer to my social standing.

The idea of talking to this detective, or even having to bring him back to my place, didn't fill me with a sense of impending dread.

Patrick suggested we take our tacos upstairs to the break room and chat a little, while on lunch.

"I promise this won't count as our first date, but it'll give us a chance to get to know each other a little bit better, so when I do ask you out, you'll already know your answer," he said with a wink, and I gave a polite smile. I wished that his flirting filled me with the same heat Harrison's attention did.

In the hour we chatted and flirted, I learned that he came from a big Irish family and eventually wanted to be the police chief. I really appreciated that he had high aspirations but a very humble background, like me.

His upbringing wasn't as sordid or tragic as mine, but a man like him would appreciate the work that I had put into my career without looking down on me because of how I started.

Finding a new crush, which I was still confident was the advice Sabrina would give me, was exactly what I needed.

No, the detective didn't make my heart race every time I looked at him, and I probably wouldn't be distracted from my work by intrusive thoughts about what his cock tasted like or how it would feel when he thrust deep inside of me. But wasn't that a good thing? I was here to work, not to have inappropriate daydreams.

Being with someone like him would make it far easier for me to separate my work from my personal life. He may even be enough of a reason for me to have a personal life.

"Let me take you out on Friday," he said as he clasped my hand in his. "I know this great little pub. When you're done with work, I can pick you up. We'll have a couple of drinks, get some fish and chips, and just see where the night takes us."

Patrick's offer was tempting, but there was no way for me to know what my hours would be like on Friday. And considering the tense relationship between Harrison and me currently, I didn't really feel comfortable asking to leave at a reasonable hour on a Friday night.

I was about to tell him no when Harrison stopped in front of the break room and barked at me to get my ass back to my desk.

His jaw was clenched as he stared daggers at the detective.

I had no idea why he was so upset with me, but I wasn't in a position to ask. Perhaps his mother or his fiancée had said something about me not meeting their expectations for his secretary.

Since Cynthia was out, had he expected me to fill her role, even though it was outside my responsibilities as his paralegal? I knew Mrs. Lakeson had asked me to but I didn't think that meant fetching coffee for his obnoxious fiancée.

Shooting the detective an apologetic glance, I rushed over to my desk.

I had just unlocked the drawer to grab the files when Mr. Astrid demanded that I come into his office.

"Close the door and lock it," he said as I walked in.

He didn't bother looking up from the stack of papers he was setting aside on his desk.

I did as he demanded and turned to face him.

He still didn't look at me.

"Is there something you need?" I asked.

"Yes, Ms. Carmichael. I need to know why you feel it's appropriate to flirt at the workplace."

Ms. Carmichael, is it?

Fine, Mr. Astrid.

I bristled at his accusation.

How dare he say things like that to me as if he wasn't the one who had accosted me in the bathroom? Yeah, I was in there when I wasn't supposed to be, but he'd been just as unprofessional, if not more so, by kissing and licking my body and putting his hands on me.

"Sir, I was on my lunch break. That is personal time, not professional."

"That still does not mean that it is okay for you to flirt with a detective while in this office."

"With all due respect, sir, who I flirt with and when, so long as I am not on the clock, is absolutely none of your business."

Finally he looked up at me, and the anger behind his brilliant blue eyes made my heart race. I took an involuntary step back toward the door.

"It is my fucking business if you choose to act like a cat in heat in the middle of my office. How did you meet Detective Doyle? Did he approach you at your desk?"

"It's none of your business how I met him."

He rose from his desk and walked around it, staring me down. "Would you like to run that by me again, Ms. Carmichael?"

My breath came in short pants as he stalked toward me.

I braced myself against the solid wood door behind me.

"No," I said, pressing my palms flat against the cool surface of the door. "I stand by what I said."

Mr. Astrid stood in front of me and flattened his hands on the door on either side of my head, boxing me in.

There was no place for me to escape.

"I'm already extremely annoyed. You don't want to know what happens if I reach pissed off. Now I'm going to ask you one more time. Did Detective Doyle approach you at your desk?"

I would rather be stripped naked and dragged through the streets of Manhattan over shards of broken glass than tell him I matched with Patrick on Tinder.

"I don't see how it is any of your busin—any of your concern how I met him."

His eyes narrowed. "You don't see why I would be concerned that an Irish detective suddenly takes an interest in you a week after you are assigned to work on a confidential Irish mafia case?"

I threw my shoulders back. If it weren't for me matching with Patrick on Tinder, my ego might have been bruised. "First of all, he's a cop not a criminal. Second of all, it may have escaped your notice but I'm actually considered desirable by most—"

His mouth slammed down on mine, stealing my breath. It was like being swept under a deep, dark current. I was instantly overwhelmed. He wrapped his arm around my waist, while his other hand cupped the back of my head, holding me so tightly I was lifted off the floor.

My lips were pressed against my teeth as his tongue took possession of my mouth. He wasn't kissing me, he was devouring me. There was an angry desperation to it, as if he had been holding back for days and was finally letting the torrent of emotion loose.

It took all my strength to push against his chest and break the contact.

I held my fingertips to my bruised lips, staring wide-eyed at him. "We agreed to keep things professional between us."

"I never agreed to that."

"It's not your career we'd be setting a match to."

His sharp gaze went from my lips to the open button on the collar of my shirt before he leaned back and shrugged out of his suit jacket. "I'll protect you from any fallout should we be discovered."

I shook my head. "I wonder how many women were foolish enough to believe that line."

"If you are implying I make a habit of fucking my paralegals, let me assure you, you're the first."

"A dubious honor. One that I will have to decline, *Mr. Astrid.*"

He unbuttoned his cuffs. "That's an unfortunate answer, *Ms. Carmichael,* since I have no intention of giving you a choice in the matter."

CHAPTER 15

HARRISON

Something inside of me snapped seeing Detective Doyle's hands on her.

The fact that he had more of a right to touch her than I did, didn't help.

I was her boss.

I had a fiancée, at least as far as New York society was now concerned.

Even if I wasn't her boss, we worked together in the same office.

There was every reason why I should keep my hands off her.

And there was only one reason why I had no intention of doing so...

She was mine.

Fuck it. Fuck all of it.

Yes, mine.

For the first time in my life, I was delirious with almost villainous glee that I was a man with a personal fortune that numbered into the billions at my disposal.

I had power and wealth.

As far as society was concerned, regardless of the scandal of my birth, I was untouchable.

Which meant if I wanted Edwina Carmichael for my own, I was going to take her.

And any man who got in my way would risk my wrath.

She turned and grasped the doorknob to my closed office door which she had failed to lock. She was only able to open it a few inches before my flattened palm against the door slammed it shut.

Pressing my body against her back, I demanded, "Turn around."

She shook her head. "No. Let me out."

"No."

She rattled the doorknob. "This isn't funny. Let me out."

My hand spanned her waist. "I'm not laughing. I gave you an order."

Instead of obeying, she ducked under my arm and stumbled to the other side of the office. I locked the door before pivoting to face her.

Her arms crossed over her middle. "This has gone way too far. Clearly your lunch with your mother and your *fiancée* has stressed you out, because you are crossing the line."

I rolled up my sleeve. "Don't talk about my mother or that other woman. This is about us."

She blinked, her mouth falling open. Stretching out her arm to gesture toward the door, she said, "I can't talk about that monster you call a mother or the horrible woman you are *marrying* but you can comment on me"—she pointed at her own chest— "innocently talking to a man on my lunch break?"

I rolled up my other sleeve. "There was nothing innocent about your conversation. He wanted to fuck you."

She flinched at my harsh words, before firing back, "And how is that any different from you?"

Secretly I loved how she gave as good as she got. There was a fire inside of her. The kind of fire that only came from fighting for every crumb life had given you. She may be intimidated by my position as DA and the power I held over her future career, but she wouldn't be cowed by me.

My cock hardened even further, thinking what all that fire would feel like harnessed beneath me in bed.

The corner of my mouth lifted in a mirthless smile as I stalked toward her. "Oh, there's a difference. He *wanted* to fuck you. I'm *going* to fuck you. Right here and now."

Eddie shoved a chair in my path as she scurried behind my desk. "You're out of your mind."

With a kick, I sent the chair crashing against the filing cabinets. "Close. I'm actually out of patience. Bend over my desk."

Her head lowered to scan the massive expanse of my antique, mahogany executive desk. "You can't be serious."

"Disobey me and see what happens."

Her eyes widened. "This is illegal. It's harassment."

I grinned as I reached for my belt buckle. "You're free to file an HR complaint—afterward. Now I want to see you lift that skirt and bare your ass."

I circled around the desk.

She skittered backward, circling around the desk, trying to keep me at arm's length. "I'll scream."

I lunged, snatching her around the waist.

Her body crashed against mine. I pushed my fingers into her golden hair and wrenched her head back. "That door is reinforced steel for security purposes. This is a hundred-year-old building with solid, foot-thick walls."

My lips hovered over hers. "So go ahead and scream, babygirl."

The moment she gasped, I claimed her mouth again.

Pushing my tongue deep inside, she tasted like sweet peppers and hot sauce. I twisted my fist in her hair and wrapped my other arm more securely around her waist, pulling her hips against my hard cock.

My tongue fought with hers as I bruised her lips with the violence of my kiss.

We were both breathless when I broke free.

Before she had a chance to regroup, I lifted her by the waist and seated her on the edge of my desk. Forcing her legs open, I stepped between them as I shoved her skirt up.

She tried to push the hem back down. "Stop! What are you doing?"

Brushing her hands away, I reached under her hem and tore at her panties.

She cried out. "Oh my God! Stop! Wait!"

I wrapped a hand around her neck and pulled her close. "I'm going to find out if your pussy tastes as sweet as your lips."

After giving her a quick, hard kiss, I pushed her onto her back.

She tried to rise, but I kept her in place with a palm to the center of her chest. "Be a good girl and lie still before you anger me further."

Tears filled her eyes. "Please, you can't do this." She sniffed. "*We* can't do this. It's inappropriate and wrong."

I kneeled in front of the desk as I wrapped my arms around her thighs. "I'm the law here. I decide what is and isn't wrong."

Fuck me. Her sweet pussy had a light dusting of short, blonde curls.

My baby was a natural blonde.

That might not seem like a big deal but in my world, where I was constantly surrounded by vain, artificial women whose breasts were filled with silicone and lips with filler, this was an unbelievable turn on.

Rubbing my stubbled cheek against her inner thigh, I parted

her pussy lips with my fingers. Leaning forward, I swept my tongue over her.

Staring up over her flat stomach, I winked at her. "Just as sweet... and wet."

She fisted the hem of her skirt and tried to push it between my chin and her naked pussy.

I wrapped my hand around her wrist and held her still as I flicked my tongue over her clit.

Her gasp was the sexiest sound I'd ever heard in my life.

Keeping my grip on her wrist, I pushed her hand between her legs. "Hold your pussy lips open for me."

"I can't. No. We—"

I sank my teeth into the soft flesh of her inner thigh. Not enough to break the skin, but enough to make my point.

Her hips bucked as she cried out.

"Do as you're told."

Her hand trembled in my grasp as she used her fingers to hold herself open for me.

I then feasted.

Licking. Sucking. Laving.

I teased her sensitive nub; she stopped struggling and her protests turned into soft moans.

Her body trembled as her orgasm swept over her. "Oh God! Oh! Oh! Oh!"

I sucked on her clit harder, skimming her flesh with the edges of my teeth, savoring every tremble and moan.

Before she had a chance to recover, I flipped her onto her stomach with her legs dangling over the edge of the desktop.

Bunching her skirt at her lower back, I ran my palm over the soft curves of her ass. "Now it's time for your punishment."

She pushed up on her hands and turned to stare at me over her shoulder. "What? Punishment?"

I lifted my arm high and swept my open palm down onto her ass.

My other hand covered her mouth at the moment she was about to scream. Keeping it there, I spanked her again and again. Watching her flesh tense and jiggle before and after each strike.

She danced up onto her toes, her fingers curling into fists.

Her tears wet my hand as I continued to cover her mouth.

I spanked her several more times, refusing to relent until her flesh glowed a bright, cherry red.

Her body going limp against my desk, her shoulders vibrated with her silent sobs.

Releasing her mouth, I leaned over and brushed her hair back over her shoulder, exposing her flushed, tear-wet cheek. I rasped against her ear, "Next time, I'll use my belt."

She sniffed. "Why are you doing this to me?"

It was a legitimate question.

One I had no answer for, at least not one she would accept.

Still, she deserved one.

I stepped behind her and lowered my zipper. Reaching inside my trousers, I pulled my aching cock free. Grasping the thick length, I ran my hand up and down the shaft several times before I positioned myself behind her.

Wrapping one hand around her hip to keep her anchored in place, I bent at the knees and placed the tip of my cock at her tight entrance.

Eddie's back bowed as she shot her torso up.

Before she could object, I commanded, "Brace yourself, sweetheart. This is going to hurt."

I then thrust straight to the hilt, showing her no mercy. There was a primal satisfaction in feeling her body stretch and strain around my cock as it struggled to accept me.

"You're too big! Take it out!"

"Your body will learn to adjust to my cock."

"No! It won't! I don't care if you ruin my career. You're never touching me again."

I pulled back and thrust again.

Slowly her inner muscles relaxed as I pressed in deep.

I ran my hand over her back to fist her hair. Forcing her to arch her back further, I reached inside of her blouse and cupped her breast with my free hand, pinching her nipple through the silk of her bra. "I'm warning you right now. There is no fucking way you're keeping this sweet pussy from me, babygirl."

With her body bowed in my grasp, I thrust harder and faster. Pounding into her small, tight body like my own salvation depended on it.

I knew making a woman orgasm from just fucking was often difficult but I was determined to wrench a second climax from her.

And yes, with my cock.

My ego was that unapologetically inflated.

She slammed the top of the desk with the flat of her palm as her body clutched around me. "Oh! No! Oh! Oh! Oh!"

I leaned over her shoulder and bit her earlobe. "Come for baby. Now. That's an order from your boss."

Her body jerked as she trembled and moaned.

Mission accomplished.

With her reluctantly sated, I tightened my grip on her hair and unleashed on her body.

I fucked her so fiercely, my heavy desk shifted under us across the carpet.

I couldn't get enough of the feel of her punished skin against my lower abdomen. Of her tight muscles clenching my cock. Of her deep-throated moans. Of how her whole body trembled when she came.

I spanked her ass several times as my balls tightened. "Fuck, baby. You're being such a good girl for me. So goddamn tight around my cock."

My shaft swelled then I came, pouring my come into her pussy.

She fell forward onto my desktop with me following, covering her back.

After several breathless moments, I slowly pulled free from her heat.

Leaving her, I shoved my cock into my pants and buckled my belt, then crossed to the bathroom and prepared a warm washcloth.

She hadn't moved by the time I returned.

Settling my hand between her legs, I let the warmth of the cloth soothe her bruised cunt.

After a few moments, she pushed my hand away and rose.

Her cheeks were flushed. Her hair a wild mess of hand-ruffled curls. Her blouse was wrinkled and there were black smudges below her eyes where her mascara had smeared.

She was easily the most beautiful creature I had ever laid eyes on.

Eddie pushed down her skirt and smoothed her blouse. She then ran a hand over her cheeks as her fingertips skimmed below her lash line to wipe away the makeup smudges.

Without saying a word, she crossed to the office door and unlocked it.

With her hand on the doorknob, she turned to face me. Thrusting out her chin, she said, "I quit."

CHAPTER 16

EDDIE

I quit.

Two words I never thought I would utter after landing a dream job as a paralegal in the district attorney's office.

Without looking back, I snatched my purse from my lower desk drawer and walked as fast as I dared without drawing attention to the elevator bays.

I pressed the elevator button several times even after it lit up.

Harrison had already put his suit jacket back on and was storming after me. With his brow lowered and his jaw clenched, he looked like an enraged bull. "Ms. Carmichael. I need a word with you before you leave."

I pressed the elevator button several more times, as if the inanimate machine would realize my distress and hurry to my floor.

As he closed the distance between us, I panicked and headed for the stairs. Taking off my heels, I broke out into a run the moment I was concealed inside the stairwell. I was already two flights down by the time he reached the upper landing.

"Eddie, get back here."

I stopped a moment to stare up at him but didn't trust myself to speak. I just put my head back down and continued to run down the stairs.

When I burst out of the building, I paused just long enough to put my shoes back on. It was my intention to head directly to the subway but I was stopped by a uniformed police officer. "Are you Edwina Carmichael?"

My heart skipped a beat.

Holy hell.

Had he actually sent the police after me?

The cop stared at me. "Miss? Are you Eddie Carmichael?"

Tossing a look over my shoulder, I realized I had no choice but to respond. "Yes, Officer. Is there a problem?"

He stretched out his arm to block my path in that supposedly non-threatening manner cops are taught to corral a person without touching them. "I'm going to need you to come with me."

I squared my shoulders. "I know my rights. Am I being charged with something?"

The officer frowned and then gave a nervous laugh. "I'm sorry, Miss. There must be a misunderstanding. You're not in trouble."

Still on guard, I asked, "Then what is this about?"

He gestured with his head. "DA Astrid radioed down that you were exiting the building and heading to the subway, unaware that he had arranged for the car service."

Again, I looked behind me, then stretched my neck back to stare up at the cold, blank windows of the office building. Was he standing in front of one of those windows watching me? Or was he still in pursuit?

"Thank you, Officer, but I'll just take the subway."

Again he gently blocked my path. "Sorry, Miss. Orders are

orders. I hope you understand. It is your safety that DA Astrid is concerned about, after all."

I wasn't going to stand and argue the point. "Fine."

Pivoting on my heel, I headed toward the black sedan where a driver was already standing at attention, ready to open the back passenger-side door.

Before I could enter, another police officer joined us. He was holding out a large, folded wool coat. "One moment, Miss Carmichael. DA Astrid said you forgot your coat."

His coat.

Again, I looked up at the dark windows above me. Their reflection only showed the facades of the surrounding buildings without giving a hint of who may be on the other side. Staring down.

As much as I wanted to toss the coat onto the dirty sidewalk, I didn't want to cause a scene. So I took it with a tight smile of gratitude before stepping into the car.

I refused to think about what had just happened the entire ride to my building.

It wasn't until I was safely in my apartment that I finally collapsed onto my mattress and curled into a ball.

My clothes smelled like his cologne.

I had fucked my boss.

My soon-to-be-married boss.

No, worse than that. If I had only just fucked him that would be bad enough, but what we had done wasn't just sex. It was an intense, world-rocking, mind-blowing experience.

The way he forced me to submit to his demands.

How he pried my legs open and licked me as if I were his last meal, giving me the best orgasm of my life.

Then the way he spanked me. Each humiliating strike of his hand causing a rush of hot heat over my skin and between my legs.

The feel of his hand covering my mouth as he punished my pussy with the size of his cock and the brute violence of his thrusts. Thank God he'd prevented me from crying out. If he hadn't, I wasn't sure I would have been able to stop myself from begging him to spank me harder, to fuck me harder, to take me harder.

The flicking of his tongue over my clit, and how I wouldn't have been able to stop myself from crying out filthy, taboo words in pleasure.

That I wanted him to dominate me. That I relished the way he forced me to submit.

That I wanted the sting against my scalp as he grabbed my hair while he thrust in deep.

That I wanted him to hold me down even as I fought him.

That I wanted to be his dirty whore, if only to hear him call me his good girl afterward.

I quit.

Two words.

My only choice.

No one survived staying that close to a fire without burning to ash.

CHAPTER 17

HARRISON

I quit.

Just two words.

The greatest sexual experience of my life and that was all she had to say.

I quit.

It was unacceptable of course. She wasn't allowed to quit.

I wouldn't let her.

After assuring my driver took her home and that the usual two car police surveillance was on her apartment, I'd resigned myself to giving her one day off.

One day to become accustomed to the idea that she was now mine.

One day away from me.

Twenty-four hours.

That was all I was willing to give her.

Not only did I need her in my bed.

I needed her at the office. We still had work to do, and clearly it wasn't bullshit that she was the best paralegal I'd ever been assigned. Her legal research was far superior to some of the attorneys in my employ.

She would make an exceptional attorney one day.

And I had every intention of making that happen.

There wasn't a doubt in my mind she was living in that rat-infested hellhole to save money for law school. She probably had her mind set on some affordable, half-assed legal education that was reasonably priced and would teach her just enough to pass the bar without throwing her into a lifetime's worth of debt.

Well, that dream of hers was over.

I was going to see to it that she was accepted at New York University School of Law. I would also pay for every penny of her tuition. I could arrange for her to go to Yale, my alma mater, but Connecticut was too far away from me. NYU Law was ranked fifth in the nation and would get her a degree she could be proud of.

But first, I needed to get her back into the office... and my bed.

In the meantime, I was forced to play the groom gallant for Mary Quinn Astrid and her doppelgänger and soulless protege—my fiancée.

It was all a waste of time, energy, and money.

I should have been in the office instead of in another over-done ballroom dripping with gold and diamonds, where people who wore designer clothes—that were probably handmade by starving children in third-world countries—while drinking hundreds of thousands of dollars worth of overpriced wine got to feel good about themselves for deigning to admit the existence of people that needed their money more than they did.

Another asinine charity event that could have given so much more had they simply cancelled the party and donated its budget, along with the invitees' donations, to the people or cause they were supposed to be helping.

The hypocrisy of these events was stifling.

But Mary Quinn Astrid insisted my attendance was mandatory. There were connections I needed to make at this party, people who would eventually become the donors that made my campaigns possible.

The English language did not currently have words to adequately express my distaste for this entire system. But it was what we had, so I had to work within it. Even with all the money in my investment portfolio that I had quadrupled since inheriting my trust fund, I couldn't dismantle the system from the outside.

To make this night even more intolerable, I was to spend the majority of it with Catherine on my arm.

I understood why we needed to be seen together at public events. I just wished she didn't insist on *talking* while at the events. Her topic of choice tonight was about the importance of God only knew what.

I'd stopped listening when she complained about how some people were so incompetent at their jobs they could not discern the difference between ivory, cream, ivory-creme, white, off-white, eggshell, and about fifty other shades of white fabric that she was considering having her wedding dress made from.

The only thing she had said all night that had merit was the possibility of buying a second home in Aspen. All I could do was pray that she'd decide to live there full-time.

It probably didn't help that my mind kept going back to Eddie.

I had tried calling her several times throughout the day, but her phone went straight to voicemail. Fortunately, the police officer in civilian attire I had placed on her floor had assured me she was home and safe. Since demanding the police presence in front of her building and in her immediate neighborhood, they had nabbed four probation violators, three dealers, two outstanding warrants for domestic abuse and one pimp.

Captain Raydar had applauded me for the *tip* I had given him and the chance to boost his precinct's closure numbers. There was no point in telling him of my personal angle. Let him think the confidential nature of the favor I requested was due to information I couldn't share with him from a case.

The sex was a surprise. Not only that it happened—I had never crossed that line before—but how intense it was. I understood that she needed time to process what happened, and under normal circumstances, I would have insisted that she take that time.

Preferably naked and next to me in bed, spending hours debating our arrangement, what it meant and what it didn't mean, and the boundaries we wanted to establish, all while resting between rounds of more incredible sex.

But at least she'd taken the car back to her crack shack of an apartment. God only knew what could have happened to her between leaving my office and getting there.

Distance-wise, it may not have been far, but danger-wise, the difference was practically insurmountable. The more I thought about it, the more I did not like her living there.

I was liking my intention of giving her twenty-four hours to process and recover even less.

"Ugh, my glass has been empty for five whole minutes," Catherine complained, stomping her foot like a child. "Who's in charge of this event? Who hired these waiters? They are completely unqualified for their positions. They should be grateful that they are even allowed to be in this beautiful room, let alone this country. So where are they? Why aren't they doing their jobs? How can my glass *still* be empty?"

Never mind that there were several servers going around

with full trays of champagne. Not to mention that the bar for cocktails, where all she had to do was walk up to get another martini, was right behind her…

Pointing that out seemed like an exercise in futility, and I did not have the patience. Instead, I took the opportunity to be rid of her for a few moments and offered to refill her drink. While waiting in line at the bar, I sent another text to Eddie demanding that she respond immediately to at least tell me that she was okay and if she planned on coming into work tomorrow, that there were things that we needed to discuss.

I wasn't stupid enough to put what had happened in my office in writing in a text message.

God only knew who could see her phone, especially that Detective Doyle she'd been flirting with. Although I had seen to it that he wouldn't have much free time for a new romance. Not with the new assignment he'd been given that would require him to work most nights on Staten Island as part of a joint task force to combat escalating crime on the ferries.

An abuse of power? Perhaps. Not that I gave a damn.

"Harrison, it's a pleasure to see you here tonight." My father clapped my shoulder as he stood next to me in line.

"Mother didn't give me an option." I gave him a half smile, knowing he could see the boredom all over my face.

"Yeah," he said. "I didn't get one either. But I'm making the most of it. After your scandal broke, she is insisting that we be seen out as much as possible at events, like it wasn't a huge scandal, and we are perfectly fine."

"Are you?" I asked.

"Am I what?"

"Perfectly fine. I know my parentage wasn't a secret and hasn't been for decades for you, but that doesn't mean the public attention wouldn't cause problems for you."

"No, the wives like to gossip but it hasn't hurt my business at all."

"That's good to hear," I said, not really believing him, but I let it go.

I was going to ask my father something else, maybe about what it was like to live in a loveless, business-contract marriage since I knew he and my mother weren't exactly a romantic match either, but I was interrupted by the emcee getting on the stage to announce that everyone was here under false pretenses.

Confused, my father and I both looked up at the stage where my mother was standing next to the emcee, and an icy feeling of dread settled in my stomach. I wasn't sure what she was doing up there, but I was positive that I was not going to like it.

She took the mic from the emcee and started spouting on about who knew what...chance encounters...true love overcoming...blah blah blah blah blah blah bullshit. Then she reached out her hand, and Catherine took it, smiling shyly at the audience.

That was the moment I realized that her white cocktail dress, embedded with Swarovski crystals that shone in the spotlight, was not a coincidence. It was a carefully curated outfit meant to make her appear sweet and innocent. Bridal.

My mother wiped away a pretend tear and said that it was her honor to welcome Catherine into the family and to announce the engagement of this beautiful, perfect woman and her son.

Fuck my life.

I had not agreed to any of this.

I was not ready to announce the engagement.

I wasn't even one hundred percent sure if I was going to go through with it. But now it didn't matter. The bell had been rung, so to speak, and every single person with a billion-dollar net worth in the greater New York City area was in this one overly pompous ballroom applauding my engagement. There was no escaping it now.

Catherine stepped off the stage and ran into my arms, laying what I guessed she assumed was a passionate kiss on my lips.

She tasted bitter, like stale wine and a crushed aspirin. Her lips were cold and slimy with gloss. It was by far the most unpleasant experience I had ever had kissing anybody, and that included Mildred Windsor the summer of ninth grade when she had braces and had just finished eating garlic bread.

There was no salvaging this moment. I had to go with it, so I dipped her and deepened the kiss, hating every single second of the display we were putting on.

When I righted her, she acted a little dizzy and flustered, which meant she was an amazing actress because that kiss may have looked hot and steamy from the outside, but in reality, it was like kissing a cold, alcoholic fish with a pain pill addiction.

As was expected of me, for the next ten minutes I smiled politely to the few waves sent my way, and accepted congratulatory handshakes and well wishes.

Then I left.

I was halfway down the stairs of the hotel when my mother caught up to me, grabbing my arm.

"Where do you think you are going?"

"Back to work," I said. "I have already lost far too much time on frivolous parties and opulent lunches."

"No, your obligation tonight is right here," she snarled. "Business can wait. You are just like your father and every other man like you. You don't understand this is just as important. This is how you make your fortune."

I took a deep breath to calm my anger before focusing back on her.

"I am not a businessman. I do not spend my day moving numbers to make me richer. I do not create money out of thin air. I do not manufacture a product, I do not sell anything. I am the district attorney. My job is to put criminals behind bars. I don't know if you've looked around lately, Mother, but New York is not limited to Fifth or Park Avenues. There are real problems in this city that need to be addressed."

"Who do you think you are, Superman?" Her face twisted in rage, or at least as much as it could considering the most recent Botox injections. "There is nothing you can do to protect New York tonight. Lawyers' offices are closed, and there are no judges currently awake. Actually, that's not true. The only judges awake that you need to concern yourself with tonight, the only criminals you need to concern yourself with tonight, are those inside the ballroom who will fund your next campaign. And while we're out here talking, we need to discuss your wedding guest list. That little whore at your desk is not invited."

My hands clenched into fists. "Don't you dare call—"

I stopped myself just in time as Mary Quinn Astrid's eyes lit up with unholy interest. Like the unfeeling shark she was, she smelled blood in the water.

There was no fucking way I was leading her back to Eddie.

Tightening my lips over my bared teeth, I finished, "Anyone on my staff a whore or this entire fiasco you've orchestrated is finished. Do you understand me?"

"I am your mother. Show me some respect."

"I'll show it to you when you earn it."

She placed her hands on her hips. "You get rid of that trollop working for you or I will."

"Remember who you're threatening, Mother. I'm not some cowering waiter or maid in your employ."

"You have your position because of me, and I can take it away just as easily."

"I have my position because I'm a damn good attorney who earned it."

She huffed. "I'm not having this fight with you in public, Harrison. You may not care about our reputation but I—"

"Don't you fucking talk to me about reputations."

She gasped as she grabbed the strand of pearls around her neck. "Don't you curse at me!"

I threw up my hand and once more turned toward the door. "This conversation is over."

She gripped my upper arm, sinking her well-manicured claws into me. "We still need to discuss your wedding guest list!"

"I would never subject anybody who works with me to the atrocity that you are no doubt going to throw with Catherine. I have done my duty for tonight. I'm leaving."

"How will it look? What will people say?"

"Tell them my office has an emergency, and I must go." I tried pulling my arm from her grip, but her acrylic nails sank in deeper, threatening to rip into the fabric of my coat.

"What will Catherine and I tell all of your guests?"

"I don't have any guests in there, Mother. It's a charity event. Even if it wasn't, this impromptu engagement party is yours and Catherine's to deal with. Tell them whatever you want. I do not give a fuck."

"You are just as bad as your sister."

I knew if I riled her up any more and didn't give her a story she could sell, she would take it out on Rose.

I took a deep breath and said through clenched teeth, "Just tell everybody that I'm working on one of the biggest cases in the country, and a witness came forward, and I had to go. Tell them that I'm working on keeping everybody in that room safe."

"I don't—"

"I need to get back to work." I spoke over her, pulling my arm from her talons. "So I can help make this city a safer place. This engagement party is not about me. It's not even about Catherine and me. It is about you salvaging your reputation. I agreed to let you set up this marriage to that end. Now you can go inside and tell everyone how hard I'm working to keep them safe and make yourself the martyr. I don't give a fuck."

I didn't give her a chance to respond.

What she was going to say didn't really matter. I refused to listen to it.

My car service was waiting just outside the hotel. I got in the back, and we took off. I had no intention of going back to the office to get more work done. I needed to see her.

"Take me to Ms. Carmichael's apartment," I told the driver.

Thankfully, he had been one of the ones shuttling her to and from the office the past week, so he knew where he was going. We were there in under thirty minutes, and in that time, I tried calling her again. I even sent her a few more texts.

The text messages remained unread, and the calls went straight to voicemail.

I didn't appreciate being ignored. I pushed aside the cold, clammy feeling running up my spine, wondering if she was safe and if she was okay, needing to know that nothing happened to her on her way home yesterday.

When we got to her building, I ran up the disgusting stairs to her apartment, and knocked.

There was no answer.

I pounded the door harder.

"Open the door, or I'll break it down," I ground out.

There was no response. The assigned officer approached with a wary look as his hand reached back to what was certainly a concealed weapon.

Reaching into my jacket pocket, I flipped open my wallet and flashed my DA badge. I then gestured toward the door. "Reluctant witness."

The guy nodded and moved one flight down.

I knocked again. "Do not test me. This thing is only being

held together by dust and scum. I could break through it without a second thought."

Finally, I heard some movement behind the door before it cracked open.

Eddie's face peeked out the door from behind the chain.

"Leave me alone," she warned.

CHAPTER 18

HARRISON

"Open the door," I demanded.

"Leave," she said.

"Open the door. I need to talk to you. It's urgent."

She rolled her eyes, and I had to suppress the urge to remind her what happened to bad girls who mouthed off. The temptation to threaten her with another spanking was definitely there, but I didn't want her to think that was why I was here.

There was no way I could lay my hands on her ass and not fuck her again.

But before that happened, we needed to talk.

She opened the door, and I first noticed the soft light coming from around the apartment. There was the warm, glowing light of single, spaced-out flames, and the cloying, sweet scent of cheap imitation vanilla. There were no lights on anywhere, just a handful of candles spread around the room.

My rage was instantaneous.

While I had been giving her space, she had called that piece of shit Doyle.

I twisted my right fist into my left palm. "Well, isn't this a cozy, romantic setting. Am I interrupting a date with the detective? Did you try to hide him in the closet, or is he in the back bedroom?"

"There is no back bedroom. There is no front bedroom either," she said, wrapping a large, worn blanket around herself, making me wonder what she could possibly have on underneath it.

Some scandalous, sexy lingerie for her date? Did he know that as he licked that pussy the little extra saltiness he would be tasting was me?

I ignored her and pushed my way into her home, looking for the detective or whatever man she was hiding there. All I could think was, how dare she have someone here for a date after having sex with me. The way she moaned and shook under me, the way her tight little pussy had clamped down around my cock while I fucked her, I would have thought she'd be too sore to take another lover so quickly.

Maybe she had this date planned. I didn't know much about her. Maybe she was in a relationship, and he couldn't satisfy her the way I could. I liked that thought. It made me feel stronger and possessive. I liked the idea that I could be taking her from a lesser man.

"Mr. Astrid, I told you no one else is here. Please leave," she pleaded.

"Harrison," I snapped back. "Where did you hide him?"

"Okay, fine, Harrison. There is nobody else in this apartment. It is just me. Now, what do you want?"

"I want to know why you're not answering your phone."

"Because the battery died," she said, like it was obvious.

"Then you should plug it in and recharge it. It should be on. You should be reachable at all hours."

I looked around some more, not really believing that she was alone. "Why are the lights all off?" My breath floated in front of my face. "And why is it so cold in here?"

I took another look around the apartment, not looking for a person, just taking in my surroundings. It was the saddest thing I had ever seen. The apartment looked like the beginning of a commercial asking for donations.

This brilliant, beautiful woman was living in squalor.

"Because my landlord decided that his tenants didn't need electricity today." She looked exhausted, like the fight in her had just drained out.

For a second, I felt guilty. Had I done that, had I been the one to break her?

No, I wasn't the one who touched her electricity. I wasn't the one freezing her out.

"What do you mean the landlord decided?" I asked.

"I mean, the landlord has been turning off the heat or the water or the electricity every couple of days for the last few months."

"Why would your landlord turn off any of the utilities to the building? There are laws to protect you and other tenants from that. He could face not only fines but serious jail time for this type of abuse."

"You think I don't know that? I would bet money that even he knows it too, but that doesn't mean he cares. We could take him to court, but nothing would ever come of it except I would lose what little shelter from the elements I have."

She pulled the blanket tighter around her, and I realized she wasn't hiding her clothes underneath. She was hiding the fact that she had my wool coat on, despite being inside.

She was cold.

This apartment was frigid, and I was in a tuxedo with a long cashmere coat over it. I was insulated from the elements, and I was cold. I could only imagine how cold she must have been.

This had to end now.

"Is there a specific reason he's torturing his tenants?" I asked.

It could be an issue where the electricity pulled too much energy into the wiring, which needed to be updated. There were grants for older buildings that would handle that, but maybe he wasn't aware. Or maybe a transformer needed to be fixed or there was something that could be handled quickly.

"Because he wants us to leave so he can sell it to some investor who's going to flip it and turn it into overpriced condos. Probably already has a buyer or group of buyers lined up, some yuppies who think this is an up-and-coming neighborhood and are okay with the idea of gentrifying it." She said it as if that was the most basic thing in the world and not extremely illegal. "Why are you here, Harrison?"

"So then, why do you still live here?" The question had to be asked.

"Because this is where I live, this is what I have to deal with, and this is what a lot of people who weren't born with a trust fund have to deal with."

"No, it's not. What your landlord is doing is illegal. Just because you were born without privilege does not mean you have lesser rights than those of us who were. What's his name?"

I asked this while looking around, taking my phone out of my breast pocket, ready to start the process to bring her landlord here immediately. It was hard not to notice how little she had in this apartment.

Paralegals did not earn a lot, but she should have been making more than to live like this. She should have been making more than enough to afford at least a warm studio in a better area, with a real kitchen and an actual bed.

She laughed.

Apparently, what I had said was hilarious. She actually

doubled over laughing, clutching her stomach. After a few moments, she calmed down and wiped a tear from her eye.

"I'm not telling you his name. Now, please. Leave. You've seen how the other half lives. It's terrible. Your little field trip to the other side of the tracks has concluded, and you can just leave me to it in peace."

She shifted to stand directly in front of me like she was trying to keep my attention on her and not around the small room and the tattered, mismatched furniture that had probably already been battered and threadbare before she dragged it up the three stories to this shit hole.

"Okay, have it your way. Don't tell me. I have resources to fix this on my own."

I dialed Captain Raydar, knowing he would see this as another tip instead of the personal favor it was. After giving him the address, I told him I wanted the landlord found and brought to Eddie's apartment in cuffs if necessary within the next fifteen minutes.

Disconnecting the call, I turned to my stubborn little paralegal. "Pack a bag. Now."

I watched as her mouth opened, then closed, opened, and then closed again, like she was searching for something to say.

"Don't argue with me," I said. "Pack your things, or I will."

Clutching the edges, she crossed her arms within the blanket. "You can't just waltz in here and demand I move. That's not how this works. You are my boss, not my father or my boyfriend. In fact, you're not even my boss anymore. I quit, remember?"

"Nice try. I'll drag you out of here naked under that coat if necessary. I'm more than capable of providing a wardrobe..." My gaze scanned over her. "And anything else you may need."

She winced. "Thanks, but I don't need a sugar daddy."

Fuck. Instant hard on. Just the idea of those pretty lips calling me her daddy as I spanked her ass and pulled her hair had me so aroused, I was almost willing to fuck her on the floor.

I grabbed her chin and lifted her face to mine. "I wouldn't test me, little one. Hearing you call me daddy while my cock is buried deep inside of you is just the kind of dirty kink I get off on."

She gasped and stared up at me, speechless. Good. My patience was wearing thin. It had already been a long, unproductive day.

To be honest, I had never understood why men liked having their women call them daddy. It always felt a bit creepy, but how her cheeks reddened made it worth it. I rather liked the idea of providing for her, protecting her like she was mine. Not my child, obviously, but I liked the idea of punishing her and spoiling her and being the one she came to for everything.

She still stood there, not moving, so I started prowling around her apartment, grabbing clothes and other things, shoving them into the worn tote bag that was on the floor.

"Tonight, we're getting you moved into a new place. Tomorrow morning, you are taking my black card, and you will go to Saks, and you'll buy a new wardrobe that is suitable to be a paralegal at my desk."

"The hell I am. I'm not letting you treat me like some bought and paid for whore. I didn't even use that card to buy lunch."

Her arms folded in front of her chest, and she stuck out her jaw like being stubborn was some sort of virtue.

Really, she looked like a petulant child. Maybe I would have her call me daddy.

"Only I'm allowed to call you my dirty little whore and only when I'm fucking you. If I hear you refer to yourself as a whore again, I'll take off my belt, understood?"

She tilted her head to the side. "What's the matter? Does the truth hurt?"

I tossed what I had been holding to the floor and stormed toward her.

She backed up so quickly she slammed against the wall by the window. The flash of red, blue, and white lights from the cop cars below played across her pale face.

"No, but that cute, insubordinate ass of yours is about to hurt."

"Stop saying such things!"

Before I could respond, there was a loud bang on her door.

I opened it to see a very short, round man in a ripped, formerly white tank top and tragically threadbare jeans.

"Bitch, you called the police on me?" he barked, pointing his finger past me at Eddie. "The electricity will be out for the rest of the week and I'll be sure to let the other tenants know you're to blame."

"Are you the owner of this building?" I asked.

I had intended to be reasonable. I was just going to name-drop a few people and tell him that he had a week to clean this shit up before they came to inspect. Then I saw his smug, arrogant, filthy, shameless demeanor. He really was doing this intentionally and acting like he was going to get away with it, probably because he had for so long.

Fuck this guy. This wasn't a landlord struggling. This was a slumlord.

As soon as I finished the case against the O'Murphy clan, I was coming after slumlords with a vengeance.

"Yes, and you're trespassing cuz you're not on the fucking lease for this apartment."

The foul odor radiating from his mouth was enough to turn my stomach and make me want to take a step back.

"Do you know who I am?" I asked. "Or better yet, do you know how many laws this building is in violation of, and that's before you even count the very illegal tactics to force your residents out?"

"I don't care who the fuck you are. I don't care if you're some cop or some spoiled little pussy-bitch who watched one too many episodes of *Suits*, and now thinks they know the law."

"I'm a district attorney. And I will not rest until you spend the rest of your life behind bars."

Anger ran through my veins. Anger at my mother, my friends and their fucked-up connections, and at my fucking paralegal who still wasn't packing.

Luckily for me, I had the perfect target in front of me.

"I ain't doing shit. Your little girlfriend's getting kicked out cuz she ain't on the lease. And if you think having those cops parked outside is intimidating me, you can fuck off."

"No, she is leaving voluntarily, and you are going to spend the next several months in court, where I will personally make your life a living hell. By the time I am done with you, the city of New York will own this building and you won't get a penny. In fact, you are going to spend the rest of your miserable little life paying off the fees I throw at you."

"You can't do—"

"I can, and I will." I took a step closer to the filthy rat of a man in front of me, holding my breath as I spoke. "You had better hope no one dies or even gets so much as the fucking sniffles while you've had the heat off, or I will make sure you are charged with manslaughter and criminally negligent homicide. Do you hear me?"

The color in the man's pock-marked face drained, and he took a few steps back while he looked around, his mouth opening and closing like he was trying to find the words to explain or excuse this atrocity.

"Expect a visit from the housing authority. Turn the fucking electricity back on. Now." I slammed the door in his face, turned to look at Eddie, and yelled, "Why aren't you packed yet?"

"Did you seriously just get me kicked out of my apartment? I have nowhere else to go."

"I have already explained that I have an apartment lined up for you."

"And I explained I'm not going to stay at your place and be your whore. I'm not going to be your dirty little secret. I'm not going to be your little kept woman in a hotel room."

I rolled my eyes and looked at her. "Stop being so dramatic. We're leaving now. I'm not putting you in a hotel or my apartment. There is somewhere else I can let you stay while I get this shit show sorted."

"You can't just—"

Her words were cut off when I gave up, picked her up, threw her over my shoulder, and carried her out of the building.

CHAPTER 19

EDDIE

The second Harrison put me in the back seat of his sedan, I slid across and tried to get out of the car through the other door.

Apparently, the driver was on Harrison's side and he locked it. I shot the driver a dirty look and sat there with my arms crossed, stuck in the Mercedes-Benz.

"Where are you taking me?" I asked through clenched teeth.

He didn't respond, just stared at his phone, typing occasionally, refusing to look at me or answer my questions.

The Mercedes pulled into traffic. The apartment buildings went from rundown, seven- and eight-story tenements, to industrial-style high-rises covered in glass, to older but well-maintained brownstone buildings. It was a journey across the economic spectrum, ending in old money New York, where baroque motifs gave the entire block a beautifully elegant, historical feel.

We arrived at a brownstone building that looked to be about fifteen or so stories high and had a uniformed doorman standing in front of the glass doors, waiting to open them for us.

I wasn't sure where we were, the Upper East or Upper West Side, but I knew I didn't belong here. I crossed my arms over my chest and looked at Harrison, waiting for him to explain himself or at least tell me where we were.

He grabbed his leather laptop case and the tote bag filled with my clothes and got out of the car.

I didn't follow.

As far as I was concerned, there was no reason to get out of the car.

He leaned down and peered inside with a furrowed brow. "Eddie, get out of the car and follow me inside, or I will pick you up and throw you over my shoulder again. I do not have time for your childish antics."

One look at this man, and I knew he wasn't bluffing. He would absolutely pick me up and throw me over his shoulder like a petulant child. Again.

And I didn't think anyone walking along the streets here would be any more inclined to stop him than they would be in my neighborhood. If anything, they'd chastise me for disturbing the peace.

God forbid my kidnapping inconvenience anyone else.

I knew I was being dramatic, but I was cold, hungry, unemployed, and now homeless. That earned me the right to a pissy attitude in my book. With an annoyed huff, I slid out of the car and followed Harrison into the building.

The lobby alone was stunning, with a beautiful marble mosaic on the floor as well as other Gilded Age details like the fleur-de-lis in the molding and the stunning design painted around the base of the crystal chandelier that hung down from the two-story ceiling.

The doorman greeted Harrison by name and asked if his guest needed to sign in. I assumed that meant me.

"No, thank you," Harrison said to the doorman. "It would be best for all involved if nobody knew she was here. However, she will be leaving each morning for work and returning late. Please see that the other doormen are aware of her presence and know which apartment she's in."

"Yes, sir, Mr. Astrid," the doorman responded, then tipped his hat to me and called me Miss. I was not aware people still tipped their hats. Maybe the rich paid extra for outdated chivalry.

"I'm putting you in apartment fifteen oh seven," Harrison said. "At least until we can find something more permanent."

"I don't know what you think is going to happen here. But I am not okay with having you pay for an apartment for me or put me up in your little sex den."

"I'm not entirely sure what a sex den is," Harrison said, quirking a brow at me. "This is an investment building for me. I'm putting you in a furnished apartment that is usually rented out to corporate clients for long-term visiting executives."

"It's not like I can afford any better place to live. Where I live now is affordable."

"That was my next question," Harrison said. "Why are you living in the slums? Paralegals make more than crackheads. Are you dealing with some type of addiction, a gambling debt, or something?"

"Sort of," I admitted.

Harrison looked at me, his eyes wide. He was not expecting that answer, so I clarified.

"I bet on my future with a high-interest student loan backed by the federal government, designed to keep the poor where they are while letting them dream of more," I said, not bothering to hide my bitterness. "I'm trying not to start my career half a million dollars in debt, so I'm trying to pay off my undergraduate degree while also saving for law school."

"You're smart enough for scholarships," he said.

I couldn't help but laugh again at the arrogance and the complete lack of awareness of what reality was like for other people. It continued to astonish me.

First, he actually thought people gave a fuck about housing court. The idea he had that it was designed to protect the tenants and not the landlords was hilarious. And now he thought that scholarships were easy to come by or that they would actually make a dent in the cost of higher education. Or that even if you got one to pay for your tuition, it didn't matter because you still needed money for food, rent, books, and countless other necessities.

"Why are you doing this?" I asked, not having the energy to enlighten this privileged dick about how the world worked for the rest of us.

"Because I need you at work, I need you doing your job, and I need to know that you're safe. I can't have my paralegal, the only one who knows the case that I'm working on, in danger."

"I'm not your paralegal anymore."

"Agree to disagree."

He led me to the apartment, and when he opened the door, it took my breath away.

I didn't know what I expected, but it wasn't this wide-open floor plan with massive bay windows and state-of-the-art kitchen appliances. It actually had a full kitchen. Not just a mini fridge and a hot plate tucked into one corner of the apartment, but a full kitchen with an oven and everything. The living room was massive, and then another hallway told me there was at least one separate bedroom and bathroom, if not more.

"Take a look around. Let me know if there's anything else you'll need."

I spun around the living room and indulged for a moment in

the fantasy of staying somewhere like this place. I dreamed for a moment that a home like this could actually be my life.

Then I turned and headed for the door before it hurt too much.

"Where do you think you're going?" Harrison asked.

"Home, assuming I still have one. If not, I guess I'll have to see if I can stay with a friend. Since you got me evicted and all."

"No, you're staying here," he said slowly, like I didn't understand.

I reached for the front door. "No, I'm not."

Harrison grabbed my wrist, not hard enough to hurt, but firmly enough to let me know that he wasn't letting me out of the apartment. He got between me and the door, blocking the only path I knew out.

"Let me go, Mr. *Astrid*," I said.

"I told you not to call me that," he repeated.

"Fine, let me go, *Harrison*."

"Better, but no."

"I'm not your whore. You do not get to trade an apartment for sexual favors."

"I never said you were my whore. I never treated you like my whore. Do you want to talk about what happened yesterday? Fine. If you want me to spank you again like the brat you're being, I am more than happy to oblige, but you are not leaving this apartment."

"I need..." My words trailed off as I tried to figure out what I needed.

I needed to know that I had earned my success honestly. I needed to not be attracted to a man who was not only my boss but engaged to be married to another woman. I needed to feel in control again, something I hadn't felt since the moment I met him. I needed to get away from him and his seductive influence.

I needed him out of my life.

His hand moved to my face, cupping my jaw and tilting my head up so my gaze met his. "Tell me what you need."

That warm, floaty feeling started to build in my core again, and I didn't know how to tell him I needed to run as far away from him as possible. So I didn't say anything.

"Okay, let me tell you what I need, and we can go from there."

I nodded.

"What I need is very simple here, Eddie. I need to know that you are safe and will make it to work on time. I need this day to be over because it has been unbelievably long and wretched. I need you to let me do this for you right now. We can talk about it again tomorrow, and we can work out something more permanent, but I need to know that you are not going to freeze to death in your sleep. Or be accosted by crack addicts trying to sell your kidneys for a hit."

"Fine," I said, giving in. "I will stay for now."

My eyes flashed down to his lips and then back to his eyes. We were standing close enough for the warmth of his body to radiate into mine, for the scent of the whiskey that he had drunk earlier to waft between us.

"Good, now let's discuss what I want," he stated.

My mouth went dry. Was this the part where he treated me like a whore who needed to serve him to earn my keep? Since my heart was in my throat, I just nodded.

His thumb moved over my lower lip. "I need you under me. I need to feel this sweet mouth wrapped around my cock. I need to hear you moan again."

He pushed his thumb into my mouth, forcing me to suck it.

As he mesmerized me with the lust-filled look in his gaze, I could almost feel the sting of his hand on my ass like some sort of pleasurable, phantom pain.

Heat pooled between my legs. The dirty truth of it was, I wanted to be his whore. I wanted him to force me to my knees.

I wanted it... but it was the last thing I needed.

Tightening my abdominal muscles to brace for his inevitable rage, I wrapped my hand around his wrist and gently pulled his thumb out of my mouth.

I took a step back... and then poked the beast. "How does it feel to want?" I challenged.

CHAPTER 20

HARRISON

*T*here was the barest of moments when what she'd said didn't register.

Someplace in my mind asserted that she couldn't possibly have just said what I thought I heard.

To challenge me in that way would be akin to a kitten going up to a lion and biting its paw just to get a rise out of him.

Bold. Intriguing. Sexy. Confident.

Sure, it was all those things, but it was also the very definition of *begging for it.*

The apartment was silent, except for the muted sounds of the city filtering through the windows.

Very calmly, I shrugged out of my coat, folded it in half, and draped it over the nearest chair. I then unbuckled and flipped open the leather satchel I used as a laptop bag and pulled out the small, black plastic bag nestled inside.

Turning my back to her, I dumped the sack's contents out onto the hall table, cracking open the hard plastic packaging of one item, while tearing off the tag of another.

Finally, the silence was too much for her. "In case it wasn't clear, that was your cue to leave. I said I'd stay here for the night but that's only because you made going back to my own apartment a little tricky. Once the dust clears, I'm sure I'll be able to convince my landlord to forget about it."

I kept my back turned as I unhooked my gold cuff links and untied my tuxedo bow tie before tossing them both in the expensive Murano glass bowl.

She sighed heavily. "I'm hoping I can rely on you for a decent referral after all this. I would appreciate it if you could look past our... personal differences... and focus on my work product. I'll need something when I start searching for another position."

She was twisting the knife but I continued to ignore her as I unbuckled my belt and whipped it through the loops before wrapping it in a circle and tossing it on top of the other contents of the bowl.

Truth be told, my rage was such that I didn't trust myself with the belt around her.

She sighed again. "Are you going to say anything?"

I straightened my shoulders and tilted my head to one side, then the other, cracking my neck. "Yes... Run."

"What?"

I shrugged out of my tuxedo jacket. "I suggest you run because you are not going to like what happens when I catch you."

Her audible gasp was all I heard before she took off down the hallway, leaving only her crumpled blanket on the floor in her wake.

Gathering the items I had purchased earlier, I followed.

Before I could turn the corner, she had slammed the nearest bedroom door shut.

I had planned on doing this in the main bedroom but one of the guest rooms would suffice.

Without bothering to knock, I stepped back and kicked the door open.

Eddie was standing in the center of the room but she quickly scurried to the far corner. "I know you're mad—"

I denied it. "Mad? Babygirl, I'm looking at mad in the rearview mirror."

The items I was holding got tossed into the center of the bed.

Her eyes widened at the lube, butt plug, spider gag and other toys.

"Hell no!"

The corner of my mouth lifted as I untucked my tuxedo shirt and pulled it over my head. "Screaming here will help you even less than back at my office."

She started for the doorway.

I blocked her path, kicking the door shut. "Not so fast."

"Harrison. Let's talk about this."

I shook my head. "Too late. I wanted to talk. You said no."

"I've changed my mind."

I stalked toward her. "So have I. Take off your clothes."

"What happens if I say no?"

I shrugged. "I tear them off."

"You can't do this."

I tilted my head to the side, observing her. "Tell you what, babygirl. Prove to me you're not turned on right now at the idea of being forced to submit to me, and I'll turn right around and leave."

She swallowed. "Of course, I'm not turned on. You're my boss —former boss. You have a fiancée—"

"A fake fiancée as part of a business agreement."

"What's the difference?"

"For one, I have no intention of fucking her. Unlike my intentions toward you."

She crossed her arms. "Well, that's not going to happen because I've already told you I'm not turned on."

"I'm afraid I'm going to need to see some evidence proving it."

"How am I supposed to—"

I flicked my eyes down then back up.

She shook her head. "Oh, no! No way."

"Do you want to get out of here or not?"

Her gaze traveled around the room.

I smirked. "You're wasting your time. The only way out is through me—or under me."

"I could sue you for this."

"I'll save you the time. How much do you want as a settlement? A million? Two? Ten? I'll pay it."

Her shoulders slumped. "How am I supposed to prove it to you?"

"Turn around and place your hands on the wall."

After a moment's hesitation, she did as she was told.

I approached her, already smelling the warmth of her skin and the faint remnants of her perfume.

She was wearing a gray hoodie with *I Heart NY* on it and a pair of leggings.

Stepping behind her, I ordered, "Kick off your sneakers."

She inhaled a trembling breath but slipped out of her simple canvas sneakers.

Standing close but not touching her, I said, "Now slide off your leggings."

She turned her head to glance at me over her shoulder.

I barked, "Face the wall."

She whipped her head forward again. Then she slipped her thumbs into the waistband of her leggings and slowly bent in half as she pulled them down over her hips and thighs until they pooled at her feet.

She hissed the moment my hands spanned her naked hips under the long hem of her hoodie.

"Step out of your leggings and push your hips back."

Her breathing was labored as she slowly did as I commanded.

Aching to touch her, but refusing myself the pleasure until she admitted defeat, I kicked her leggings away and nudged her legs open further with my foot.

She was now doubled over, her palms pressed against the wall with her hips pushed out.

I knelt behind her.

"What are you—"

I cut her off. "I didn't give you permission to speak."

After placing my hands on the backs of her thighs, I leaned forward and ran my tongue over her sweet, fully aroused pussy. I moaned. "Tastes like winning."

"It doesn't prove anything."

I caressed her pussy, teasing her clit with the two middle fingers of my right hand. "It proves everything."

Rising, I stretched my arm out and grabbed the silver metal butt plug. Leaning over her bent-over body, I said, "Open your mouth."

Eddie whimpered but did as she was told.

I pushed the wide plug between her lips and rolled it over her tongue. "Good girl. Get it nice and wet because next it's going up your tight little asshole."

She tried to shake her head and talk around the plug. "No! I'de neber—"

"Shhh. Don't talk with your mouth full."

After pulling the plug free, I laid a restraining hand on her lower back. "Push out your hips."

I ran the rounded tip of the plug between her cheeks.

She clenched.

Shifting my hand from her back, I spanked her several times. "Do. Not. Clench."

She sniffed. "Please, I don't want you to stick anything in my ass."

I leaned over her and nipped at her earlobe before whispering, "How does it feel to want?"

Before she could react, I pressed the tip of the butt plug against her puckered hole.

She shifted her hips forward.

"Do you want another spanking?"

"No."

"Then push your hips out and don't clench."

Watching as the delicate skin around her hole resisted, I pushed harder until the plug finally slipped past her tight muscle ring.

"Ow! Ow! Ow! No! Take it out."

I tapped the circular, fake-diamond handle of the plug before giving it a twist.

The movement caused her to rise up on her toes, pushing her ass higher in the air. She protested even louder. "Please! It's too full. It hurts."

I chuckled. "This is just your trial plug. Wait until I force you to accept the inflatable one."

A tremor wracked her body.

I reached onto the bed and picked up another toy. "Now turn around and get on your knees."

She obeyed but not without a wince as she tried to move with the intrusion deep inside her ass.

"Take off your hoodie."

I was pleased to see she didn't have a bra on. I held up the spider gag. "Now be a good girl and open your mouth nice and wide."

A tear slid over her cheek before she licked her lips and then opened her mouth.

I gingerly placed the metal prongs into her mouth, prying her lips open, before buckling it behind her neck. Taking a step back, I slowly lowered my zipper and pulled out my already erect cock.

Her eyes widened.

I grasped her chin. "You're going to suck my cock like a good little whore, or I'm going to get my belt and make you wish you had. Understood?"

She nodded, more tears falling down her cheeks.

I traced her lips with the head of my cock before pushing it into her mouth. I threw my head back and groaned, trying to resist the urge to make her deep-throat me right then and there.

Her hands pushed against my thighs while I slowly thrust into her mouth.

The gag prevented her from biting down or closing her lips.

I had complete control over her.

Her shoulders hitched and she gurgled and gagged each time the tip of my cock pressed against the back of her throat.

I stroked her hair before twisting my fist into it. "Do you like being forced to submit to me, baby? Do you like me forcing my cock down your throat?"

She moaned before nodding.

I smiled. Goddamn, she was the perfect woman for me. I thrust in deeper, gagging her.

Her tongue swept the sensitive underside of my shaft as I increased the pace. I applied pressure on her head, pushing her forward. "That's it, babygirl. Take my cock in your sweet mouth. I want to feel your nose against my stomach."

Her eyes widened as she tried to plead with me despite the gag and my cock down her throat.

Ignoring her pleas, I pressed harder. Pushing past her gag reflex until the ring of muscle at the back of her throat clenched around the head of my shaft. "Fuck yeah, baby. That's it. Swallow me."

I pushed in the last few inches until her chin brushed my balls and the tip of her cute nose hit my stomach.

Another time, I would last longer and savor the feeling, but not tonight. Tonight her submission and the feel of her throat was too wickedly amazing.

I thrust several more times before I eased back and grasped my saliva-slicked cock to release a warm stream of come onto her tongue.

I leaned down and helped her to her feet before I pushed her back to sit on the edge of the bed. After grabbing her legs and spreading them, I gave her an order. "I'm going to lick this delicious pussy and when I'm done, I better see my come still melting on your tongue."

Kneeling before her, I flicked my tongue over her clit and didn't relent until her hips bucked and her body trembled with her release.

When I rose over her body, her mouth was still open from the gag. My come pooled in the center of her tongue. I pushed my fingers past her lips and coated them with my own release.

I then flipped her onto her stomach. By now I was already hard again.

I unbuckled the spider gag and asked, "Are you ready to take my cock up your tight ass?"

The moment the gag fell away, she looked over her shoulder. "Please, Harrison. You can't!"

Pulling her up onto her knees, I spanked her ass several times for good measure with my free hand before I tugged on the handle of her butt plug.

Eddie groaned and fell forward onto her forearms to bury her head in the coverlet.

I watched her asshole stretch around the plug and resist as I slowly pulled it out.

Eddie moaned as the pressure increased.

Finally, her asshole gave way and the plug popped out. The moment it did, I swept my come-coated fingers over her still gaping hole.

Preparing her.

Stepping close to the edge of the bed, my cock brushed her ass cheeks as the fronts of my thighs brushed the backs of hers. I ran my hand over her back and twisted her long locks in my hand.

I wrenched on her hair and growled, "What do you say?"

She whimpered. "Don't make me say it."

I notched the tip of my cock in her still slightly gaping hole that was now a tempting cream pie. "Say it. Show me what a good little whore you are. Beg me to fuck your ass."

She shifted her hips as she rasped, "I'm scared."

I reached around her and cupped her breast, pinching her nipple, already knowing how much she liked that. "You should be. This is going to hurt like hell, but I know you're going to like the pain. Aren't you, baby?"

Her body jerked under my grasp and my filthy promise.

"Oh God! Treat me like your little whore. Fuck my... fuck my ass."

I thrust forward.

Her scream mingled with my guttural groan of pleasure.

Tightening my hold on her hair, I gripped her hip and thrust again. Pushing her past her limits as my cock stretched her asshole. Watching her little hole stretch around my girth was the single sexiest thing I had ever witnessed.

I thrust again, each time pressing into her deeper. "Where's my cock, baby?"

She moaned. "In my ass."

"Does it hurt, babygirl?"

She breathed heavily, her smooth back glowing with a slick sheen of sweat. "Yes. Oh God, it hurts."

I pounded in several more times. "Do you want me to come in your ass?"

"Yes, please, please, please come!"

I spanked her right cheek. "That's not what I asked."

"Yes, please come in my ass."

"Why?"

"Because I'm your good little whore."

Still I held off for several more minutes to press my fingers against her clit, needing to feel her come one more time before I did.

The moment her body stiffened then trembled, I let out a roar and smashed my hips against her ass as I spilled my hot come deep inside of her.

* * *

EDDIE MOANED when I swept her into my arms after stripping out of the rest of my clothes.

I kissed her forehead. "Shhh, babygirl. It's okay. I've got you. I started a nice warm shower for us."

Her head rested against my shoulder. "This was wrong," she whispered. "You were my boss. You're a married man."

I carried her over the bathroom threshold. "No, sweetheart. It wasn't wrong and I'm not married. That woman is nothing more than a business deal. I've told you that. *And I am still your boss.*"

She shook her head which I ignored, keeping her in my arms while I stepped under the hot stream of water.

Swiping the loose curls and water away from her face, she looked up at me. "We can't keep doing this. It needs to be over. You understand that, right? I've already lost my job and my home. How much more do you want to ruin my life before you realize you have to leave me alone?"

I looked down at her beautiful face and didn't answer.

Because there was no way I was going to say, out loud, that I had no problem destroying every facet of her life and my own if it meant keeping her.

CHAPTER 21

EDDIE

*H*e was gone by the time I woke up.
Next to my pillow was a note.

SEE YOU AT THE OFFICE. *Don't even think about not showing up.*

Remember, I have one of the largest police forces in the world at my disposal.

And I won't hesitate to use them to find you.

Harrison

WELL, *good morning to you too.*

I crumpled the note and tossed it in the bedside garbage bin.

Then I fell back against the pillows as I pulled the sheet up over my naked breasts.

I didn't even know how to begin processing what happened last night.

Being with Harrison was like surviving a midnight tornado

and then needing a FEMA disaster report after the storm to take stock of what the fuck happened during the darkness and chaos.

It wasn't even useful to consider the whole boss-employee dynamic at this point. Clearly the man wasn't the least bit concerned about the consequences of a relationship with me to either of our careers.

And if I were honest, deep down, as much as I used it as a shield to keep him at bay, I knew he wouldn't really allow my entire career to be ruined by this. Harrison was an arrogant, domineering, possessive, demanding tyrant at times but he was also an intelligent, compassionate man who lived by a higher set of morals than the typical trust fund baby.

There was no way to be certain, but I had to believe he would make sure I landed on my feet if I were forced from the DA's office by a scandal.

So that left just us.

Well, not really just us. Strictly speaking, I was currently in a threesome.

Me, Harrison, and his horrible fiancée.

Try as I might to conjure up righteous anger for that despicable woman, I had lived in New York long enough to know that society marriages where there was no love lost happened all the time.

It didn't mean I wanted to be his mistress. Hell, no. But it did mean I didn't feel the usual moral guilt I would if the man were truly cheating on a woman he professed to love and wanted to marry.

Of course, that meant there was no way whatsoever that what we were doing was going to last. I might be willing to turn a blind eye to the whole fake fiancée thing but only for so long. The moment that man said I do, as far as I was concerned he was entering into a binding contract.

Whether that was with society or God was for someone far

more religious than me to decide. I just knew that as a future attorney, I respected contracts and I wouldn't be a party to breaking one. Fake relationship or not.

Okay, fiancée processed in the tornado report.

Which again brought me back to us.

There was a doomsday clock attached to this relationship. For most women that would have been a deal breaker but it wasn't like I was on the hunt for a husband. I was only twenty-four. Marriage was the furthest thing from my mind, especially with law school and my career to pursue.

And it wasn't like Harrison would be the first boyfriend in history to have a doomsday clock attached to him. Women dated men they knew they'd never marry in a million years all the time. They did it for all kinds of reasons. For the sex, for the money, for the fun of it. Just because I never had didn't mean I wasn't capable of it.

That was when a small voice inside my head warned me, *You're not capable of it.*

Although the illicit nature of our relationship might be adding to the sexy, taboo nature of it, there was no denying I was heading into dangerous territory.

Harrison was tapping into parts of my personality I never knew existed.

Dark, scary corners of my personality that relished in being called a dirty whore while being forced to submit to ever-increasing, degrading, brutal sex.

We had only had sex twice and both times it was twisted and depraved and mind-blowing. Never in my life had sex been this all-consuming experience where I was able to leave all my usual chaotic and distracted thoughts behind and focus only on my body.

In my limited experience, sex was okay but it didn't erase from my mind the length of my to-do list, or that work e-mail I needed to send, or that bill I needed to pay, or that phone call I needed to return. Unless it was sex with Harrison.

I'd fucked the man half naked, bent over his desk in the middle of the day!

And even knowing that, I didn't have enough sense to worry about whether someone was going to burst through the door at any moment. All I could think about was his hands, his mouth, his cock.

What the hell was wrong with me?

And that was before we'd even given any thought to the whole birth control thing.

That would definitely need to be a discussion with him. The pill wasn't an option for me, and we had already taken a huge risk having gone bareback in his office.

My cheeks warmed as I remembered the feel of him fucking my ass. At least *that* way I didn't have to worry about getting pregnant. Still, he would need to start using condoms.

That was, if I continued down this super dark and twisty path with him.

So. Disaster report thus far wasn't too bad.

My job was there if I wanted it and probably secure regardless if I continued to sleep with him or not.

The fiancée wasn't a concern until she was the wife, but it meant that this relationship had no chance of going anywhere. It was an absolute dead end.

The relationship was dangerous and taboo but also offered incredible orgasms and the experience of a lifetime. I needed to face it. There was no minimizing what it felt like to be on the receiving end of such intense, lustful attention from a man like Harrison and I was not likely to ever experience it again.

Then there were the perks...

Maybe, just maybe, Harrison had a point: I didn't need to live like a pauper. I could afford a little more if I were careful. Definitely not an apartment like this, but there were programs available to help lower-income residents find suitable accommodations, as well as more grants available than I had really been applying for.

Maybe I didn't need to do absolutely everything by myself.

If Harrison Astrid, one of the wealthiest men in the city, was offering to give me a hand up, why wouldn't I take it?

The system was rigged. Everyone knew the system was rigged. There was no getting around it. The chances of me being able to pull myself from complete poverty to prosperity or even comfort without help were slim to none.

I would have been livid with her if someone had given Sabrina this opportunity and she was stubborn enough not to take it. I would have marched her cute little butt back to whoever gave her that offer and forced her to accept it.

Why wouldn't I do the same for myself?

Amazing sex. A secure job. And a great apartment with hot running water and electricity in a safe neighborhood for a month or so while I saved up to rent a new place.

I could do worse...

I managed to be showered, dressed and ready to go about five minutes before the buzzer in the apartment rang, letting me know my ride had arrived.

I went downstairs to greet the driver. Next to the gilded doors in the opulent lobby was another doorman in the same uniform as the one last night. He tipped his hat to me and opened one of the lobby doors, then ran ahead of me and opened the car door as well.

I made a mental note to myself that just because I could afford more than my studio apartment, it didn't mean that I should get used to this level of luxury.

Though it *was* nice.

When I got to work Harrison was already there, his door closed.

Too nervous and unsure to knock on it, I quietly slipped behind my desk and fired up my computer. There was already a stack of files on my desk as well as my usual coffee order so I went ahead and got to work.

About an hour in, his door swung open.

With a start, I turned and just stared.

His gaze narrowed as he stared back.

Neither of us said a word for what felt like an eternity.

My cheeks began to warm, visions of the previous night flashing through my mind's eye. It didn't help that at the same time, I caught sight of his massive desk just past his right hip.

My cheeks burned hotter.

Clearing my throat, I rose and shuffled the stack of files on my desk, giving them my full attention.

Refusing to look up, I spoke in a rush to fill the awkward void. "I went through the first three files that you laid on my desk, highlighting all the pertinent information and making notes on cases that we need to check for precedents, and laws we need to review. I have also double-checked the chain of custody forms and highlighted a few irregularities that definitely need to be followed up on. There is some kind of a pattern, I just can't tell what it is quite yet."

Harrison nodded. "Come into my office. I have some more files for you."

I froze. I gave him a bright smile that made my jaw hurt as I rushed to sit down again and tap on the space bar of my computer. "Actually, I'm expecting an important e-mail at any moment. Perhaps you could just leave the files like you did this morning?"

Harrison stepped back and gestured with his arm. "Get in here."

Glancing around to make sure that no one observed his stern command, I grabbed a notebook and pen and dutifully crossed the threshold into his lair.

Office. I meant office.

I stopped in front of his desk and lifted the notepad, focusing on the small, pale blue lines on the page. "Yes, sir."

He stood close behind me. "Turn around, Eddie."

I tightened the space between my shoulder blades.

It had been so easy this morning, secure beneath the bedcovers, for me to be all blasé about what was happening, acting like I was a modern woman who could handle a casual liaison.

It was an entirely different proposition to remain that way in his presence.

In his presence, nothing felt easy breezy.

This close to him, it was as if there wasn't enough oxygen in the room. The man radiated testosterone, power, and energy. The idea of a relationship on my terms seemed as laughable and impossible as a purple-and-pink polka-dotted sky.

Who was I kidding?

I wasn't the one in control. Never had been. I could fight it all I liked. I could talk back and try to walk away but in the end, Harrison was the one in control. And worse, he not only knew it, but he also knew how much I secretly loved it.

I swallowed as I pretended to make a note on my pad. "Are the files behind me?"

"No."

"Are there any files?"

"No."

I tried to suck air into my tight lungs. The silence stretched out.

He sighed. "If you don't turn around, I'll have no choice but to assume it's because you want me to push you face down on my desk and fuck you from behind."

169

I turned around so quickly I got a head rush.

The corner of his mouth lifted. "Good girl."

I opened my mouth but he stopped me.

He placed a finger under my chin and lifted my head up. "I have no doubt that feverishly intelligent brain of yours has been turning over every filthy moment from last night and the day before."

I bit my lower lip, the blush in my cheeks spreading over my neck.

He continued. "And I look forward to the naked mock trial we will be having later tonight when I will successfully refute all your arguments and accusations."

Naked mock trial? My inner thighs clenched at visions of him cross-examining me with a belt in his hand. I flushed hotter.

"In the meantime, I have several meetings I need to attend. You have two days' worth of work to catch up on. I will be back late but I expect to find you still here. We'll review your work and then leave together. Is that understood?"

All I could do was nod like an obedient child.

He kissed me on the forehead before grabbing his leather laptop satchel and coat and leaving. Opening his office door, he threw out, "My black card is in your center drawer. Use it for lunch and dinner. Do *not* leave this building."

I bristled at his high-handed order.

As if reading my mind, he paused. "Don't defy me on this, Eddie, or there will be consequences."

With that, he was gone.

Well, good morning to you too.

CHAPTER 22

EDDIE

I hadn't been planning on leaving, but there was a big difference between it being my decision or his.

With an indignant huff, I returned to my desk, muttering about arrogant, domineering bosses who ordered people around.

I lost myself in my work, just shutting out absolutely everything that was happening with Harrison, with the apartment, with my new outlook on what I did and didn't deserve—all of it.

I turned it all off and focused on my work so intently that I didn't notice when someone was hovering over my desk until an envelope dropped onto the top of the stack of papers I was working on.

I looked up to see Evil Barbie from the day before yesterday.

"Can I help you?" I asked.

"Yes, you can do your job," she said with her hands on her hips like she was scolding a small child. "Once Harrison and I are married, I'm going to insist that he get a better secretary."

"I'm not a secretary." I smiled up at her. "His secretary is on vacation. I'm a paralegal."

"As if there's any difference." she said, waving off anything I said. "Look, I need you to do something. I don't care if you think it's beneath you since I'm just the fiancée, but you need to do it, or I will get you fired."

I hated this woman with everything I had, but I knew it would be much faster just to smile and agree to whatever it was that she was here for.

"How can I help you, ma'am?"

I may have added the "ma'am" just to annoy her, and with the way her puffed-up Botox lips twisted into a snarl, I knew it worked.

It may have been petty, but I enjoyed the little hint of vindication I got from getting on her nerves. It was catty and a bit mean, especially since I was the woman sleeping with her fiancé, but I never said I was perfect, and I certainly didn't pretend to be.

"I need to speak to my fiancé."

"Mr. Astrid is in a meeting."

"I don't care if he's in a meeting. Go get him."

"I'm afraid Mr. Astrid is not in the building. He took a meeting somewhere else, and I don't know where he is."

"How can you not know where he is?"

"Because," I said evenly and slowly as if speaking to a child. "I am not his secretary, nor am I his mother. Have you tried calling his phone?"

"It's your job to know where he is." She stomped her probably ridiculously expensive stiletto at me.

"It really isn't," I said.

"Well, I'm not leaving until you tell me where he is. I don't know why you think you get to keep my fiancé from me. Who do you even think you are? I don't care if you're his secretary or his paralegal or whatever. I'm going to be his wife. That means I will always be more important because unlike you, I'm good enough for him. You are probably just some little charity case he's taking pity on."

Her words stung more than she could possibly know. No, I did not have this job because I was a charity case. I had this job because I was the best paralegal here, but her calling me a charity case hit a nerve harder than she could know.

"Ma'am, as I have already stated, I do not know where Mr. Astrid currently is. I have not seen nor heard from him since he left this morning and I'm not expecting him back in the office during business hours today."

"That's not acceptable," she screeched, loud enough that several of the others in the bullpen all stopped to look at us.

I took a deep breath to maintain my composure.

"I apologize if you don't find that acceptable, but that's all I have to tell you. I don't know anything else. I am happy to take a message if you would like, or I could try calling his cell phone if you don't have the number."

"Of course I have my fiancé's cell phone number." The way her eyes darted to the floor and then to the space right over my left shoulder told me she didn't.

"Right," I said, giving her a pleasant smile and praying this woman would just leave already.

Instead, she leaned down, hovering over my desk, the smell of her expensive perfume smothering the air around me. "Look, you little street urchin, I don't know who you think you are, but you cannot keep him from me."

"I'm not trying to keep him from you. I'm telling you he's not here. Is there a message you'd like me to give him?" I spoke slowly and condescendingly, hoping that she would finally get the point.

"Fine." She huffed. "Tell him I was here looking for him and give him these to approve." She tapped a long, manicured fingernail on the thick envelope on top of my desk.

"Absolutely, I will see that he gets it." I carefully moved it to the side out of my way.

"Good," she said. "It's the announcements for our engagement and copies of the wedding invitations for him to approve. I will hear about it when he gets home if you don't give them to him. I will have you fired."

She turned on her heel and stomped away, leaving only an invisible trail of the cloyingly sweet, toxic scent of her perfume.

"Oh my God, girl, who was that?" One of the other paralegals, whose name I never remembered, stood in front of my desk.

"I believe that was Mr. Astrid's fiancée," I said.

"What did she want?"

"She was just dropping off some things for Mr. Astrid to look over. I'm guessing they got their signals crossed, because she was under the impression that he was here."

"But why was she yelling at you?"

I just shrugged. I had no other answer. I had absolutely no idea why I was the one she decided to aim her venom at.

"God, for the way that she was going after you, you'd think you were fucking her man or something."

I pretended to cough on a sip of coffee, hoping it would hide the telltale signs of my guilt. I pressed my fingertips to my cheeks as if it were the coughing fit that made them flushed.

"Yeah, I don't know, maybe her bikini wax was a little rough this morning?" I joked, and the other paralegal laughed, placing her hand on her chest as she walked back to her own desk.

The more I thought about it, the more I wondered if I were the asshole in this situation?

If I asked people on Reddit who was the victim—the paralegal screwing her boss or the entitled rich bitch that was being cheated on—I wasn't entirely sure I would be seen as the victim anymore.

Yeah, she was a grade-A Karen, but maybe she knew.

Instinctively maybe she knew the reason her fiancé wasn't at home last night wasn't because he was late at work but because he was with me.

Did he go home last night and crawl into bed with her after leaving the one he'd fucked me in?

I no longer felt vindicated by my pettiness toward her.

She was the victim whether she consciously knew it or not.

I was the villain.

I had knowingly, willingly, had sex with a man who belonged to someone else.

Twice.

It was one thing when I was entertaining fantasies of him before I knew he was engaged, but for me to let it go this far knowing that he belonged to someone else was deplorable. I had become the worst kind of woman.

My bullshit reasoning this morning was nothing more than the future lawyer in me arguing my own innocence, even though I knew I was guilty as sin. Maybe I should switch sides and become a defense attorney?

I was the other woman who was fucking a man that could help her career.

It wasn't as if he had given me a chance to say no. But I knew that was no more of an excuse than one a criminal driving the getaway car would make, claiming innocence because they weren't the one inside robbing the bank.

I was just as guilty.

If I had truly said no, truly shown him I didn't want to have sex, then there wasn't a doubt in my mind he would have stopped.

He didn't because he knew I wanted it. Knew I wanted to be forced to my knees. Knew I wanted to be dominated by him. Knew I was just as attracted and drawn to him as he was to me.

In the moment, it didn't matter who else I was hurting by my actions, and I was no better than any of the people that I had helped prosecute.

I had knowingly let my ambition, my own wants and needs, cloud my better judgment, and I'd acted in my own interest regardless of the pain and harm my actions inflicted on others.

Adultery may not have been punishable by law in the United States anymore, but if it had been, I would have turned myself in.

My entire adult life was spent working toward becoming a lawyer. I wanted to stand in front of the bar after passing the exam and have those great men and women look at me and say that I was their ethical equal.

Of course, I knew not all lawyers were ethical, in fact, some were downright shady, but that wasn't me. I had always believed that ethics meant doing the right thing because it was the right thing, not because someone was watching.

My gut twisted painfully, and I knew that I couldn't accept any of this anymore.

I couldn't do it.

I looked down at my phone.

It was 4:45, and I had already done well over the amount of work that could be expected for a single day.

If Harrison was not back in the next fifteen minutes, I was clocking out at 5:00 p.m. with my colleagues.

The second 5:00 p.m. hit, the office around me got louder.

The other paralegals and a few of the secretaries packed up for the night and for the first time since I started working here, I followed suit.

Harrison may have requested, no, *demanded*, that I stay late at work, but I knew that if we were alone in his office again there was no way I would be able to resist him.

Especially after knowing how his mouth felt on my skin and how he felt inside of me. I considered myself a strong woman, but even I had limits.

There was no way for me to take back what had already happened, but I could at least do everything in my power to make sure it never happened again.

In the elevator, I grabbed my phone to call the car service, but at the last minute I thought better of it and called someone else instead.

CHAPTER 23

EDDIE

*W*hen I walked up to the third floor, dodging a few mice and some paper bags that looked very suspect, I found Sabrina standing outside of her door wearing a parka and holding two steaming, disposable cups.

"What's that?" I asked, wrapping my arms around my middle, trying to keep my body heat in my thin coat.

I was considering, not for the first time, ripping open the seams of the paltry coat and shoving the matted polyester filling from my pillows into the lining for warmth. The flat pillows rarely kept me comfortable anyway. Maybe they could have a new life keeping me from freezing to death.

Why had I been so stubborn as to leave Harrison's coat behind at the office?

"Hot chocolate from the café down the block," she said. "Landlord douche-face turned on the electric but now is claiming the heat is broken, and I was too cold to stand there to make the good stuff."

"It looks hot, so it already is the good stuff. The chocolate is just a bonus at this point."

"That's exactly what I was thinking. You want to tell me what happened?"

"No, not even a little bit," I said, moving past her to unlock the door to my apartment.

I looked around and realized for the first time that maybe this was where I belonged. Going from the luxury apartment to this made me realize how bad this place really was. I had always known it was horrible, and that when Harrison saw it, he would see me differently. But just a taste of what life could have been like was enough to see my reality in a new light.

This apartment wasn't a stepping stone. It was exactly where I was meant to be, in the filth with all of the other people who put their pleasures above common sense and the needs of others.

This was what I deserved, and the fact that I had deluded myself enough to think anything else was just pathetic.

"Are you sure you don't want to tell me?" Sabrina asked, handing me the paper cup of hot chocolate.

"Yeah, I'm sure. I just can't talk about it right now." I took a deep breath and set my bag on the floor in front of the mattress that made my back hurt.

"Take a sip of your hot chocolate," she said.

I assumed she was telling me to try some new amazing seasonal flavor like white chocolate peppermint or something festive. Instead, I was assaulted by the stringent taste of vodka.

"What the fuck?" I gasped after I just managed to swallow it.

"I only had enough spare change for one hot chocolate, so I asked for two cups, and I figured you'd need a drink, so... I improvised."

I took another sip, this time not choking because I knew what to expect. I let the warmth of the melted chocolate, fueled by the heat of the alcohol, warm me from the inside out.

"It was a good call," I said, "but next time, how about a little bit of a warning? And maybe whiskey or rum instead?"

"Where's the fun in that?" She gave me an impish grin.

"Sadist," I mumbled into my cup before taking another sip.

"Maybe," Sabrina said, stroking her chin like she was thinking about the possibility that she was, in fact, a sadist, making us both laugh.

"So, are you going to tell me about the guy?" she asked.

"Not right now. I'm still too sober," I lamented.

"Well, I actually have a shift in about fifteen minutes." This time her smile was half-hearted. "So, sadly, yours is the only hot chocolate that is spiked."

"Sabrina, if you have to go to work, then go to work. You don't need to babysit me. I'm a big girl, I can take care of myself."

"All evidence to the contrary, sweet cheeks," she said, taking another long sip from her own cup.

"I don't see how you are much better. You are living in the same infected, cold, damp, Dark Ages hellhole I am."

"I'm still better at adulting."

"How do you figure that?" I scoffed.

"I have a bed frame, which means I am a more adultier adult. Therefore, I win."

She had a very valid point.

"Now, Reader's Digest version of the boy in question. Do I get to sharpen my knives? Do I *need* to sharpen my knives?"

We sat there in silence for a moment while I considered what I could tell her, what I should tell her, and what I wanted to tell her.

Part of me wanted to lay it all out and let her be my judge, jury, and executioner.

Sabrina, although absolutely amazing, had had her share of run-ins with unfaithful men. It seemed like the culinary industry was more polluted with liars, cheaters, and assholes than the criminal justice system.

Or maybe it was just that people everywhere sucked.

I didn't know anymore. All I knew was that I definitely wasn't above it.

I thought about telling her about the swanky apartment Harrison had put me in, about how he had talked to our landlord, and that I was probably going to have to find a new place to live as soon as he bothered to get off his ass to file eviction paperwork.

The sad part was my landlord didn't even need to file eviction paperwork. He could just call the police because while I had a subleasing agreement, he hadn't exactly agreed to it and I wasn't on the lease.

"Can you at least tell me who the guy is?" Sabrina asked, pulling me out of my thoughts.

"What guy?"

"The one you spent the night with last night. The boys downstairs said that some rich asshole yelled at the landlord and threatened him if he didn't get the power back on, then carried you out of here like a sack of potatoes. They joked that it was the first time they'd seen a body being carried out of here while it was still kicking and screaming."

"That was my boss," I said. "He didn't like that I was staying at a place without heat. Apparently, he's convinced the case we're working on is the biggest of his career."

"Okay, so then why was he here, and how did he know you didn't have heat?"

"I wasn't answering my phone because it was dead, so he came to ask a question, and he got all uppity because it's an election year. And apparently, if his paralegal is so underpaid that she freezes to death while working for him, it might look bad."

"Right…" Sabrina gave me that look, that signature Sabrina *I am squinting at you and trying to see if I am buying your bullshit* look.

"Yeah, he's one of those trust fund babies." I shrugged. "And I think his opponent is middle class and trying to use his family money against him. So he's worried that his opponent will say that he's not paying me enough and that he's profiting off my suffering blah blah blah, which is stupid. He doesn't pay me. The taxpayers do. Even lowly paralegals are public servants that work for the government."

"I guess that makes sense." Sabrina shrugged, then took another sip of her hot chocolate. "So, is that where you were last night? At his place?"

"No, that would be wildly inappropriate." I laughed and stared into my already perfectly stirred hot chocolate to avoid eye contact.

"He's also engaged. I spent last night at an apartment that is used for witness protection," I lied.

Wow, I guessed when a person headed down the path to hell, the rest of the vices started coming easy, like lying to my best friend.

"He let me just stay the night, thinking the heat and electric would be back on today. Clearly, he was wrong, but I think they are probably moving someone into that apartment tonight." I shrugged. "It was nice while it lasted." I took another pull from the very boozy chocolate.

Sabrina nodded and stood up, heading toward the door.

"Well, I have to get to work but before that I'm dropping off some stuff at my sister's. I'm going to stay there until the heat is back on. Want to come with? We can take turns sharing the sofa. With lots of blankets, the floor isn't too bad."

"I'm good. Tell your sister I said hi," I called out to her retreating back. She waved to me without turning around, to indicate she heard.

I finished my drink, the rich chocolate and cheap vodka

swirling in my stomach and staving off some of my hunger, at least. I hadn't had lunch or dinner.

It was early, but I didn't have any food. The heat was still off, so I figured the best thing I could do was to build myself a cocoon of blankets to keep warm and just go to sleep and deal with tomorrow when tomorrow came.

I crawled into bed, still dressed in my work clothes, not willing to risk the brittle cold to get naked and put on more cozy pajamas.

* * *

I DIDN'T KNOW how long I'd been asleep when my head started pounding.

I knew we could only afford the cheap vodka, which meant the hangover was going to be brutal. It took a moment for me to realize the pounding wasn't coming from my head. It was coming from my front door.

The door was locked, the chain was secure, and I was not getting out of my cocoon of blankets.

I may not have been super warm, but I was at least warmer than I would be outside of my nest of blankets. Just sticking one toe out told me that the apartment was frigid and I needed to stay exactly where I was. Whoever was at the door would get bored and go away eventually, I told myself as I closed my eyes and buried my head under the pillow, hoping to muffle the sound.

The pounding didn't stop.

It slowed down but got harder, like whoever was trying to get my attention wasn't knocking anymore but throwing themselves against the door.

Once. Twice. By the third time, there was a sickening crack.

I looked up to see what was left of my door falling into the room inches from my face.

"What the fuck do you think you're doing?" I sat up instantly, regretting the cold air that hit my back as my heat bubble popped.

"What am I doing?" Harrison asked, stepping into the apartment. "What the fuck are you doing? I told you to wait for me. I told you not to leave the office."

"Well, your fiancée came and said you had dinner plans, so I figured I should just go home," I lied, again.

"What are you talking about?"

"Your fiancée showed up at the office today demanding to know where you were because she wanted to make sure you're available for dinner and to drop off the wedding invitations and announcement for your approval. I left them on Cynthia's desk, so if there's nothing else." I lay back down and pulled the blankets over me.

"Why did you come back here? Why didn't you at least go back to the apartment I gave you?"

"Because this is where I live. This is who I am, and pretending to be some Fifth Avenue princess is just going to make it that much harder when I have to come back here. Assuming you don't get me evicted first? In which case, I need to start looking for a nice, comfortable cardboard box. Have any of your rich friends recently bought a refrigerator?"

"Get up. I'm taking you back to the apartment."

"How would your fiancée feel if she knew that you were fucking your paralegal? I would say at least it's not as cliche as fucking your secretary, but she doesn't know the difference."

"Honestly, she shouldn't care," he said. "I've repeatedly told you. Our engagement isn't a romantic one. It's just business."

"Does she know that?" I asked.

"I don't give a fuck what she knows or doesn't know. It's a business arrangement. I need you there, where you're safe and aren't going to die of hypothermia."

I snorted. "And where you have easy access to my pussy. No thanks. You need to leave." I pulled the covers up over my head.

"Absolutely. Finally, we are in agreement. Get your ass up, and we will leave."

"You need to leave without me." I poked my head back out. "I refuse to be some side chick that you're fucking and cheating on your fiancée with."

"It's not cheating when she and I are not in a romantic relationship, but fine, we don't have to have sex. That's fine. Deny how much you want me all you like. Fucking me is not a stipulation of you being in that apartment. Get your ass up, and let's go. I'm hungry. I want food and to actually eat somewhere where I'm not going to have to fight off cockroaches the size of dogs for a slice of pizza."

"I'm not going with you, *Mr. Astrid.*"

"Really, we're back to that?" He started to pace around my tiny apartment. He would take two steps in one direction and have to turn around again. It would have been funny if his being here didn't hurt.

"Apparently," I quipped. I looked down at the floor to where the pieces of my door were lying and sat straight up. "How am I supposed to keep this place warm now that you broke my door?" I screamed.

"I don't know if you've noticed this or not, but it actually got warmer after I broke the door. Get up. We're leaving now."

"No." I dug my nails into one of the blankets, trying to keep myself from doing something stupid, like taking a swing at him or throwing myself into his arms.

"Get up now, or I will pick you up and drag you out of here again."

"Leave."

"Fine," he said.

I thought that meant that he was going to leave, so I lay back down to try to find some warmth in my little nest of bedding.

Instead, he grabbed my arm and pulled me to my feet.

CHAPTER 24

HARRISON

*T*his woman.

This stubborn, pig-headed, obstinate woman was going to be the death of me.

If anyone else, and I do mean anyone else, had given me the attitude she had, I would have left them here to freeze to death.

Her feet tangled in the bedding she had been wrapped in and she stumbled and fell against me, the blankets dropping away as she ended up pressed to my chest.

She was trembling in my arms, and I didn't know if it was from rage or the cold.

"What do you think you're doing?" she shrieked.

It's both.

"Do you think you can just walk in here and take whatever the fuck you want? This place is mine. It's not much, especially not compared to what you have, but it is mine, not yours. You don't get to just barge in here and—"

I cut off her yells with a brutal, almost barbaric kiss.

She tried to break it, but I wouldn't let her.

I needed to feel her against me. I needed to warm her up and protect her from her own obstinance. Mostly, I needed an outlet for my rage.

She was going to obey.

I needed her to understand what I couldn't say. I needed her to know that I had somehow grown attached.

I didn't love people, not in an emotional way.

I loved my sisters in a way that came from the familial duty I felt toward them. I loved my father in the way that I was grateful for the lessons he taught me even though he didn't have to once he found out that I was a bastard, not his heir. I even loved my mother in some convoluted way that ensured I put up with her meddling and antics time and time again.

Romantic love was something that I was not made for.

I had found women attractive before, and I wanted to fuck them. I had a few female friends whose company I enjoyed but had no interest in anything even resembling intimacy with them.

Until her, never had I found a woman that I wanted to possess so completely, mind and body. So, I was unpracticed in how to express the affection that had somehow grown so quickly between us.

Eddie was the first woman in the office whose physical appearance I had noticed, and yes, when I saw her in my bathroom, I wanted her.

I'd been willing to pay anything to have her before I knew she was a paralegal, but then when I found out that that beautiful body, that angelic face framed by those golden locks, also possessed the brain that had put together some of the most eloquently worded and poignant arguments that I had ever seen, I was fascinated. She had made connections between cases that most experienced lawyers wouldn't have seen in a million years if they were staring directly at them.

The way her brain worked was enthralling.

I didn't possess the words needed to convince her that I

didn't want the harpy that my mother had arranged for me to marry.

I wanted her not because of some savior complex but because, despite the differences in our backgrounds, careers, ages, and everything in her, I had found my equal.

I have had peers before, I've had colleagues and mentors I've admired, but I had never had someone in my life that I saw as my equal in every way that mattered.

Maybe this was all timing.

Maybe it was because she walked into my office bathroom at a time when I was feeling out of control, and I reached for something that was there.

Maybe this was just an infatuation that would burn out in time.

I didn't know.

There was no way for me to know because this had never happened before.

But I needed to find out.

Every fiber of my being screamed to not let this woman walk out of my life. So no matter the danger and obstacles, I was willing to take a risk and claim her as my own.

That didn't mean she was.

If she said no, then that was that. I would respect her decision.

I had no idea how I was going to, but I would at the very least try.

Because I truly respected her, I meant it when I said the apartment was hers to use, and it was not conditional. The references I was prepared to give her for law school or any job she wanted were not conditional either. It would be a crime to deprive the legal world of her mind. There was no way, no matter how this ended, that I would do less than everything in my power to *help* her career, not hinder it.

She took a small step back and looked up at me, her hair wild from sleep, her lips kiss-bruised and slightly open as her breath came out in tiny little pants. Her eyes shone a brilliant green as they stared back at me, her pupils blown wide. She might have more control than I did. She might have possessed a greater ability to keep her hormones in check than I did, but she was just as affected by me as I was by her.

I cupped her face. "You need to understand. I'm aware of the risks and I don't give a damn. For the first time in my life, I've found something, someone, who is worth more to me than my career. *You.* And I—"

This time, she was the one to cut off my words with a kiss.

She took one step toward me, reached out, laced her fingers in my hair, and yanked me down so my lips met hers.

My hands went to her hips and I pulled her up, her legs wrapping around my middle. I walked us to the wall, pressing her body against the drywall so she could brace herself against it while my hands ran down her body over her clothes, from her breasts to her waist.

I wanted to strip her bare, devour every inch of her body. I couldn't, not in here. It was too cold, and the open doorway exposed us to anyone walking down the hallway. I wouldn't make her uncomfortable just to satiate my own carnal desire.

"I need to hear you say it," I said, running my mouth up the slender column of her neck.

"Say what," she breathed.

I licked the outer shell of her ear before nipping her earlobe with my teeth. "I need to hear you say that you want this as much as I do."

I was about to let her go when she slid her fingers through my hair again and pulled me closer. "Fuck the risks."

I sealed my lips over hers again, and I knew I should have

gotten her out of here. I knew I should have been a gentleman and waited, but I needed her more than I needed to breathe.

Waiting until we got to the other apartment, or even to the car, wasn't an option I was willing to entertain.

I dropped her feet to the floor and turned her around, pushing her against the wall and pressing my body to hers.

She was still wearing the same clothes she'd had on at work, and I loved it. The cute pencil skirt, the professional-looking, white, fitted button-down, now a little wrinkled and disheveled from sleep.

It reminded me of what she was like when I took her in the office.

It was taboo and forbidden, and it made me want her more.

"Here's what's going to happen," I whispered in her ear. "I'm going to lift this skirt, and I'm going to fuck you against this wall hard and fast. It won't be sweet or gentle. I'm going to fuck you like the bad girl you are, and you are going to take it. When I fill you with my come, you're going to pull this skirt down, straighten your top, and march that sweet ass downstairs and get in the car. Do you understand me?"

"Yes," she breathed out.

"Yes, what?"

"Yes, sir," she said with a gasp.

"Are you wet for me?" I asked.

She didn't say anything. She just nodded, pressing her forehead into the wall.

I pulled her hair from her face on one side so I could see how red her cheeks were. Whether it was arousal or embarrassment, I really didn't care.

She was going to take my cock like a good girl and do as she was told.

I reached down and roughly yanked up her skirt.

My cock had been rock hard since the second I had walked into this apartment.

The second she'd fought back, I was ready to take her against this wall.

She had tried to fight me.

Tried to fight the inevitability of us.

Eddie didn't want to want me, but that wasn't going to stop me. Nothing could stop me at this moment.

She had tried to fight our attraction, and I had won.

I grabbed her panties and yanked them to the side, not bothering to pet her little clit or to make sure that her cunt was ready for me.

I knew it was. I knew she was wet for me when I broke down her door.

It wouldn't be the first time fighting me had made her wet. Or me hard.

She was made to be owned by me, so the last thing I needed to do was to check and see if she was ready. She would always be ready.

I grabbed her hips, tilting them back, and shoved my way in.

She was so wet, so hot, and still so tight, the slick of her velvet heat gripping my cock. She moaned at my first thrust and arched her back, urging me to go deeper.

I fucked her hard and fast with everything I had.

This was meant to be a punishment. I'd intended to rile her up and leave her wanting, but I just couldn't do it. I reached around to her front, working my hand into her shirt so I could pinch her nipples while I fucked her.

"Do you like your punishment, my dirty little whore?"

"Yes," she panted.

"If you like this so much, why do you fight me so hard? This could be so much better if you didn't have to fucking fight me every time you wanted my cock," I rumbled.

I wasn't even sure I believed my own words.

The reason this was so intense and so carnal was because she didn't just give in, she didn't just drop to her knees, ready to serve me like every other woman had as soon as they heard my last name.

Eddie made me earn it with her. She didn't want to want me the way she did.

Her desire for me was carnal, not financial.

Like mine for her, it was something more than just a quick release of tension.

She was my prize, and I was claiming her.

I had earned her. She was mine.

"Prove it," I growled. "Come on my cock."

I didn't know if it was because I demanded it or if she needed it as much as I did, but my words were enough to push her over the edge.

Her tight body squeezed my cock, pulsing around it as she arched her back, biting her bottom lip to muffle a scream of pleasure.

The intensity made my vision white out for a moment as I filled her with stream after stream of my come.

It took me a moment to regain my bearings, but when I did, all I wanted to do was lie Eddie down somewhere safe and wrap my arms around her. I wanted her safe, warm, and with me, always.

"Fuck," she gasped as I let her down and she straightened her skirt. "That was more intense than in the office."

Her words brought me out of my anger- and lust-filled haze.

She brought me back down to earth as the volatile mix of emotions and desire receded.

Reality, far colder than her apartment, hit me.

Goddammit. Fuck.

She was willing, but that did not make this appropriate.

It did not make this okay. It didn't even make this legal.

What was worse was what I had done after I had broken her door.

Any one of the crackheads who lived in this building could have walked by and seen us. They could have filmed us and used it to blackmail her or me, or they could have done something much worse.

I had broken the door of her apartment, putting her in danger.

I couldn't be like this to her.

She deserved so much better. This wasn't right.

It wasn't fair to her.

My engagement may just be a business deal, but it was still binding, and it still meant that I could never give her what she deserved.

I could give her a quick fuck. I could even set her up in a penthouse apartment and pay for law school, but I could never give her a true home. I would always be demanding more from her than I could give of myself.

Even now, I was enough of a prick to deny her a date with someone else despite the fact that I was engaged. That would never change. I would never be okay seeing her with another man. Ever. And yet, she would have to live with the knowledge that each night I left her bed to return to the house I shared with another woman. She would have to live with seeing my photo in the newspapers with Catherine on my arm, not her.

She would have to accept the consequences of a baby if we continued to fuck without protection. I would of course financially support the child but even if I openly claimed them, they would still be a bastard.

I had just put this beautiful creature that I admired so much in a lose-lose situation.

I zipped up my pants while she straightened her shirt and skirt and grabbed her purse before I led her downstairs.

After sending one of the police officers upstairs to guard her apartment until I got her door fixed, we got into the car without saying a word.

Flipping through my contacts, I sent a quick text to my maintenance man and instructed him to replace the door immediately. When we arrived at the apartment I had set her up in, I made sure she went in and was safe.

And then I did the worst thing a man could do after sex.

Without a single word.

I left.

CHAPTER 25

HARRISON

I went back to my empty penthouse and got fucking drunk.

I had pulled all-nighters before, but it was always for a case, never a woman. Though, I had never met a woman like Edwina Carmichael.

After three sleepless nights capped off with half a bottle of whiskey that Luc had gifted me some time ago, I was nursing a pretty intense hangover.

And still didn't have the solution to how I could keep Eddie without ruining her life.

There was only one thing to do.

I would present my case to Edwina.

We would establish professional and personal boundaries.

I would lay out everything, what I wanted from her professionally and personally. It was paramount I make it perfectly clear she could reject my proposal, but if she rejected it then changed her mind later—that would be it.

She would be mine.

No more excuses or hesitations.

No more dilemma over work, or even the reality of my loveless marriage.

Mine.

The more I considered my options, the more I liked the things we could do once those boundaries were set. The spanking and the rough fuck over my desk were reckless and couldn't happen again. But they could happen over the weekend in my home office.

I liked the idea of her working in the nude. Pacing back and forth in front of me, reading case law while I watched her full, perky tits shake with each step.

Or better yet, while I dealt with tedious weekend calls that seemed to last for hours, she could be on her knees, keeping my cock warm with her sweet lips.

Of course, I would pay her for her work on the weekends from my personal account, not taxpayer funds. Just because I was resolved to pay for her future law school degree as well as her apartment and all other expenses, didn't mean she shouldn't be paid for her work.

If she allowed it, it would be the perfect arrangement.

"Mr. Astrid, good morning."

A surprisingly chipper and absolutely annoying voice greeted me at the elevator.

"Hi, I am Gretchen. I will be your paralegal. I know your secretary is out, so I took the liberty of getting your coffee. The last girl didn't give me the key to the desk, she said I had to get it from you so I could start work?"

"I'm sorry, who are you?" I asked, walking to my office, in desperate need of aspirin and for the annoying, chipper bird squawking at my side to fly off.

"I'm Gretchen, your new paralegal."

"No." I slammed my office door in the girl's face, before grabbing my phone and calling over to Mrs. Lakeson.

"Good morning, Mr. Astrid. Can I help you with something?"

"Put Edwina back on my desk. Now."

"She came in this morning saying that it was best if you two didn't work together. She said something about an incident with your fiancée. I hadn't heard you were engaged. Congratulations."

"I don't care what happened between Edwina and Catherine," I barked. I think her name was Catherine, who could remember. "I want her back on my desk."

"Mr. Astrid, we have plenty of other paralegals…"

"That I am sure the others will be fine with, but send Edwina to my desk now, or I will fire the squeaky toy currently on my desk and every other paralegal you send to me until she's the only one left. She will be assigned back to my desk in the next fifteen minutes or else."

I slammed my phone down and made a note to Cynthia to send Mrs. Lakeson an apology basket of whatever the fuck she liked as soon as Cynthia was back.

The fact that so far she would only have to send one was proof of how well Eddie and I worked together.

Mrs. Lakeson, to her credit, worked quickly.

The phone at the paralegal desk rang within two minutes, and then a moment after that, the squeaky one was gone. It took another twenty minutes for Eddie to be back where she belonged.

She had done it to bait me, and it fucking worked.

"Ms. Carmichael." I stretched my arm out to motion to the interior of my office. "A moment."

She marched over the threshold, arms crossed over her chest. Her expression carved out of stone. The very definition of resting bitch face.

She was pissed. Understood.

I closed the door and approached my desk.

She looked at me for only a moment with narrowed eyes before turning and swinging the door open.

Okay, I was becoming less understanding.

Without saying a word, I pivoted and, keeping my gaze on her, decisively slammed the door shut. Then I locked it.

I raised my eyebrow. Clearly she was angry. I would let her speak her mind first.

Then I would bend her over this desk and remind her who she answered to.

My resolution to not indulge in such risky behavior at the office again immediately forgotten in the face of her disobedient attitude.

"Well, you called?" she asked, tapping her foot on the carpet.

"You look like you have something to say, and so do I. You have the floor."

"Since you've made it impossible for me to work elsewhere and keep my job, I wanted to make a few things clear," she said, standing tall, ready to make her case.

I imagined just for a moment that this was how she would look in front of a judge and jury, ready to make her opening arguments. She was going to be a force to be reckoned with, and I couldn't wait to behold it—when her icy gaze was lasered in on someone else.

"By all means." I motioned to the chair in front of my desk.

She looked at it for a moment and then stayed where she was. Her arms still tightly crossed over her chest. Her body language screaming that she was closed off to me completely.

"Fine." She took a breath and started her statement. "What happened last night will never happen again. Never. If I have to work for you, fine, I will work for you, but that is it. You will never touch me again. *I hate you.* I hate men *like* you. I hate that you think that you can just pull rank and decide where I work and how I spend my time. I hate that you broke into my home, dragged me out of there, and put me somewhere more convenient for you to fuck, as if my purpose in life is to serve your cock."

I clenched my jaw, not liking what she was implying but enjoying the mental image of her on her knees serving my cock.

Still, I let her continue.

"You say over and over that's not why you're doing it, but what else could it possibly be? This professional relationship may have gotten started on the wrong foot. Fine, I'll take responsibility for that one."

She admitted partial guilt, a rookie mistake.

"But all of that ends now. You do not own me. From this point forward, I work for you, but that is it."

"Are you done?" I asked, leaning back into my leather seat.

I looked her up and down and wondered if she knew she had started off wrapped around herself to seem small, but by the time she was done, her feet were shoulder-width apart, her hands on her hips and her chest pushed forward.

In the span of only a few moments, she went from meek and closed off to a classic power pose. Damn, she was going to make a fine attorney one day.

"I am," she said. "I should get back to work."

"No, you had your turn, and I listened. Now you'll hear me. I don't care if you hate me. In fact, I encourage it because anger gets things done. You can hate me all you want as long as you take that energy and channel it into your work. And you don't want me to touch you anymore? That's absolutely fine. You will regret those words, but I swear I will never lay a finger on you again—unless you beg for it. But do not mistake my generosity for some misguided, lecherous intent."

She made a motion like she was going to speak again, and I raised my hand to stop her.

"No, you had the floor, you said your piece, now it's my turn. You will stay in that apartment. Not because I want to fuck you but because it's safe. I don't know if you just haven't been paying attention to your work or if you are a little slower when it comes to common sense, but we are working on bringing down an extremely dangerous mafia organization. There is a reason I have only one paralegal working on this, and I'm not willing to bring on another. Do you think it's a coincidence that my secretary is on vacation, and I didn't get a temp at that desk?"

Actually, I didn't get a temp because I couldn't stand them. Each of them were not only incompetent but just as chipper as the paralegal I'd just had removed from Eddie's desk. But she didn't need to know that.

She stood staring at me for a few moments, not saying anything, her brow furrowed like she was confused by something.

"It's not a coincidence, Ms. Carmichael. I asked for the best of the best. I saw your work in the other case, and when I saw your name listed as Eddie, I thought you were a man. Not because I needed a man to do this work but because I thought a man would be safer. Turned out I was wrong, and I was not about to dismiss you because of your gender. I'm still not, because you are one of the brightest minds on the paralegal team. That is what I need for this case. But the fact is that this case does put you in a position where you could be in danger. And I think last night I proved exactly how easy it would be to get to you in that filthy, cheap apartment."

"I..."

"I'm still not finished, Ms. Carmichael." I stood, forcing her to look up at me.

I didn't move closer to her, but I didn't have to. "Here is what's going to happen. You are going to accept the driver and come to work every single morning. You are going to use my black American Express to order lunch for you and me every single day because it is not safe for you right now to randomly roam the streets of New York City. The same will happen with dinner. You clearly don't have any self-preservation instincts, so precautions must be taken. At the end of the day, you will take the car that I have assigned to you and head back to the apartment, where you will be safe. You will double-lock the doors, you will not tell anyone where you are, and —let me make this last part completely clear, Ms. Carmichael—you will never, ever insinuate that I was doing this out of anything other than concern in a professional capacity."

"But–"

"You don't want to continue our sexual relationship, that is fine."

The last thing it was... was fine.

I also had no intention of stopping my pursuit of her. I would just have to be more strategic about it.

By the time I had finished my argument, I was out of breath. I'd talked to her like a witness or opposing counsel.

She looked at me and straightened her spine, then nodded. "I understand, and I think what you just said is the best action moving forward. I will be at my desk continuing my work until noon, when I will come in to get your lunch order. Is there anything else?" she said.

I took a deep breath through my nose and shook my head, dismissing her.

She turned on her heel, unlocked the door, and marched to her desk, leaving my door open. True to her word, she pulled the files from her file cabinet and got to work.

What just happened was unfortunate, but it was the best professional move.

If she had reacted in any other way, if she had smiled or cried or shown any type of emotion other than cold understanding and professionalism, then what I felt for her would have died.

Fuck, I loved not only the fight in her but how she carried herself with dignity.

It made our private moments where I broke both down and forced her to submit to the demands of my cock that much more intense.

There was absolutely no way I could possibly keep my vow never to touch her again. Even now, while sitting at my desk staring at the computer screen, my cock was rock hard for her.

I only had two choices: keep my distance or make her beg.

She was going to look so pretty on her knees begging me.

CHAPTER 26

EDDIE

"Can you explain something to me?" I asked, moving the files from my desk to the coffee table in Harrison's office.

The other paralegals left at five. A few of the more ambitious prosecutors and paralegals stayed on until seven but now it was eight, and I was fairly certain that Harrison and I were the only ones left in the building other than the janitors.

The janitors preferred being able to clean the bullpens uninterrupted, so for the past few days this week, Harrison and I had started working together in his office, first grabbing dinner, and then going over the files from a little after 7:00 until we gave in for the night, usually sometime between eleven and midnight. Even then, it was only when the driver sent him a message saying his on-call shift was ending soon.

After our little "talk," I had worried things would be tense and awkward. They were for the first few hours. Then we both fell into a rhythm with the work, and the personal no longer mattered. At least, not while we were in the office.

When I was back in that fancy apartment enjoying the over-the-top luxuries like electricity and hot running water, that was when the personal mattered. Each night this week I'd worked myself to the point of exhaustion, then unwound with a glass of wine from a bottle I found in the kitchen.

It was older than I was, red, and I couldn't read the label, so I knew it was good. I would sip my single glass while soaking in a tub full of water as hot as I could stand it and let my mind wander to Harrison.

I would think about how it felt when he touched me, when he kissed me. How had no one ever before made me feel so wanted, needed, and safe enough to surrender my control?

"Is there something in one of the files you don't understand?" he asked, cocking his head as he looked at me over his computer. I shot him back a bored expression, praying he didn't see the guilt from my thoughts painted all over my face.

"I think I have proven time and time again that I understand the legal work despite not having been to law school yet."

"Okay." He lifted his hands in surrender. "Why is it you insist upon ordering from the cheap takeaway place down the street when I could just as easily have food delivered from literally any other restaurant in the city? Because that's what I don't understand. I could have authentic, healthy, amazing egg rolls delivered fresh and hot and not in paper bags that are literally dripping with grease."

I rolled my eyes at Harrison. "Okay, I am only going to try to explain this one more time. The food from Ye's Apothecary and Blue Willow is best experienced in the amazing atmosphere that they create. The experience and the quality of the food greatly diminish the second it leaves the building. However, the takeaway chow mein and egg rolls and heavily battered sweet and sour pork from Wong's are all just as good in the office as they are if you were eating them from the cardboard containers directly in front of the restaurant."

"I don't think you're making the point you think you're making," Harrison said, folding his arms. "But back to your question, what is it you don't understand?"

"These files, you've clearly been gathering information on this family for years. Why are you only putting it together now, and more importantly, why haven't you actually made an official move? I mean, you have so much evidence of laws being broken and police officers who may or may not be dirty. It's just, it stacks up, and I don't understand what you're waiting for?"

Harrison moved from his desk to the couch, sitting directly opposite me while rubbing the back of his neck.

I could have sat on the chairs facing the couch, but after sitting all day in the swivel chair with my back straight, I preferred to sit on the floor in front of the table with my legs folded under me. At least until after we ate, and then I would usually end up sitting on a couch next to Harrison as we went over the things that I had found that day and the things that he was adding throughout his meetings and his findings.

"It's complicated," he said.

"You know, I've heard I'm actually kind of smart, maybe I'll understand." I was mostly teasing, but the look he gave me said that wasn't how he took it.

"I'll explain it, but I need your word that what is said in this room never leaves this room."

"Nothing you have said in this room has ever left this room, at least as far as I'm concerned." I was honestly a little hurt he thought I would betray his trust like that. We may not be sleeping together anymore, but there was still a level of professionalism that I couldn't believe he thought I would cross.

"I have been looking at this outfit for a very long time, and initially, I stopped because I came across the evidence of what happened to the last prosecutor."

"They killed their last prosecutor," I said, staring at him with my mouth open.

"No, he dropped the case because they killed his family. They kidnapped his daughter and his wife and threatened their lives, saying they would only be returned safely if all charges were dropped."

"And he tried to call their bluff, and didn't drop the charges?" I clarified.

"No, he did," Harrison said as he sat back. "All charges were dropped immediately, and from what I can tell, he went so far as to destroy evidence. But it didn't matter, they killed the man's wife and sold his daughter. They still haven't found her. And did a few other unspeakable things. It didn't matter that the prosecutor had dropped everything, they still followed through just to prove a point."

"Okay… that explains why you would back off, but—"

"Actually, no, when I found that out, I was even more determined. I figured I would have to be the one to bring them down since my family is wealthy enough to always have security. They were protected. I thought we were untouchable until I found out that the Irish mob worked with another family. A family I thought was legitimate."

"What do you mean?" I asked, not following.

"The family of a friend of mine from school. A man I thought to be honorable and as aboveboard as the one percent of the one percent got. I found ties between the mob and his father. If his father was working with them, then I wasn't just dealing with a bunch of thugs, and I wasn't as convinced I could keep my family safe."

"Oh." Anyone else and I would be positive he dropped it just because his friend was involved, but the way his fingers tightened into a fist at his side and his shoulders tensed made me think that he was angry. A favor wouldn't make him angry.

"I asked him about it, and he confirmed all of the rumors. My friend told me that he had already made plans to distance his legacy and his business from the mob but while his father was in power, he wasn't able to do that. He needed to get control of more of the business, and then sever all ties. He wanted to be separated from these men before someone finally brought charges that stuck, and his empire was taken down with theirs."

"Did you believe him? That he wanted to separate from them?" I asked.

"Yes. With the men I went to school with, it was always best to trust but verify. When I looked into what he was saying, I found out that he was right. If I were to take down this mob, there would be no way to stop the damage from spreading. At that time the two were too closely linked, and if I took on one, I had better be ready to take on them both. So I decided what I was going to do was give him time, not a lot, but enough so if he wanted to, he could sever those ties. I was giving him time to prove himself because I didn't believe that he should be brought down by the actions of his father. Not to mention his family's legitimate business has a bigger GDP than most countries and putting more people out of work and on the streets is not my intent."

I nodded, kind of understanding where he was coming from, at least in theory. "So your friend, he has severed those ties, and now you're free to go after them without hurting him?"

"Kind of. It's actually gotten a little bit more complicated. He has made the move to separate the ties, which is great, but more importantly, he married my sister. And now I'm worried that this group might try to retaliate for the loss of business by grabbing my sister. So now it's not a matter of just keeping New York safe, it's a matter of keeping my family safe."

Harrison sat back and pressed his palms into his eyes. The stress of these long nights were clearly starting to weigh on him.

211

"Okay," I said, nodding.

"What do you mean okay?"

"Just that, I mean, okay, let's get the scumbags off the streets before they go after the people important to you or, really, anybody else. Even the people who aren't lucky enough to have the district attorney as a brother still deserve that protection. So let's build this case and lock up the bad guys."

He looked up at me, then smiled and nodded and placed the order for greasy Chinese food, and we got back to work.

We worked for a few more hours, uncovering different trails, adding to the files of names and dates that were growing. First looking for dirty cops, and the politicians they had influenced, possible crimes they may or may not have been linked to including everything from racketeering and blackmail to mugging, drug possession with the intent to distribute, and whispers of human trafficking. There was so much this family was tied to I was afraid to ask why his friend's family worked with them. I was pretty sure at this point I honestly did not want to know.

"Do you know when you're going to press charges?" I asked, mostly for the excuse to look up from the paper and blink. This work really did take four times as long when it wasn't done digitally.

"As soon as I have a clear view of who is involved and enough evidence to make sure that I can get a fair trial. I want to make sure that I know each judge they've paid off, every prosecutor that they have blackmailed. I need to know it all so I can assemble the best team and force any compromised judges to recuse themselves. This case needs to be beyond airtight because it will go to trial."

"And you need to make sure that the evidence provides proof beyond a shadow of a doubt so they don't walk, and you can't prosecute them later," I said.

"Exactly," he replied, looking at me for a moment.

The phone on the desk rang, and Harrison moved to answer it. When he hung up, he looked at me and told me that security had our dinner.

"Did you want to run down to get it, or do you want me to?" he asked.

"I'll go get it. I need a break," I said, standing up and trying to brush the wrinkles from my pants. "If I keep staring at these papers for another couple minutes, I'm going to go blind, so I'll go ahead and grab the food."

By the time I got to the elevator, went downstairs, got our dinner, and came back up, Harrison was lying on his couch with his eyes closed and thumbs pressed into the corners of his eyes.

"Are you okay?"

"Yeah, just a headache starting." He sat up. I nodded and set the food down on the side of the table and then picked up all the folders and moved them to his desk.

"We need those," he said.

"Not right now, we don't," I said. "We need a break or we're going to burn out and we're going to miss something. So let's just have dinner and talk about anything else for a couple of minutes and once we are done, we'll get back to it."

He opened his mouth like he was going to argue but then nodded in defeat. He started unpacking the boxes while I took a seat on the couch next to him. We ate in silence for a moment, like neither one of us knew how to talk about anything other than work.

"Why aren't you in law school?" he asked, making me choke a little bit on my sweet and sour pork.

"That was subtle," I said. "I love how you just ease into the difficult questions like that." I laughed and he gave me a rueful smile.

"But really, why aren't you in law school?"

"Because it took me longer to finish my undergraduate degree than I was anticipating," I said.

"What do you mean?"

"I mean I needed a specific number of credits to get my degree."

"No, I know what that means, I'm asking you why it took you longer and why, since you have your degree, you're working here instead of going to law school?"

"Because law school costs more money than I currently have and I'm not able to survive on just student loans and the measly financial aid I was getting for my BA, which meant I had to spread out my classes and take on more student loans which increased my debt, and I had to begin making payments."

"Did you qualify for full aid?"

"Yeah, it covered the classes, but it wasn't enough to also cover books, food and housing. So I quit." I shrugged.

"You just quit?"

"Well no, I postponed applying to law school so I can work, pay on my loans, save up some money and still have some to live on. Then I plan to take law school classes one at a time and pay for them as I go," I said.

"And that's why you lived in that shithole apartment." He made the connection himself. "So you could save up in order to apply to law school faster."

"Exactly."

"Okay, I guess that makes sense."

"Well, now it's my turn to ask a very personal and invasive question out of nowhere."

"Okay?"

"It's only fair," I said with a smile, and he nodded and waved me on.

"What is your favorite color?"

"What?" He laughed, dropping his chopsticks in his chow

mein noodles. "That's your invasive personal question, what's my favorite color?"

"I figure it must be extremely embarrassing because when I look around here, everything is beige. So you either love the color beige or you are deeply embarrassed by your favorite color. Is it pink? It's pink, isn't it? It's like baby pink, you just love baby pink."

Harrison started laughing so hard he had to put his cardboard container down. His laugh was robust, and I didn't think I had ever actually heard it before. I meant we were working on a massive mob case, so I guessed there wasn't a lot of time for jokes, but I wasn't expecting such a full-bodied, robust laugh from such a serious man.

"I don't think I actually have a favorite color anymore."

"Counselor, I object. Everybody has a favorite color. Just because you haven't thought about it in years does not mean that you do not have a favorite color."

"Overruled," he said.

"I'll rephrase," I said. "When you were seven, and someone asked you what your favorite color was, what would you say?"

"Relevance?" he asked.

"Because I want to know."

"When I was younger, I said the color red. But now that I'm an adult I think it's actually changed."

"Oh, so you do have a favorite color?"

"At the moment, green, but not just any green, the deep emerald that's still so impossibly bright it looks like it cannot possibly be real."

The way he was staring into my eyes, I knew he was looking at them, looking at me. Just the color of my eyes had such an impact that he'd noticed. It wasn't my legs, it wasn't my breasts, it wasn't even the Cupid's bow of my lip that he found attractive. It was the color of my eyes.

"You test my control. Do you know that, Eddie?"

I shook my head.

"I am a man of my word, and I said I wouldn't touch you again, but you test my control."

The way he was looking at me, the way he made me feel, I couldn't remember why being with him was a bad idea. How could anything that felt this right be bad?

"What if I didn't want you to keep that promise? What if those words were said out of anger and self-preservation, and I didn't mean them?"

"Eddie." He said my name like a prayer and leaned in like he was going to kiss me again. I wanted him to kiss me. I desperately wanted to feel the press of his lips on mine again.

"Harrison!" A shrill voice came from the bullpen.

We looked through the door and watched his mother and fiancée, both dressed in formal gowns, marching toward his office.

CHAPTER 27

HARRISON

I jumped away from Eddie the second I saw my mother in a formal gown stomping toward my office, with Catherine a few steps behind.

The way the two women glared at me like I had committed some great offense, like turning down a Birkin bag or burning vintage Prada, made me realize I must have forgotten something.

"I think I should go," Eddie said.

"Yes, quick, run, save yourself," I said under my breath. She looked at me with the top corner of her lips curling into a smirk.

"You, trampy little secretary, leave immediately," my mother said, scowling at her.

I stared at my mother, not wanting to give her the impression she had any control in my office. "Apologize."

Mary's lips twisted into a grimace. "I'm not apologizing to *the staff!*"

Eddie struggled to hold the misaligned pile of files and potential trial exhibits in her arms while also reaching for her pen and cell phone. "It's not necessary."

I crossed my arms over my chest. "I disagree. Apologize, Mother, or I'll have you thrown out."

Mary's eyes widened.

The room was filled with tense silence for several heartbeats.

Then with an indignant huff and a dismissive twist of her wrist, Mary grumbled. "Sorry, whatever your name is, I didn't mean to offend your sensitive blue-collar morals."

I rubbed my eyes as I muttered to Eddie, "That's as good as it will get."

"Honestly, Harrison, it's fine. If you don't mind, it's late, and I'm not going to be any more use to you tonight. Do you mind if we pick this up in the morning?"

I knew the question was purely for my mother's benefit, putting me in a better position of power while still letting her escape whatever chiffon terror was about to go down in this room.

"Okay, get some rest. I'll see you in the morning, Eddie," I said.

She called down to the driver as she scurried out the door, pressing herself to the wall to avoid touching Mary and Catherine, who didn't move to make way for her at all.

Catherine sneered at her as she overtly looked Eddie up and down, then called out to her retreating back. "Harrison? That's Mr. Astrid to you."

"What brings you to my office so late?" I interrupted.

"You were supposed to be at the Astrid Foundation Ball hours ago." My mother stomped her foot and put her hands on her hips.

"I don't recall RSVPing to any events," I said. "I have work to do that benefits the people here."

"You don't RSVP to an event your family is hosting," she said between clenched teeth. "Your secretary should have reminded you of your obligation. This was supposed to be one of the outings to further cement you and Catherine as a couple in the public's eye. Have you even bothered looking at the wedding invitations yet?"

"My secretary is on vacation, and I choose not to have a temp replace her," I said as I moved back to my desk and started separating the folders. Some would need to be on Eddie's desk in the morning. Others I would handle myself.

I made a mental note to grab an air-gapped computer. We couldn't risk it ever connecting to the internet, but maybe it would be better if we could use it to organize files digitally and store them on a hard drive. She was right. Doing this all old school was tedious, and the risk of losing a paper in the wrong file was a little too real.

"Harrison." My mother scowled. "You knew about this event. You had agreed to go to this event to announce your engagement when we had lunch the other day."

I thought back to a few weeks ago when I met Catherine for the first time, and we had worked out the details of our engagement. She was right. She had mentioned this event, and if Cynthia hadn't been on vacation, then it would have been on my calendar, and I would have known about it. I relied on my secretary too much. I added a mental note to tell her to get herself one of the gift baskets when she bought one for Mrs. Lakeson.

"Catherine, dear, why don't you go take a seat at one of the desks out there? Give me a moment to speak to my son," my mother said sweetly, patting Catherine on the arm.

Catherine didn't say anything. She glared at me, and then she looked around the room with her lips curled in disgust before she turned on her heel and walked through the bullpen.

My mother gently closed the door behind her and then turned to face me. The last shreds of a pleasant demeanor had vanished. All that was left was the real Mary Quinn Astrid, the hatred in her eyes, and the disapproving sneer. That look used to be accompanied by lines on her forehead and around her eyes and mouth, but Botox had taken care of that years ago.

"Harrison Phillip Astrid," my mother said. "You are being incredibly stupid."

"Excuse me," I said, standing from my desk.

"You heard me. You know, I never thought that you would make the same stupid mistakes as every other man. I always knew you weren't perfect. Lord knows I knew that. You have a temper like your father and are just as willful as your sisters."

"I think you mean like my mother," I spat back.

"No, I might get angry, but I don't act irrationally. I don't act out of stupidity and emotions like you're doing. I think things through, which is why I told you that leaking the news about your true parentage was inadvisable. But did you listen to me? No, you didn't. And what happened?"

I didn't answer her. I wasn't willing to vindicate her or give her the satisfaction of being right again.

"What happened, Harrison." She leaned down, placing her hands on my desk.

"You know what happened," I said.

"I know what happened, but do you? Because you dropped in public opinion. I told you that the scandal would turn voters against you, but you said no, the people wouldn't care. It would make you even more approachable to the common man. Did it? No! It made you fodder for Page Six for a month, and now the voters don't take you seriously. They look at you, and they don't see an Astrid. They don't see a master of the universe. They see another scandal right between the drunk pop star and the spoiled heiress."

"What's your point, Mother?"

"My point is that you agreed to let me fix this for you. You agreed to let me handle the public opinion and repair your reputation. The best way for me to do that is to show the people who you are, that you are not just another rich, lazy little bitch with Daddy's money. No, you are a real person. I do that by marrying you off to Catherine, making a solid match, and then she will be able to make you likable again to put you back in our society's good graces." Her face got redder as she spoke, not that you could see it anywhere except where her thick foundation had started to crack.

"I know this. I have already agreed to marry her. What more do you want?"

"It's not enough that you marry her. You have to be seen with her, you have to go to these events, and you have to get your things together. You are not stupid. You are not like your sisters, defiant little brats that they are. You are smart. You know what needs to be done. I need you to do it."

I hated when she talked about Amelia and Rose like that. I hated how she looked down on them just because they were women. The hypocrisy and the misogyny were incredible. It wasn't like she would ever allow them to work or to do anything outside the home other than be pawns and marry whomever my mother decided.

"Fine, I apologize for missing the event. I will not miss the next one," I said.

"It's not just this event, you stupid boy. You need to be seen with Catherine. You need people to believe that you two are a couple, and when it comes out that you're sleeping with your secretary, no one will be able to save you from that."

"Excuse me?" Now, she had gone too far.

"Are you not paying attention? Haven't you seen what this 'Me Too' movement has done? It's empowered these girls to think that if they bed a powerful man, they can blackmail them, and now people will actually believe them when they say that they were sexually harassed. There are ramifications for this even if you work in the public sector. You cannot be seen with her."

"Are you accusing me of sexually assaulting my paralegal?"

"No, I'm accusing you of being stupid enough to let her lead you around by your pants. You're being short-sighted and ridiculous. Even if everything is consensual, she could change her mind. She could start saying all types of things, and even if she doesn't, even if she is a good person or she really likes you, now what's to say that'll stay the same when you get her pregnant?"

My heart started thundering in my ears. Pregnant. I had already thought of that. I doubted she'd had health insurance before working here, and I didn't know if her insurance had kicked in yet. Even if it had, that didn't necessarily mean she was on birth control.

She was right. This horrible shrew of a woman standing in front of me was right. My actions toward Eddie were undermining the wedding. My union with Catherine was a tool, but I had to wield it properly to reap the benefits. If not, it could backfire, and then there would be no saving my career, regardless of the criminals I got off the streets.

"Fine," I said.

"Good, now that is straight. All you have to do is fire the tart, and you will be able to focus. Women like that don't belong in this office anyway."

Had she just left it alone, I wouldn't have said anything. I would have let her have her little victory, but I would not tolerate her speaking about Eddie like that. Eddie didn't need me to protect her from my mother, but I was going to do it anyway.

"Since I have you here, I think it's high time we get a few other things straight." I stood to my full height, and took a few steps closer to my mother, towering over her. "You do not dictate who I do and don't work with. You have no authority in

222

this office, and you will not barge in here unannounced again. I don't care if it's in the middle of the day or after hours. It will not happen again."

"I am still your mother. You will show respect."

"No, you are the slut who cheated on her husband and made me a bastard. You are also the conniving bitch who abused my sister and embarrassed my father. Don't think for a second, I don't have files and files of proof that you are also a criminal—"

"I am a law-abiding citizen. You have nothing on me."

"You committed financial fraud when you manipulated the purchase of several businesses to make it look like the Manwarrings were targeting the DuBoises. You were also a conspirator in the kidnapping of Olivia Manwarring. That is financial fraud, conspiracy in the kidnapping, and there is the little matter of insider trading. Not to mention the bruises you have left on Amelia her entire life."

"You wouldn't."

"Oh, no. I would. I really would, but as it stands, bringing charges against you would be a headache for me as well as the people I care about. But if you ever speak disrespectfully to Eddie or anyone else in this office again, I will buy stock in Advil and press charges on behalf of the city of New York. I will also have a little sidebar with Manwarring Enterprises and DuBois Investments about suing you, and just for shits and giggles, I will get Olivia Manwarring to sue you for damages."

Watching the blood drain from my mother's face was even more satisfying than it was when a hardened career criminal realized it was over for them.

"You would only drag your own name through the mud." Her lips trembled as she spoke.

"No, I wouldn't. I have been paying attention, Mother. Just because I have refused to stoop to your level thus far doesn't mean that I can't spin this and show that I am the hero son standing up for justice, holding the aristocracy to the same laws as everyone else. I will get a statue in Central Park and a clear path to the presidency."

I wasn't bluffing. The files were already backed up to a secure drive.

"Son, you are making a mistake. I am untouchable." She twisted her lips into a cruel smirk. "I have the best attorney in the state. He will mop the floor with you."

"No, he won't. Not when he reads the charges. The family lawyer represents the family. This goes public, the divorce filing will follow, and the lawyer stays with Dad. Your assets will all be seized. The only representation you will get is a public defender fresh from law school and wet behind the ears. He won't even know how to argue for bail. Not that he'll need to when I show how much of a flight risk you are."

"You can't."

"I can, but I won't unless provoked. Now get out of my office." I turned my back to her and looked out the window. It was dark enough that the only things I could see were my mother's and my reflections. A multitude of emotions flickered over her face: shock, doubt, anger, and finally, determination. She turned and marched out of my office.

Just when I thought it was over, shouts erupted right outside my door.

"This is all your fault, you stupid little whore," my mother yelled. I didn't think I had ever heard my mother yell like that at anyone who wasn't staff with an NDA or family.

CHAPTER 28

HARRISON

I ran out into the bullpen to see my mother's hand wrapped around Eddie's arm and Catherine looking on with a smug smile.

Fuck my life.

"Did you want to add assault charges to the list, Mother?" I asked.

"This is all her fault." My mother dug her nails into Edwina's arm, and she let out a whimper of pain that woke up something deep inside me.

"Let me go." Edwina tried to pull out of my mother's grip, but her acrylic talons dug in deeper. I swore I could see a drop of blood starting to form.

"Let her go immediately," I shouted. I didn't think I had ever shouted before, not out of anger, not at my mother.

The second her talons were out of Eddie's skin, Eddie ran to me, moving behind me, trusting me to protect her.

That felt good, too good.

"Be gone when I get back," I told the two women before ushering Eddie into my office. "Are you okay?"

Tears started to spill down her cheeks, and I whipped them away with my thumb.

"I'm sorry, I just realized that I still had files on my desk, and it wasn't locked. It still isn't, and the driver wasn't here yet, so I thought I could sneak back up and just lock it without being seen, then found that bottle blonde bitch sitting at my desk and she started accusing me of things and then your mother came out..."

I pulled her into my arms and held her for a moment. It felt good to hold her, to protect her, so I closed my eyes and savored it, trying to commit to memory exactly what this felt like.

We waited about fifteen minutes in silence and when we left my office they were gone. Eddie ran over to her desk and locked the drawers, and I walked her to the car.

Later, my mind was racing with everything that had happened, debating what the best course of action was going forward. I weighed what I wanted versus what I needed over and over. Every angle was meticulously examined in my head as I lay alone in bed.

What would happen if I continued the affair with Eddie and we got caught in my office after hours. There were so many fantasies of what we could do during those late nights, I didn't think it would be possible to not fool around in my office.

What would happen to her if she got pregnant and Catherine or my mother decided to launch a smear campaign? Eddie's entire career would be tainted by my feelings for her, she wouldn't be able to escape it.

Alternatively, what would happen if everything went right? If we were never caught, what would that look like? I would still be living a hypocritical double life with this secret over my head, and Eddie would be alone. She would have me when I was able to be with her, but it would be a secret.

Eddie deserved more.

She deserved a man who could proudly have her on his arm, who could shower her with gifts and affection and not have to hide. She deserved a man who could eventually give her a wedding and a family.

$$* \, * \, *$$

THE SUNLIGHT WAS STREAMING through my windows when I realized what I had to do.

When I got to the office, Eddie was already there going through her desk.

"I have some calls to make this morning, but then I need you to come into my office. Bring with you the files on Judge Harrison and Judge White."

"Yes, sir." She gave me a sweet smile, making my chest ache.

It only intensified my foul mood. I wasn't a man accustomed to not getting what I wanted, let alone having precisely what I wanted within my reach but denied the pleasure of it. While my decision was the right one, it didn't mean I had to like it.

I slammed the door to my office harder than I intended, making me feel like an even bigger asshole, just adding to my miserable mood.

The phone calls took two hours, and in that time, I had made two attorneys cry, and another was probably writing their letter of resignation.

It was already well known I didn't tolerate incompetence well on a good day, but the mood I was in had me acting borderline unprofessional and a little belligerent. I hit the intercom on my desk that usually went to Cynthia's desk but had been moved to Eddie's for the moment.

"Eddie, can you come in here please?" I was going to be brief and explain that we had to keep this professional, and then we were going to get to work.

It should have been simple enough, but then why did it make my stomach tighten? My chest hurt, and I was filled with dread for the entire situation.

"Do you have the files I asked for?" I inquired when Eddie walked into my office.

"I have one of them," she said. "I can't find the file on Judge White."

"What do you mean you can't find the file?"

"It's not on my desk. It's not in any of the drawers. It's not with the other files."

"This is very sensitive information, Ms. Carmichael," I bit out.

"I understand that, which is why I'm telling you the file is missing."

"Well, it didn't just get up and walk away on its own. Where is it?"

"Honestly, I think your mother or your fiancée took it out of my desk last night."

"That is absolutely ridiculous." I stood from my desk and started pacing in front of the large window, pressing my fingertips to my temples.

"Harrison, I don't know where this file went. I don't have another explanation," she said.

"Do not blame my mother or fiancée for incompetence and lack of professionalism," I ground out, far harsher than I should have.

"Don't raise your voice to me, and do you really want to open the door to the conversation on professionalism?" she snapped.

I hated how much I loved it when she stood up for herself and fought back. I pressed my lips together to stop myself from saying something. I could throw out another argument, and she would rebuff it just as quickly, and by the end of the fight, I would have her bent over my desk, taking my cock.

"Look, I don't know what's going on between you, your

mother, and your fiancée, and it's not my business. We have agreed that this would remain a professional relationship." Her words stung more than they should have.

She was right.

We had agreed that this would remain professional, And I had come to the same conclusion again the night before, but that didn't mean I liked it or liked being reminded of it.

"But when I came back upstairs last night, your fiancée was going through my desk." Her voice was lower and forcibly calm. She was trying not to escalate the situation. It was the smart thing to do, but it wasn't enough. I didn't need this situation de-escalated. I needed it over.

"I don't have time for this," I bit out. "People make mistakes, and the fact that you won't own up to and admit that you lost his file and instead try to blame my family is juvenile and unprofessional. I don't know what I expected from a simple paralegal."

I watched her eyes harden and her jaw clench as I continued to speak.

"It takes a certain level of character to admit when you are wrong, and I am very disappointed that you do not possess that maturity yet. However, I do. I fully take responsibility and admit that I was wrong. We cannot work well together. I want you to pack up your desk. I'm going to call Ms. Lakeson immediately and have you reassigned. Get out of my office."

Eddie stared at me for a moment, her eyes starting to water but her posture going completely stiff.

I expected her to say something.

I thought she was going to fight…to give me an excuse to react in a very unprofessional way to calm her down.

Instead, she just nodded, turned, and left.

The problem was handled.

Instead of relief, there was only anger.

With a clenched fist, I punched a hole in the wall.

CHAPTER 29

HARRISON

*B*y the end of the following week, my mood had managed to get worse. I was shouting at people left and right, refusing to return calls, working by myself day and night. I couldn't remember the last time I slept. The only reason I had even gone home each night was to shower and change my suit. I was glad that Cynthia agreed to extend her two-week vacation another week because if she had returned to me like this, she would have quit in a minute. She probably would have flipped me off as she strolled out of the office, and I would have deserved it.

Finally, it was Friday, and a few people in the office had hinted that if I did not actually take the weekend off to relax, the entire district attorney's office might just get up and walk out.

I hoped it was a joke, but honestly, at this point, I really wouldn't blame everybody if they did leave. I made another note for Cynthia to upgrade the coffee station in the break room at my expense. It wasn't really a solution, but it was a gesture.

I left my office during lunch and just took a walk around a nearby park. Trying to clear my mind a little. I needed the break to get away from the stress of work but mostly from seeing Eddie at a different lawyer's desk day in and day out.

She had been assigned to a very promising up-and-coming prosecutor who, I was surprised, hadn't just moved onto the corporate sector yet. Maybe he just wasn't done making a name for himself. Having Eddie on his desk was definitely going to help him do that. It was a good place for her. It was a place where she could learn a lot and advance her career, but it also put her in my direct line of sight every single time I left or came back to my office.

The walk during lunch had cleared my head a little bit and helped me refocus. I was genuinely feeling better and like I could maybe be productive for a few hours before I had to leave to attend a private dinner with my fiancée where she and I would discuss exactly how our marriage would work and what was and was not expected of each other. And then I saw Eddie at her desk, flirting with that fucking Detective Doyle again.

A hot spike of anger flushed through my body, so intense I saw red. I tightened my fist and had to stop myself from assaulting a police officer in my own office. Instead, I turned and marched into my office, closing and locking the door and then moving back to my private bathroom, splashing cold water on my face.

Walking into this room was a mistake, though. All I could see was Eddie the first time we met when she was in here with her blouse pulled up over her head, in the middle of changing.

Or even the second time I caught her in here with her shirt off and her perfect breasts exposed. That was the first time I discovered exactly how wet her pussy could get for me.

I couldn't be in the office. Without looking at anyone else, I grabbed my coat and headed straight for the elevator.

It was getting harder and harder to breathe. My hands were

balled into fists, trying to curb the shaking that wouldn't stop until the elevator doors closed and I was alone.

With a quick text message, I told my driver to meet me downstairs, and I left the building without looking back.

The second I got outside into the cold, fresh air, the pressure in my lungs eased a bit, but it wasn't enough. I got into the back seat of the car before the driver had even come to a full stop.

"The penthouse," I barked and then put up the partition.

The panic attack started fast. I couldn't remember the last time it was this bad. Before Eddie came into my life, I hadn't had a panic attack since school days. But now it felt like everything was out of control.

There was more work on my plate than I could handle by myself, and that had never happened before. I needed help, but there was no one that I could trust to help because I couldn't control myself around the one paralegal that was on my level.

I couldn't even control my social calendar. My mother was adding more and more events where I was supposed to be seen with Catherine to make a good impression and secure my future. I couldn't control Eddie. The woman I wanted was openly flirting with another man in the office, and there was nothing I could do about it.

It was her right to flirt with whoever she wanted to. I didn't own her, although I really wanted to.

The irony of the entire situation was not lost on me. I refused to be with Eddie the way I wanted because the best-case scenario for her was that she didn't get to live a full life. So, I'd let her go so she could live that life. But seeing her living it, seeing her flirting with another man, sent me into a tailspin so intense I didn't know how I was going to make it through the day. I couldn't watch her live the life she had every right to live.

The car slowed to a stop, and I looked up. We weren't anywhere close to my penthouse. I considered just getting out and making a run for it, but there were so many people on the streets it would have been inadvisable. The last thing I needed was for the Page Six headline to say "Golden Bastard Loses Grip on Re-Election Golden Egg."

That would kill my career along with any chance I ever had of running for any type of public office again. If I let that happen, I would be lucky to land a job as a part-time attorney at a third-rate legal clinic.

I bent down, tucking my head in between my knees, and tried to block out the rest of the world as I ran the numbers.

Five things I could see. I could see the black leather of my shoes, I could see the dark gray carpet on the floor of the car, I could see the glint of the metal rails that held the driver's seat, I could see the back of the leather seat in front of me, and I could see the seam on the front of my pants.

Four things I could touch. I could touch the soft wool of my suit, I could touch the smooth, heated leather of the seat I was sitting on, I could touch the rough woven material of the seat belt across my lap, and I could touch the cool, sleek silk of my tie.

Three things I could hear. I could hear the soft classical music that the driver was listening to in the front seat, I could hear the traffic next to the car, and I could hear a woman shouting at a man on the sidewalk for stealing her cab.

Two things I could smell. I could smell the rich leather polish that the driver used on these seats, and I could smell the hot dogs from a cart right on the other side of my window.

And finally, one thing I could taste. I could taste the saltwater running down my face. Slowly, I reached up and touched my face, brushing the tears away. I hadn't noticed that I had started to cry. I just prayed that the tears didn't start flowing until I was already in the back of the car, hidden away from prying eyes.

I took several deep breaths as the car finally started to move again. I got myself together, wiping my eyes, straightening my tie, and sitting upright. The cold mask of indifference slid back over my features, and it was enough to get back to my apartment.

It took another twenty minutes before I was in my apartment in the Financial District, high above the hustle and bustle of the New York City streets. I was so far up it almost seemed calmer up here, looking out over the world at all of the problems that seemed smaller from this perspective. It was one of the reasons I loved this apartment so much.

I considered for a moment making an appointment with my physical trainer, to see if I couldn't work out some of this anxiety, tension, and lack of control in a boxing class. It was actually why I started boxing, and lately, I'd been too busy to make it to the gym.

For a brief moment, I did consider making an appointment with the therapist I had used when I was younger. But I couldn't risk it getting out that I was in therapy. There wasn't anything wrong with being in therapy. Logically, I knew that, but I also knew that the stigma was still there, and it was just another mistake I was making that could be used as fodder on Page Six. I couldn't do that. Hiring an escort had the same risk.

The thought of another woman in my bed made me a little sick.

Instead, I set an alarm on my phone and did something I hadn't done in far too long. I took off my suit and went to bed.

Four empty hours later, I awoke feeling calmer. I was still overwhelmed, I was still stressed, but I was more in control. And that was what I needed to be.

It had occurred to me to cancel the dinner with Catherine and instead see if Luc or Marksen were up for a drink, or maybe even call my sisters and relive one of the nights we had when Amelia had made her escape from my mother's clutches.

There were a few nights when the three of us would just hang out, watch movies, and eat pizza like we were born into a normal family.

The alarm on my phone sounded, reminding me that I had an appointment that, although I was not looking forward to it, needed to happen. Catherine and I needed to lay out exactly what was and wasn't expected in our relationship and where we were going to go. It needed to happen tonight, and it needed to happen before my mother found out that we were having this meeting. This meeting would put me more in control of what was happening with my social calendar, which would be one less thing for me to stress about.

Still, I sent Amelia a text asking if she wanted to get together this weekend, and then I got dressed for my evening with Catherine.

Catherine, to her credit, did make us a reservation at some ridiculously upscale French restaurant that offered booths that were nestled into little alcoves and had curtains to give the diners a more private, intimate experience.

Although for all intents and purposes this was a business dinner, privacy was required, and it needed to look romantic.

I arrived only a few minutes after she did, and she was already seated at a table in the back corner.

"Catherine, you look lovely tonight." I greeted her appropriately.

I wasn't wrong. She did look lovely in a white sheath dress with gold earrings and necklaces. Perfectly understated. Demure, delicate, and expensive. It looked like my mother had dressed Catherine herself. Perhaps she had?

I didn't know which thought was more terrifying, that Catherine's taste was so in line with my mother's, or the distinct possibility that she actually had my mother pick out her outfit for the night.

We ordered the first round of drinks and appetizers and got down to business.

It started simply enough, talking about events and charity obligations, those that she would be able to do on her own, others that she would prefer having my presence at, and a few where my presence was not optional. All things considered, it was very reasonable. Most of the events she would handle herself, and the non-negotiable events so far were on dates that I was able to make work.

"About your secretary," she started as she finished her third glass of wine.

"Not my secretary," I said.

"Whatever." She waved her hand dismissively. "About the girl that was at your desk and any other girls on your desk or whatever after her."

"What about her?" I asked, not liking where this conversation was headed.

"You need to stop seeing her."

"Excuse me?"

"Look, I don't care who you sleep with, but it needs to be more discreet than someone at work. I don't expect you to treat this like an actual marriage because it's not one."

I knew she was right, but how she was so cold and dismissive about it made me a little sick. And I had to wonder, was this what I wanted? Did I want the same contract marriage that my father and mother had, or did I want more?

"Well, that girl, Ms. Carmichael, is no longer on my desk."

"Oh, good. I was worried that you were going to keep her on even after everything, but Mary assured me you wouldn't and that you have a very low tolerance for incompetence."

"What do you mean, everything? You mean the altercation where my mother assaulted her?"

"Well, that and that other thing. Your mother is so bad." She laughed and set her glass down roughly on the table, sloshing the dregs of the champagne around the glass.

"Oh?" I smiled at her. "What did she do this time? She always gets up to the most interesting things," I said, playing along.

My stomach twisted, and I had a feeling I knew exactly where this was going.

"Well." She leaned in like she was going to tell me some scandalous secret or let me in on the latest gossip. "While I was waiting for you and your mother, I started looking through the girl's desk, thinking she might be up to something or she might have something of yours or something incriminating, but I couldn't find anything. It was all work. Then all that stuff with your mother happened, and when you took that girl back into your office, your mother went into her desk and grabbed a couple of files."

"She stole evidence?"

"Oh no, nothing like that. She just took a couple of files, just some work things. I'm sure they were nothing. She just wanted to make sure that the girl got in trouble and got fired so she'd no longer be a threat to what we were doing here. Really, Harrison, you should know to be more careful with who you sleep with. I mean, having an affair is fine, but does it have to be as cliche as to have it with a secretary? That's almost as bad as sleeping with your yoga instructor. At least have it with somebody on your same level. If you're looking for a little discreet hookup, I'm sure I can find someone who would be interested. However, the more I think about it, we should probably start having kids right away, so maybe it's best if you don't stray, at least until we have our first child."

How could I have been so stupid? I knew that Eddie wasn't stupid. I knew she wasn't incompetent, and she understood how important those documents were. I owed her an apology. And she shouldn't accept it. I had fucked up so royally there was no way she was going to forgive me.

Although, Amelia forgave Luc for being absolutely terrible. Olivia even forgave Marksen for kidnapping and then trying to blackmail her. If they could forgive their partners for that and still love them, could Eddie forgive me for being an asshole earlier?

Even if she couldn't, did I want to deprive myself of the chance of finding a relationship like my friends had for this cold, icy woman?

"Catherine, I appreciate what you were trying to do, and I understand that in your head, you were doing the right thing. But this is not going to work."

"Of course, it's going to work. Your mother's arranged everything. It's all planned."

"No, it's not. Keep the wedding location if you want to keep the deposits. I don't really care. But I will not be marrying you, not now, not ever."

"You can't do this to me! Do you know who I am?"

I flattened my palms on the table and leaned down. "I know something way more important than that... I know *what* you are. A fucking bitch. I'm done."

I put a few hundred dollars on the table and walked out feeling suddenly lighter and more centered than I had in weeks. I was over letting myself be manipulated by Mary Quinn Astrid and her privileged insanity.

I needed to go find my girl.

CHAPTER 30

HARRISON

The crowded New York street no longer felt suffocating and congested. It felt alive, like I could tap into the energy of the city and use it to fuel anything. Like it could seep into my cells and give me life. This had to be what people meant when they said New York City was the greatest city in the world.

It was incredible. I needed to find Eddie immediately. I owed her so much and wanted to take so much more. I was finally in a position to give her everything she deserved. I would be the man she didn't know she had been missing her entire life, just as soon as she begged me to touch her. I wasn't about to start this new chapter of our lives on another broken promise.

The cold air felt somehow crisper, lighter, and freer, and I needed to take Eddie Carmichael in my arms and kiss her until I made her see things my way.

I needed to apologize to her for the things I said and for accusing her of being incompetent when she was one of the most ambitious and hardworking people I had ever known. She couldn't have been incompetent if she actually tried. She was too good, too smart, too thorough. That woman was born to be a lawyer. Until she made it into law school, she had taken the initiative to learn whatever she could by being the most dedicated paralegal.

Who did that?

She did.

I wanted her back on my desk desperately, but realistically, I knew that might not be possible. So, I wanted to give her an option, let her choose what she wanted. It was something I should have been doing from the beginning, but I hadn't given her a single choice since I had met her. I'd told her she had choices. I'd deluded myself into thinking I had given her choices, but I hadn't, not really. The options I'd presented to her were not good enough for consideration.

I just had to find her. I had to tell her everything and lay out my entire argument. I had an opening and closing statement prepared. There was no way, just no way, that she wouldn't agree that she and I were meant to be together. I was operating in good faith, and it only made sense that she would be now, too. I was ready to give her everything to help her meet her goals while she worked to help me meet mine. I didn't want her to be an accessory or a tool like Catherine. I wanted her to be my partner in everything.

The first thing I did was run back to the office. I didn't know what case she was working on, but I did know she was a workaholic, so there was a really good chance I would find her there. It was, after all, where she was most comfortable. I knew that because it was where I was most comfortable.

It was only eight in the evening, but it was a Friday night, so I shouldn't have been too surprised when I found her desk empty. The disappointment stung, but I was nothing if not resourceful.

She could be working for a lawyer who was going to court, and her work was already done, or maybe she was working with one of the men who kicked off early Friday nights but came in over the weekend.

It was fine, an unexpected hurdle, but I could use it to my advantage. It was probably better that my propositions didn't happen in the office anyway. Maybe she had gone out with friends or something?

I ran back to my office and used my admin password to view her calendar. What did privacy matter when it came to want and need?

She had confided in me over one of our late work nights that she loved organization. She preferred physical, but digital made more sense, and she didn't have to keep running out of supplies.

Using a calendar and being what she called "a little extra" with Outlook folders and things like that made her feel like she had some semblance of control. She had even taken the time to color code all of her appointments and included the due dates for bills and the deadlines to sign up for classes, even though she hadn't planned on taking any this semester.

So I knew if she had plans, they would be on that calendar.

If not, then I'd go to the apartment that I had set up for her. If she wasn't there, I would turn over every single rock in this entire city until I found her and made things right. This could not wait until Monday.

When I had her by my side where she belonged, I would woo her with all the highlighters and Post-it Notes she could ever want. I would buy her an entire office supply store if that was what she wanted. Hell, I would take her to Japan to buy fancy Japanese stationary. Anything to make her happy.

There was a single entry in the calendar for tonight, in a pale pink color, signifying that it was personal.

Date night: with Detective D at Gianna's in East Village.

I stared at the entry for a good two to three minutes, not quite understanding what it meant.

She was on a date with another man. That man. Detective Patrick Doyle.

My woman was sitting in a romantic restaurant with that dirty jackass of a detective.

Fuck, that asshole moved fast.

That detective was a dirty cop. He may not have had the last name of the Irish mob, but his mother did. He was the nephew of one of the enforcers who had committed countless crimes and had even been one of the names that appeared repeatedly on tampered evidence logs. Of course, in the precinct he used his legal name, Patrick Doyle, but he introduced himself using his nickname, Patrick D.

There was no way she could have known that this man was a danger to her, and I didn't know if he was flirting with her to see what she was working on and to try to get information or if he just realized exactly how beautiful she was, and it was a pure coincidence.

Either way, it wasn't happening. He had pushed too far, gotten too close, and tried to take what was mine. With a deep breath, I decided this was enough. There would be no more asking. There would be no begging. I was done trying to be reasonable.

Eddie was going to come to the realization that she was mine, and there wasn't a goddamned thing she could do about it.

I had enough to go after the detective. It wasn't as much as I liked. He was a slippery son of a bitch, and I wanted bail denied and a slam dunk case, but it was enough. I made the necessary calls and had a warrant for his arrest issued within minutes.

Then, I called the police commissioner and called in a favor. The man owed me several, and when I told him that we were going to go pick up not just a dirty cop but the pocket cop of a mob family, he was ready to pull out all the stops.

It had been so long since I had been on a ride-along and been part of an arrest that didn't happen in a courtroom, I'd forgotten how much fun they could be.

My body was humming with adrenaline. Part of me wanted to believe it was because the case I had worked on for so long was finally starting, but this wasn't like every other big case. This excitement had to do with Eddie being a part of it. As much as this was a big case for my career, it was going to be huge for hers.

When we got to the restaurant, I immediately saw them in a booth in the back corner. She was stunning, wearing a simple, dark blue silk blouse that made her eyes seem to glow, and a sexy little black pencil skirt that hugged her ass in just the right way.

Her golden hair was down and in loose waves, and her makeup was light, but a darker red lipstick made her lips look fuller and more kissable. They looked like they would taste like cherries, and I wanted to sink my teeth into them. But I wouldn't, not until she begged. She would be begging for more than just my kiss by the end of the night.

Jealousy burned in my gut, replacing the anticipation I had been feeling. I wanted her to dress like that for me. I wanted her to wear that silver necklace that hung in the deep "V" of her blouse right between her breasts for me. I wanted everything she was doing to be for me, not the dirty cop that she was sitting with.

They were laughing about something, and I hated not being in on the joke. The way she laughed with her whole body, her head tilting back, she looked happy and free in a way that I hadn't really seen before. The time we'd spent together was all anger and chemistry or centered on work. We worked, we fought, we fucked. We hadn't had the opportunity for much else.

I had only seen a glimpse of her being light and funny. I hadn't really seen her when she wasn't preparing for battle.

Just looking at her across the room, I wondered if I knew her at all. Could I make her feel like she felt right now? Or would being with me mean that she would feel like she was always under a microscope and always had to be on? For a moment, just a split second, I wondered if I was doing the right thing. Then I watched as his hand went around her shoulders, and he pulled her closer like he was going to kiss her, like he dared to put his dirty, lying, criminal lips on my woman.

Absolutely not.

I made my way through the restaurant, leading the team of police to the table and almost running over the mousy hostess in the process. I didn't even spare her a look, like I wasn't going to spare a thought for anyone else I destroyed on my way toward what I wanted.

"Harrison, what are you doing here?" Eddie asked when she saw me.

"Arresting your date," I said, stepping aside so the uniform behind me could take out his cuffs and start reading Doyle his rights.

Shouting over Doyle's blowhard objections and the police officer's droning voice, Eddie squared off against me. "You can't arrest him."

"I can, and I am," I said matter-of-factly.

"He hasn't done anything to you." She tried to get between her date and the officer.

"Ma'am, I'm going to need you to move." The uniform looked very uncomfortable as he tried to get around her.

"Not to me, Eddie. He has done quite a bit to the city of New York."

"Are you kidding?" She looked at me, putting her cute little hands on her cute little hips like she had authority. "You're arresting my date tonight? What would your fiancée say about this? Have you run this by your mother yet?" I kind of liked that

246

she tried to stand up to me. It would make bringing her back to earth so much more enjoyable.

"Your date is a criminal. He's the reason other criminals are still on the street. This has absolutely nothing to do with you. Move, or I will have you arrested for trying to impede justice."

"You wouldn't dare," she said through her clenched teeth.

I turned to look at one of the other uniforms and said, "Officer, detain her as well."

"Are you sure?" he asked, looking back and forth between us.

"Yes. Just because she works in my office does not mean she is above the law. She interferes with an active investigation, she should be arrested and charged."

"Harrison, you cannot be serious," she said, her eyes wide and mouth opened.

"Absolutely." I leaned in, to whisper in her ear, "You better start thinking of ways to get out of this. If you have a record, you will never get to join the bar."

The blood drained from her face as I moved back and watched as both she and Doyle were put in cuffs, their rights read as they were escorted from the building with the entire world watching.

I grabbed another uniform and whispered in his ear, telling him I wanted them separated into different precincts. He was going to a rougher area where being a cop on the wrong side of the bars would make for an interesting night. She was going to a newer precinct, one that had a new wing that was just completed but wouldn't officially be in use until next month.

She and I were going to need a little privacy as soon as I let her cool off for a while.

CHAPTER 31

EDDIE

Sitting in a jail cell contemplating murder was never something I had envisioned for my future. I knew it was a distinct possibility at some point. You didn't grow up in the neighborhoods I grew up in or with the limited resources that we'd had and not realize that jail for many people was an inevitability.

Some people ended up here because they were lazy and took shortcuts, others because they were desperate and had no other options, and some just did dumb shit.

None of those were the reason I was sitting in this cell. I was here because I'd had the audacity to develop feelings for an asshole with money and power.

I didn't know what Harrison was trying to pull, but he was right. If I were processed, I wouldn't be mad or upset, I'd be terrified. If I were processed, fingerprinted, and put into the system, then I would have a record, and the chances of me getting into the bar were slim to none.

It actually would become extremely unlikely that I would

ever be accepted into any type of law school. Grades, letters of recommendation, and my work ethic would all be worthless. Years of scrimping and saving and putting every other aspect of my life last would have been for nothing.

Harrison knew that, and I was pretty sure that was why I hadn't been processed yet. He wanted something, and he was going to hold my entire future over my head to get it. Or maybe he was just trying to prove a point.

He was such a dick.

I had just been thrown in a cell like they were throwing somebody in a drunk tank so they could sober up before sending them home.

Thankfully, this was a smaller precinct, and the women's cell was currently empty. Still, I paced back and forth in the tiny little room, waiting.

Waiting for Harrison to show up and reveal his master plan or to berate me or yell at me or do whatever other heavy-handed, privileged shit he was ready to do and then let me go.

I didn't understand why he interrupted my date with Patrick. I knew he didn't want me flirting with him before, but I thought that was just petty jealousy. Or that he thought it was unprofessional, but he hadn't said two words to me since he kicked me off of his desk.

"Hey, am I going to get a phone call?" I yelled for probably the fifteenth time.

Nobody was sitting at the desks in front of the cell, and nobody was around as far as I could see. Maybe they had just forgotten they stashed me in here, and I would be stuck until someone came into work.

"That depends. Who are you going to call?" Harrison casually strolled down the hallway with his hands tucked in his pants pockets.

"Are you charging me with something?"

"Should I be?"

"If you're not charging me, you need to let me go." I tightened my grip on the metal bars.

"Actually, I can hold you for twenty-four hours. And I just arrested your date on RICO charges, so I can keep this going for quite some time. You may be a suspect. You could have been talking about anything at that romantic little restaurant."

I moved as close to him as possible, pressing my body against the bars.

"You had no right to have me arrested."

"I had every right to have you arrested. Detective Doyle has been charged with a whole slew of charges. Well, I'm sure you know what the charges are seeing as you've been working the case with me for weeks."

I crossed my arms. "I *was* working the case with you, until you dumped me on another attorney after falsely accusing me of losing a file."

Not taking the bait, Harrison pressed on. "Did you know Doyle's mother's maiden name is O'Murphy?"

"Fuck," I said as I sat down, realizing that I had been on a date with a dirty cop.

I thought he was asking about my work to make conversation. I didn't realize he was actually trying to suss out what information Harrison already had.

"Did you two talk about the cases that you're working on?"

"He did ask," I admitted. "But I was telling him about the case I'm working on now, and even then, it was all very general information. I know not to disclose an active investigation to anyone, even an officer of the law."

"Good. Did you tell him anything about the case that we were working on?"

"No." Fuck, I had misjudged this entire situation.

"Why did you agree to go on a date with him at all?"

I shrugged my shoulders when I looked up at him. A line was forming between his brows. Something I had only ever seen happen when he was annoyed.

"Tell me, Eddie, why did you agree to go on a date with him? Do you find him attractive?"

"Not really," I admitted.

"Then why did you go out with him?"

"Because he asked," I said.

"I admit I am a little disappointed in you." His voice was stern, and hearing he was disappointed in me made my cheeks heat, and I suddenly wanted to curl in on myself and cry. I didn't, but I really wanted to. I had never felt like such a fool or a failure before.

"Look, are you going to charge me or not? Because I have a lot of things that I need to get done." I was proud of myself for saying that and not letting any of my emotions through.

"I haven't made up my mind yet." He crossed his arms in front of his chest. "But I'm willing to let you plead your case. Why should I just let you go?"

"Because I didn't do anything," I bit out as I stood back up and paced in my small cell.

"Didn't you though? Let's go over the facts, Ms. Carmichael. True or false, you broke into my office on two separate occasions to use my private bathroom?"

"What does that have to do with anything?"

"Just answer the question," he said. "True or false."

Looking back at him, I bared my teeth. "Relevance, counselor?"

"Speaks to the character of the accused, not to mention motive." He casually leaned on the edge of one of the desks. His body language said he was relaxed, maybe even a little bored, but something in his eyes made my stomach clench. He was enjoying this, laying a trap, and I didn't know what it was or how to avoid it.

"I don't want to play your little game."

"What you want is irrelevant. Answer the question. I caught you breaking into my office on two separate occasions. True or false, Ms. Carmichael."

"True."

"Both times I caught you, you were in various stages of undress. One could assume that you were trying to distract me from your break-in with your body."

"Objection. You can't speak to my motivations."

"Overruled." He waved his hand dismissively.

"Any judge would have your comments stricken from the record," I fired back, straightening my spine, ready to argue my case.

"Do you see a judge here, Ms. Carmichael? Right now, I am the only judge you get. There is no jury or record. I even had the cameras turned off. Right now, it is just you and me."

"Does that mean you are my judge, jury, and executioner? I have rights, counselor."

"You do. This little conversation isn't to determine your guilt. It's to determine your future. This debate will determine if I press charges or let you out of that cell."

He stood from the desk and ate the distance between us up in two long strides. His intense blue eyes stared down at me, and I had to crane my neck back to meet his gaze. My heart was thundering in my ears, and I wanted to shrink back, but I knew I couldn't give up ground. I gripped the bars tightly and feigned a strength I didn't know I had.

"Ask your questions."

"Is it true or false that you were previously warned away from flirting with Detective Patrick Doyle?"

"Yes, but—"

"And is it true that you agreed not to speak to him again?"

"Yes, but—" I was getting flustered.

"Is it or is it not true that you have worked several hours on the case I am currently building against the O'Murphy family."

"Yes, but—"

"Is it true that you had access to all the files, every single bit of evidence I have gathered? In fact, wouldn't it be fair to say that you are the only person other than myself to have access to everything?"

The way he growled out each word made my heart race and my cheeks flush. I had heard about his prowess in the courtroom. Some of the lawyers gossiped about him. They said he was driven and single-minded, like a warrior going to battle. They said he was all power and precision, a true alpha male. I thought I knew what they were talking about. I was wrong.

"Is it true that a few hours ago, I caught you sitting at an intimate table with Detective Patrick Doyle?"

"Yes." My voice was shaky, and I moved away from the bars, trying to at least get control of myself by looking away.

He took the keys from his pocket and opened the cell.

Marching over to me, he grabbed my throat and pressed me against the cold cinder block wall.

"Look at me." It wasn't a request. His fingers tightened, not enough to hurt, but enough to make sure I knew he was in control. He made the decisions. The only thing I could do was look into his steely eyes and obey. "Tell me the real reason you went on that date."

"I was hoping spending time with him would make me want you less." It didn't even occur to me to lie.

"Did it?"

"No." I answered honestly again.

I hadn't been able to get Harrison out of my head. It didn't help that I saw him come and go all day or that his driver still picked me up and brought me to and from work and the loaner apartment.

"I find you guilty, Ms. Carmichael. I find you guilty of disobeying, distracting, and being willfully insubordinate to me. Before I give you your sentence, I have one more question."

CHAPTER 32

EDDIE

"*H*arrison, I—" His hand tightening around my throat in warning cut off my words.

"Ms. Carmichael, if I were to reach under your skirt right now, would I find your pussy wet and aching for me?"

"Yes."

I had been wet for him from the moment he started his questioning. I didn't understand how he did it. No other man had ever affected me the way Harrison Astrid did. What he was doing should have been seen as a threat. But I wanted him. My body wanted him.

"Good." He slammed his lips to mine in a brutal kiss. It felt like he was trying to devour me, claim me, and I wanted to let him.

Every time he touched me—every single caress of his fingers, kiss of his lips, or press of his body to mine—I melted. I didn't understand. How could one man do things that, under any other circumstance, would be a turn-off if anyone else had done them? But because it was Harrison Astrid, it just made me want him more.

Then I remembered where I was.

In a jail cell where he had the audacity to hold my future over my head because I had dared to go on a date with another man after he had made it perfectly clear he didn't want me.

Fuck him. This wasn't happening on his terms. I was not going to be some little damsel in distress who gave in to him every single time he wanted to claim me.

I laced my fingers in his hair and pulled hard. When he broke the kiss to grunt something out, I took the opportunity to latch onto his neck, biting as my hands went from his hair down his chest to his pants. I was taking control of this entire situation. He was not going to use me in a jail cell to work out his frustration. I was turning the tables, and I was going to use him. How dare he think that he had the right to threaten my entire future because I went on a single date? No, I wasn't the one that was going to be punished here.

With more strength than I knew I had, I pushed Harrison back a step at a time until he hit the bench that was attached to one of the barred walls.

He sat on the bench, and I climbed onto his lap, gripping the bars on either side of his head, caging him in.

"It's my turn to ask some questions," I said.

"I already made my judgment, babygirl."

"Then consider this my appeal. True or false, counselor, the name in the files is not Detective Patrick Doyle, it's an alias used as a means to conceal the identity of a dirty cop until charges could be filed."

"True."

"So there's no way that I could have known that Detective Doyle was the man listed in those files."

"Do you often go on dates with men before getting their full names?"

"It's my turn to ask the questions, counselor," I said, grinding my hips down on his lap, on his hard cock that was barely contained by his pants.

"When you told the defendant not to speak with Detective Doyle, did you tell them why?" I asked.

"I did not," he said. His hands went to my hips, and he tried to rock me back and forth, but I tightened my core and became immovable.

"Why did you decide not to tell me the reason I shouldn't be flirting with the detective?"

"Because you should have known better. Flirting in the office is unprofessional," he said before he wrapped his hand in my hair and pulled me down so my lips met his again.

I broke the kiss and leaned back, taking my mouth out of his reach. So he started kissing my chest and working the buttons of my blouse apart one by one.

"I'm glad you said that." I wrapped my fingers in his hair, directing his lips to where I wanted them. "Because professional boundaries are important. Tell me then, counselor, was it professional when you bent your paralegal over your desk and spanked her during the workday?"

"She deserved to be punished."

"That wasn't my question. Please answer the question I asked. Was spanking your paralegal during work hours professional?"

It was getting harder to focus. His lips were wrapped around my nipple, still covered by the lace of my bra, and his cock straining to get free of his pants pressed at my core.

"No," he growled before sinking his teeth into my breast, sending a bolt of electricity down my body to my core. I wasn't going to be able to hold out for too much longer.

"Was it professional to fuck her in the office when there were other people working just on the other side of the door? Tell me, counselor, did you even bother to ensure the door was locked?"

"I have a release built into my desk to lock it without getting up."

"But was it professional behavior, counselor?"

"No," he grunted out before ripping aside the cup of my dark blue lace bra and sucking my nipple into his mouth.

It was hard to maintain my focus with the way his lips kept pulling at my breast, sending shock waves of pleasure down my body and pressure building in my core.

"And counselor, was I working with you when I behaved unprofessionally and accepted a date from a detective?"

"No."

"And why wasn't I working with you?"

He didn't answer my question. His hands just moved to my hips and pulled me closer.

"Counselor, I require a response to my question." I pulled his hair back, forcing him to release my breast and look me in the eye.

"I had you reassigned to another lawyer's desk."

"Yes, you had me reassigned to another desk, a demotion without cause."

"I had cause. Files went missing." His fingers dug into my hips, and he pulled me against his body. I had to fight to keep what little control I had. If I let my fingers touch any part of him other than the hold I had on his hair, I would have given in to him and been completely lost.

"And were they ever located?" I asked mostly out of curiosity and an attempt to refocus.

His body stiffened under me, and he let out an annoyed sigh.

"Yes, you were right. Someone else had taken them from your desk. Happy now?" He pulled the cup that still covered my other breast hard enough that it tore. It didn't matter at that moment. I could be upset about it later.

"So you dismissed me without cause," I pointed out. "Was that professional?"

"What's your point?"

"My point is that between the two of us, I was not the one that was the most unprofessional. But I'll move on."

"Good," he said, burying his face between my tits, his hands moving down to my hips on either side of where my skirt had already worked its way up my legs. He pushed it further up around my waist, baring my dark blue panties. His hands trailed up my inner thighs, and his thumb slipped under the soaking wet silk, finding my clit and starting to rub, in slow, steady circles.

There was no point in trying to hide how he affected me. He could feel it, so I let out a shaky breath and flexed my fingers, massaging his head.

"When I went on that date, were you and I in any type of sexual relationship?"

"No," he said.

"So you had no claim on me. None whatsoever."

"I wouldn't say—"

"That wasn't a question," I interrupted him.

"You and I were not engaged in a relationship, sexual or professional. We hadn't even spoken in a week. You have no claim on my free time. What or who I do after work is none of your business."

When I said that, his hands tightened on my hips, and his fingers pushed back and slid inside me, pressing against my G-spot.

I bit back a moan of pleasure.

"Is that still your stance, Ms. Carmichael?"

"I have only a few more questions, counselor," I said, ignoring what he said.

"Thank fuck," he mumbled.

"Do you think it's fair—"

"I don't give a fuck about fair," he interrupted me.

"Fine. Do you think it's ethical that you took your paralegal out of her home and forced her to relocate?"

"That was for your safety," he interrupted again.

"Let me finish," I said, pulling his hair back so he had to look into my eyes as I hovered over him, my hand moving down between our bodies to palm his hardened cock where it was tenting his overpriced designer pants.

"Do you think it was ethical to have forced me onto my knees to suck your cock, then licked my pussy until I had an orgasm that was so powerful, I almost blacked out, before fucking me within an inch of my life? Do you think it was ethical to do all that while your fiancée was sitting at home for you? In fact, where is she right now, waiting for you at some overpriced restaurant where you just so happen to have forgotten her again?"

"That's irrelevant."

"It is absolutely not irrelevant." I moved to get off of him, but he grabbed my thighs and held me in place.

"Catherine and I are no longer linked. Socially, romantically, or financially, there is nothing between us."

"She finally get tired of having a fiancé that preferred to fuck secretaries?" I used air quotes and made my voice high-pitched and nasally like she did every single time she talked down to me.

"No, I decided I didn't want a woman whose only ambition in life was to be the arm candy of a powerful man. I wanted a smart, sexy woman who challenged me. I had come to claim you when I discovered you were on a date with another man."

He pulled me into another fierce kiss that I wanted to melt into. Every fiber of my being was begging me to give in and to melt into this man. But I was not about to set that precedent.

"Claim me?" I asked, breaking our kiss and gripping his cock.

"Do you think after everything that happened, I was just waiting for you to come and make love to me?"

"Yes." He stated it like it was a fact, a simple irrevocable fact, not realizing how much fucking audacity he had.

"I find you guilty, Harrison Phillip Astrid," I said. "Guilty of arrogance, of assuming that everyone's world revolves just around you. I find you in contempt for having the disrespect of putting my entire future in jeopardy so that you could have a laugh, making me wait for you in a jail cell. How dare you. You don't get to use my body as some type of compensation for whatever imagined slights you have come up with."

I unzipped his pants, freeing his cock and stroking it roughly from root to tip several times, making sure he was fully hard and ready for me.

"So what? You think that you're going to just use me, that you're going to flip the tables and take control?"

"That's exactly what is going to happen."

I gripped the bars on either side of his head again and lowered myself onto his thick, hard cock. The stretch was just as delicious as it had been the first time. I was so wet I slid down him, taking his entire length in one smooth thrust.

His hands moved to my hips as I rocked up and down, taking him at just the right angle to hit all of my most sensitive places.

"Do you like that, Eddie? Do you like taking control and riding my cock?" he whispered in my ear.

I nodded, my eyes sliding closed as I lost myself to the sensations running through my body.

"Do you like feeling like you're in charge? Thinking you can take anything you need from me?"

Again, I nodded.

"Good girl, you can ride my cock whenever you want. Take as much of me as you can. Ride as fast or as hard as you want as long as you remember one little thing."

"What's that?" I asked with a shallow breath as I rode closer and closer to oblivion.

He picked me up, and without taking his cock out of me, he moved us so my back was against the bars, and I had to grab them with both hands as he started thrusting into me with everything he had.

"It doesn't matter who starts on top," he rumbled into my ear. "I'll always demand your complete submission in the end."

CHAPTER 33

HARRISON

For the first time ever, I woke up feeling rested. My body was calm, my mind was still, and I felt at peace. It was an unusual feeling for me. I couldn't for the life of me figure out how I had slept so well.

Then the most beautiful woman in the world, still fast asleep, wrapped her arm around my waist and pulled herself closer to me, resting her head on my shoulder. As if it had a mind of its own, my hand went to her silky blonde hair and I let my fingers slip through the soft strands. Before pulling her closer to me and then rolling so I was on my back, and she was asleep on my chest.

Closing my eyes, I thought back to the previous night, the rounds of fighting, sex, more fighting, and a lot more sex.

I, like many men in my position, have had plenty of experience, but nothing had ever compared to the primal heat between us. It was sensational. I had lost count of how many times we had argued just for it to end up with one of us kissing the other and then me pushing into her tight little body or her pushing me down so she could ride me.

My particularly favorite moment of the night was when she told me to go fuck myself, and I responded that if she said something like that to me again, I'd wash her mouth out. She said it again, and I grabbed her by the hair, forcing her to her knees and shoving my cock in her mouth. She responded by grabbing my hips and holding me still as she deep throated me with such enthusiasm and vigor it was like she was taking out her anger and frustration with me on my cock.

It was life-affirming.

After I had washed her dirty mouth out with my come, I tossed a bottle of water at her, giving her a second to catch her breath before throwing her on the bed and telling her she absolutely did not get the last word in this argument. Then diving between her thighs and using my tongue and fingers to make her come so hard that her own juices dripped from my chin.

"Good morning," she said as she opened her eyes and looked up at me.

Even first thing in the morning, she was still absolutely stunning. She didn't need designer clothes or high-end makeup to look glamorous. All she needed were her bright green eyes, soft golden hair, and pink lips that were still a little puffy and bruised from my attention.

"Good morning," I said, my voice a little gruff. "How did you sleep?"

She made a low purring sound in the back of her throat as she slid off me and stretched her arms and legs, arching her back enough that the sheet fell away from her perfect breasts.

"Good, but I am in desperate need of a shower and a cup of coffee before we go into the office."

"Oh, we're not going into the office today," I said.

She looked up at me. Her eyes got wide, and I swore there was hurt shining through them.

"I thought you said you wanted me back on your desk to help with this case."

"Oh, I do, but we're not going into the office. We're going to work from here today." I climbed out of bed and stood, completely naked. "Why don't you go hop in the shower, and I'll make the coffee. Then meet me back here, and we'll get to work," I offered while stretching my arms over my head, trying to get the rest of the sleep from my limbs.

When I didn't get an immediate answer, I turned around and caught her checking me out. Her gaze was traveling up and down my body, her eyes wide and her tongue running over her top lip. Even after everything we had done last night, she was still checking me out. My God, didn't that do great things for a man's ego?

"Counterproposal, counselor?" she said, shaking herself out of whatever fantasy was playing in her head.

She bit her lip and looked up at me as she sat up in the bed, letting the sheet pool at her waist.

"Go ahead."

* * *

"How about you go make a large pot of coffee and then come join me in the shower?" She kicked the sheet down the bed.

"Agreed."

It took all of the discipline I had to walk away from Eddie, naked and sprawled out on my bed, to go make a pot of coffee, but she needed caffeine and I wanted to provide. For the first time I realized that I wanted to get her everything. I wanted to be the one that provided for her, not because she was sleeping with me, but because I wanted her needs to be met and I wanted to be the one to do it.

There was a strange tightness in my chest that I tried to rub away while walking into the kitchen. I didn't know what this girl was doing to me, but I decided right then and there that whatever it was, I was going to let it happen. It didn't matter to me anymore that Eddie might not be good for my career. That was ridiculous, anyone who spent five minutes with her knew that she was absolutely brilliant.

Eddie was not the same type of woman that Catherine was. Catherine was made to be the wife of a strong man, she was meant to be a tool to help someone's career. She came with political ties, a pedigree that could not be argued with, and a trust fund that could build an empire. She was a Barbie made for a powerful man.

Eddie was so much more.

Eddie was the girl who didn't work to further someone else's career. She had her own. She would work tirelessly toward her own objectives, and anyone smart enough to be her partner would align their intentions with hers. Eddie would be an equal, not an accessory. I wanted to give her the chance to reach her goals and build the life she wanted at my side. If that meant that I didn't run for office, so be it. I would open up my own law firm, and she could practice whatever law she wanted to right beside me.

She was my female counterpart. In a courtroom, she would be a warrior like I was. Her arguments would be brilliant and brutal. No one would face her and win. I could see her not only having a near-flawless record but, like me, there would also be a secret tally. People would count how many lawyers went up against her and lost so badly that they left the profession or turned to something spineless like contract law.

She was the Valkyrie to my Viking—the Amazon to my Gargarean. I suddenly understood what Luc and Marksen were talking about when they called Amelia and Olivia their partners.

I didn't want to break Eddie. I wanted to help her fight and win every battle we came across.

The only thing I had left to figure out was how I was going to convince her to stay by my side.

I guessed I just had to spend the weekend showing her what a life with me could look like.

When the water started in my shower, I abandoned the coffee pot and went straight into the bathroom.

We spent over an hour in the shower, kissing and washing each other, making sure every single inch of the other one was clean. By the time we got out, I had made her come two more times, each while moaning my name, and she had used the soap to give me the most amazing hand job I had ever had.

Still, I promised her coffee, so while she took her time shrugging into my black cashmere robe, I went into the kitchen with a towel snug around my hips to make her coffee.

I went ahead and loaded up a tray with everything she could need for her coffee, as well as a little breakfast spread of some fruits and cheeses from my fridge. I wanted to make sure she had everything she needed because I did not want her leaving my bed for as long as possible.

When I set the breakfast tray down on the bedside table, she was still in the bathroom, humming happily to herself. God, I loved the way that sounded. She was comfortable in my home, and for a moment, I wondered if she would be comfortable making this her home. I loved the idea of waking up to her in my arms and hearing that adorable, off-tune humming coming from my bathroom as she got ready for work every morning.

Quickly, I went into my home office to grab the files that we needed, as well as my laptop and a tablet for her. And spread everything out on the bed.

"What's all this?" she asked, stepping out of the bathroom. The robe was hanging off her shoulders and cinched tight at her waist. I loved knowing with one single pull her body would be mine again.

"Ms. Carmichael, do you think that just because I said we weren't going into the office, you would have the day off?" I arched an eyebrow at her. She smirked right back.

"I figured at least we would be working in your home office."

"I'm sorry, is my bed suddenly not up to your standards?" I crossed my arms over my chest and had to press my lips together to keep myself from laughing.

"Oh, but Mr. Astrid, what would the other secretaries say," she said in a breathy voice before erupting into a fit of giggles.

I walked around the bed until I stood in front of her and grabbed her still-warm hair to tilt her head up and meet my eyes.

"Don't ever let me hear you calling yourself a secretary. You are so much more."

"Sorry, paralegal," she corrected.

"Come, let's get some work done and drink our coffee. Then maybe if you are a really good girl, I'll reward you for a job well done." I gently pushed her toward the bed, then handed her a cup of steaming coffee and a file.

"Yes, sir." She gave me a playful wink before taking the file from me and sipping her coffee.

CHAPTER 34

HARRISON

We worked in silence for a few hours. I was sitting against the head of the bed, my laptop balanced on my outstretched legs. Eddie was lying on her stomach, facing the foot of the bed, while she stared at files and took notes on the tablet I had given her. I typed with only one hand while the other stayed on the back of her leg. There was just no way for me to be this close to her and not touch her.

I would have thought having her this close, wearing only my robe, would be a distraction, but it had been a very productive morning. Having her so close made me feel calm and centered in a way that I hadn't felt in a long time.

"I don't get it." She turned to look at me over her shoulder.

"Get what?" I closed my laptop to give her my full attention.

She got up, swiveling to face me. The knot holding the robe together loosened, giving me a tantalizing view of her cleavage.

"These guys have been pulling this racketeering shit since the eighties," she said, settling on her knees next to me and staring at the tablet.

"Probably before that," I said as I watched the robe separate a

271

bit more, exposing more of her full breasts. I should have been sated. I'd had more sex in the last twenty-four hours than I did for the entirety of the last year, but something about her made me ravenous.

"Then why are you only now bringing up charges? Is it because they were working with the Manwarrings? Were you covering for your friends?"

"Luc Manwarring and I are friends," I admitted. I could have lied but I just simply didn't want to. "The O'Murphy clan has never really been big enough to be on my radar. Until very recently, I thought they were thugs working for the Manwarrings, doing shady shit, but not really worth the taxpayers' money to prosecute."

"Explain."

"Well, as the Manwarrings' attack dogs, they would have had the best lawyers. A court case would have dragged on for months, if not years. It's also not unreasonable to assume the Manwarrings would try to bribe the judge, assuming they didn't already have a few in their pocket. Since the shit they did was all corporate espionage and it could have only been against other corporations dealing dirty, they didn't seem like a public concern."

"Why spend millions pursuing a case against criminals when they are only harming other criminals." She nodded, understanding my thought process. "Especially when they would probably walk anyway, and then it would make you a target."

"Exactly. But now Luc is in the process of taking over for his father, and he has cut ties with the O'Murphy clan. It has brought a lot more to light. It looks like the Senior Manwarring was covering a lot more than just some intimidation."

"Like?" Eddie moved around so she was sitting cross-legged on the bed, leaning back on her arms and getting comfortable, and I wondered if she knew how tempting she was, exposing just a few more inches of skin while she discussed the merits and reasoning behind this case. My mouth was watering, and my cock started hardening for her again.

"Arson, for one, a few counts of attempted murder, suspected involvement in a few missing persons cases, kidnapping, blackmail, bribing a government official, and extortion."

"So now that your friend's family isn't protecting them, they can be brought to justice?"

"No, now that I know the extent of their crimes, they will be brought to justice." I couldn't help myself. I reached out and ran my finger from her neck down along the line of the robe, then brushed it aside to fully expose one perfect breast, her nipple instantly pebbling under the graze of my thumb.

"So now you are going to be the one to take the bad men off the streets and make New York a little safer." She was teasing me, but I liked it.

"I don't know, what's in it for me?" I teased her right back.

"How about the gratitude of the city?"

"What if I was only interested in the gratitude of a single citizen."

"The mayor?" she asked, placing a finger on her chin like she was thinking.

"No," I said, tweaking her nipple, making it hard enough to cut glass.

"The governor?"

"Try again, little one," I all but growled.

She leaned over me, letting the side of the robe open completely, as she grabbed my laptop and moved it to the side table. Then she threw her leg over my lap and straddled me, grinding her hips down over my achingly hard cock.

"What does this citizen have to do to show her appreciation?"

"This." I reached up, sliding my hands in her loose waves, and pulled her lips to mine. Her kiss was hot, passionate fire, but I wanted something else, something that was more.

I kissed her slowly, waiting for her to follow my lead. I kissed her slow and deep, and when she relaxed against my lips, I rolled her over and made love to her. It was slow, passionate, and intimate. I didn't want to control her, I didn't want to dominate her, I wanted to coax pleasure from her body, and I wanted her to love me as I was starting to love her. It was too soon to tell her how I felt, so I wanted to show her.

* * *

"You know what this means, don't you," I asked, laying on the bed with Eddie in my arms, both of us naked, covered in sweat, and completely enamored in the afterglow of what I could only describe as making love.

"No, what does this mean?" she asked, placing a sweet kiss on my chest before laying her head back down in the same spot.

"It means you're mine now, all mine."

She let out a seductive little giggle. "And what does that mean?"

"It means you're mine to protect." I kissed her shoulder. "To provide for." I placed another kiss on her shoulder. "To adore."

"Mr. Astrid," she said, looking up into my eyes. "If I didn't know any better, I'd think you were informing me that we are a couple. In a romantic relationship, not a professional one, with certain... benefits."

"Ms. Carmichael, that is exactly what I'm telling you." I leaned down and kissed her forehead.

"Harrison, you know that won't work. You need a woman like Catherine, preferably not as bitchy, but someone who can be on your arm at fancy cocktail parties, balls and galas, and other pretentious gatherings. You need a woman that can make idle chitchat with the other women of your station. That's not me. I don't know how to do that. I don't want to learn how to do it either."

"If that was what I wanted, then I would have stayed with Catherine," I said, looking her in the eye. "That's not what I want, and she was certainly not who I want."

"Then what do you want?" she asked.

"I want a brilliant, sexy woman who is as much of a fighter as I am. I want a woman who knows what it means to work, what it means to want something so bad you can taste it. I need a woman with ambitions built on more than just societal expectations."

"You want a charity case?"

"Ms. Carmichael, you couldn't be a charity case if you tried. In fact, I did try, and you refused. I had to pick you up out of that god-awful crack den of a room and drag you to somewhere that was more fitting for a woman of your stature."

"My stature?" She laughed, throwing her head back, her feet kicking a little. "Counselor, my stature indicates that I was exactly where I should have been. I was in an apartment that I could afford."

"There are New York City rats that were living better than you were," I deadpanned. "And stature has nothing to do with money, sweet girl. Your stature has to do with your importance. It has more to do with a reputation that is gained by ability and/or achievement. You aren't born into stature. You earn every single inch of it. The fact that your living arrangement didn't reflect that was appalling."

"I don't know if you're aware of this, but the housing market for a lot of New Yorkers is appalling," she said, sitting up to look at me.

I stayed lying down, stretched out in case she wanted to lay down in my arms again.

"Fine, we can address the housing situation after the O'Murphy case if that is what you want to do. But for right now, I'm going to address the housing situation of one particular New Yorker. Move in with me?"

I hadn't planned on asking something like that so soon. I had intended on persuading her to move into the apartment I had put her in before, letting her think she was still using empty corporate housing, but I didn't want her even that far away. The idea of having her live with me just seemed right.

"Harrison, what would people say? You'd be ruining my reputation. People would assume that I had slept my way to the top."

I tried not to roll my eyes.

"Eddie, you are a gorgeous woman who has chosen to take a male-dominated field by the balls. It doesn't matter if you were a cloistered nun before law school or a prostitute. People will always say that you slept your way to the top, not because it's true but because that's the only way they could justify a woman being better than they are. And if they're going to say it anyway, why not let me help you? Let me pay for law school. Let me—"

"No," she interrupted. "You're not paying for my law school." She sat up straighter. "I want to do this on my own. I need to."

"You are incredibly stubborn," I said.

"Yeah, that's what's going to make me a great lawyer," she said, giving me a little half smile. "But I need to know that I worked my way up, and I paid my own way."

"Counter proposal, counselor?" I asked.

"Go ahead." She nodded.

"Pay for law school yourself. I think it's dumb not to accept the help, but pay for it yourself. But live with me. It's no different from all the other law students who live with their parents or a partner. They don't pay rent, and neither will you. But you can still work in the office. I insist that you still work at my desk, and in the office, we will keep it professional. No one needs to know you are living here if you don't want them to. But I also insist on writing a letter of recommendation as your employer."

"I still don't think it's a good idea," she said, looking down at the bed. She stayed sitting up, chewing her bottom lip a little, and playing with her fingers.

"Well, I think it's a fantastic idea," I said. "But either way, you're staying here this weekend. Give me a chance to show you what life could be like here with me."

CHAPTER 35

HARRISON

"What do you mean they have a tendency to kidnap loved ones?" I slammed my fist on the wooden table, staring at Luc.

Eddie and I had spent most of the day together, in bed working, while I mentally prepared my arguments to convince her to move in. I was sure she was preparing hers on why she shouldn't.

I had been looking forward to our little debate, where I would stop at absolutely nothing to win. I was going to consider it her first foray into battling a real lawyer.

Then Luc called and insisted I get out of bed and meet him at the club. So here I was, dressed in a suit, sitting across from Luc as he explained that my sister, mother, and quite possibly my girlfriend were in danger.

"I'm sure that nothing will—"

"No, I'm going to need you to walk me through this again," I demanded, interrupting Luc.

He nodded and then picked up the crystal tumbler in front of him and downed the contents in a single swig.

"Apparently, the O'Murphys have been more direct with the handling of disagreements than I had originally anticipated."

"Luc, I am one of the top lawyers in the city. I am the fucking district attorney, and I couldn't follow that line of bullshit you just spouted. Tell me everything, now." I grabbed my own short, crystal glass of whiskey and shot it back, letting the burn refocus some of my energy.

"Initially, I was worried that Amelia was going to be in danger since I cut ties with the mob. I feared for her safety and for that of Olivia, so you know I had extra guards put on both of them."

"I am aware. What's your point? Has something happened to Amelia?"

"No, apparently they don't consider the loss of business from the Manwarring Corporation to be the biggest threat to them at the moment. They've caught wind of an investigation happening in your office. Apparently one of their cousins is a cop, and he was picked up on charges of conspiracy and evidence tampering."

I bit back a curse. I knew arresting the detective was going to show my hand. I just didn't realize how quickly it was going to happen and how reckless I had been.

"So you're saying they're going to start targeting people in my office?"

"No, Harrison, I'm saying they're going to target you. They seem to think that the only person in your office who would have the balls to go after them is you. Please tell me they're not right."

"They are absolutely right," I said, sitting back in my chair and crossing my arms over my chest.

Luc bit out a curse and then ran his fingers through his hair.

"Okay, the good news is that Catherine has already taken to social media and has let the entire world know that the engagement is off. Something about moving too quickly, I don't know. I wasn't paying attention when Amelia was talking about it."

I cleared my throat. "Do you often ignore my sister when she speaks?"

"I do when she's wearing lace," he said with a shit-eating grin. I rolled my eyes, not needing to hear that.

"Okay, so they're not going to come after Catherine. That's good, I guess," I said, shrugging. "Who are they going to come after then, my mother? They can have her."

"God, if only," Luc said.

He had been having just as many issues and run-ins with my mother and how she thought her children's lives should go as I had. Apparently, she was still not happy that Luc had interrupted the wedding she had intended for Amelia. But it all worked out. Amelia was happy with a man who was technically still a very beneficial match. Luc just wasn't as easy to control as Marksen would have been.

"Are there any other women in your life that you spend a lot of time with? I still have security on Amelia, and I've already spoken to your father, making sure that your mother and Rose are both protected as well."

"I've got a girlfriend, but I don't think they would know about her. It's pretty new."

"When's the last time you spoke to her?" he asked.

"I was with her when you called. She's safe in my apartment." I relaxed back in my seat, ignoring the creeping feeling something was off.

"If they don't have a target, then they're probably watching your apartment. Is there any chance that she would leave while you're gone?" Luc asked.

My first instinct was to say no. There was no reason for her to leave. Then my blood ran cold. There must have been some tell or some sign that I was internally panicking because Luc put down his glass and leaned forward, his brows drawn low over his eyes.

"What's wrong? Does she have an errand to run or something?" Luc asked.

"No," I said, "but I had just asked her to move in with me earlier today. I'm a little worried she's going to panic and run."

"Why would she panic? How long have you two been together?"

"Well, it's a little hard to say. I mean, I could make the argument that I made my intentions clear when I had her arrested last night, but—"

"You had her arrested last night?" Luc leaned back in his chair, giving me a look that was confused and a little shocked.

"Yeah, she was on a date with that detective, and so I issued the warrant for his arrest because I thought maybe he was using her to try to get information about the mob and the case. Actually, no, that's a lie." I rested my head in my hands. "I chose that time to go after him because she went on a date with him, and I was afraid that she was going to be more interested in that dirty fucking cop than she was in me," I finished, the truth burning its way from my lips.

"I'm sorry, what? You like the girl, so you had her arrested?" Luc asked. "That makes no sense. Why would a woman want you after you had her arrested?"

I eyed Luc through my fingers, sat up, and sent an inquiring look in his direction. "You interrupted my sister's wedding and had the entire world thinking that she had an affair with you when you two hadn't even said two words to each other. Markson actually kidnapped Olivia and took blackmail photos of her that made it look like she was just another party girl and not the strong businesswoman she actually is. If you two can come back from those things, then why can't I come back from a little arresting? It's not like I actually had her processed or charged."

"Well, when you put it like that." The sarcasm in his voice was thick. Then he looked at me with something I had never seen on his face before. If it were anyone else, I would have said it was concern. "You might want to call her and make sure she's okay and tell her not to leave your apartment."

I grabbed my phone and dialed her number, pressing it to my ear, ignoring the slew of no cell phone signs posted around the club. No one really paid attention to those signs anyway. Besides, on a Saturday afternoon, it was just Luc and me in this area and a few retired guys on the other side of the room.

After the third ring, my heart started thundering in my ears. After the fifth ring, it became harder to breathe. And when the call went to voicemail, a cold sweat broke out over my back.

I hung up the phone and called again.

This time, it went straight to voicemail.

No, no, this cannot be happening, my voice screamed inside of my own head.

Hand shaking, I hit the "end call" button and called my driver, telling him to pull around and pick me up immediately.

"Did she not answer?" Luc asked, stating the obvious.

"No, she didn't. I'm going to head home and make sure nothing's wrong. If they took her, if they managed to get to her, where would they have taken her?" I asked Luc, trying to stamp down the overwhelming sensation of dread that was rising in my chest.

"I don't know, but I can start making calls. Get home and make sure she's okay. Call me once you know she's safe," Luc said, clapping me on the shoulder.

I nodded and returned the gesture before practically running outside to meet my driver.

The brisk air of the New York winter did nothing to cool my

skin or stop my sweating as I dove into the back of my car and slammed the door behind me.

"The apartment, immediately," I barked at the driver.

"Yes, sir." The driver pulled into traffic and tried to maneuver around the yellow cabs and other cars on the road.

We got maybe three blocks before I had the privilege to watch a car run a red-light, T-boning another car.

"Fuck," I swore, knowing that this was going to take forever to clear. They were blocking the entire intersection, and we were three cars back, so even if I wanted to have the driver maneuver around the wreck and keep going, there was no way to do it.

I sat there for five minutes trying Eddie's phone over and over. Still no answer, each time going straight to voicemail, telling me that she either got spooked and ran and blocked my number because she didn't want to move in with me, didn't want me. Or she was taken by the goddamned Irish mafia, and it was all my fault.

Either scenario was unacceptable.

Fifteen minutes later, the traffic cops finally cleared enough of the intersection that traffic kept going, but of course, it went at a fucking crawl until we moved past the wreck because people had to stop and stare. It was like they didn't watch the accident that just happened in front of their faces.

It was another ten minutes before we pulled up in front of my building. I didn't even wait for the car to come to a full stop or the driver to open the door before I flew out of the back of the car, ran past the doorman to the elevators, and started hitting the buttons.

It was probably only three or four minutes, but it felt like hours before I was finally on my floor, in front of my apartment door. I took a few deep breaths, trying to brace myself for whatever I was going to find.

I opened the door, feeling like my stomach was in my throat. Everything looked normal.

Nothing seemed out of place. Nothing had been moved. But it was also empty. Eddie wasn't here.

I went back to the bedroom where we had spent most of our day, and there was a note sitting on the table on top of the tablet.

Harrison, in case you get back before I do, I went back to my old shithole apartment to grab some clothes. I'm still not sure about living with you full-time, but I will admit I do need to find a safer apartment, and I'm okay (if you are) staying here until I can arrange a better place.

Love Eddie

The sigh of relief that I felt was absolutely incredible.

I crumpled to the floor just to catch my breath and let the fear flow out of my body.

My phone rang, and I looked at the screen. Eddie's name was lit up. And I answered, ready to give her hell for leaving without telling me first.

"Eddie, when are you coming back?" I asked into the phone.

"Well," a deep masculine voice said. "I don't think Eddie will be coming back, at least not until you do what you're told."

"What do you want," I bit out, my stomach clenching and my heart racing.

"Don't worry, Mr. Astrid, we'll be contacting you with our demands real soon." The deep voice laughed and then disconnected the line.

CHAPTER 36

EDDIE

Harrison left to have a drink with a friend and talk about whatever it was that ridiculously rich people talked about, probably plans for world domination or something else equally as asinine.

I'd admit I did make myself giggle when he dressed in a three-piece suit. Was this friend the president or a king? What would happen if he dressed in jeans and a sweater like a normal human meeting a friend? Would the Brooks brothers roll over in their graves? Would he be instantly disinherited?

I had to wonder what casual-Harrison looked like. Not DA Astrid, or Mr. Astrid, just Harrison.

Did that person exist outside of the time he spent in bed with me?

Did other people get to see that lighter, sweet side of him? Or was the warrior always out for blood and justice the only thing other people knew?

With a smile on my face and the tension that I thought had a permanent place in my back now gone, I took the opportunity to learn a little more about Mr. Harrison Astrid by snooping around his apartment.

Under normal circumstances, I would have considered it an invasion of privacy—I would have still done it, but I would have admitted it was wrong. But he had asked me to move in with him. I thought I had a good grasp on who he was as a man, but I hadn't known him that long, and I had to be sure.

I started rummaging through his closet of never-ending suits while I let my mind wander.

There were some hard decisions that I had to make. Did I want to live with Harrison? I did, but was I ready for the things that would go along with living with Harrison? He had said no one in the office needed to know, but realistically speaking, they would find out. They always found out. Lawyers, secretaries, and paralegals were nothing but gossips, always looking for the next scandal. Minding other people's business was what made them good at their jobs.

If it came out that I was living with and sleeping with my boss, it would definitely hurt my reputation, but we weren't breaking any laws. It was an ethical gray area that I could easily argue was perfectly legal. I was a consenting adult, and Harrison was not holding my job over my head. There was no misconduct happening within the office that anyone ever needed to know about. I could go to Mrs. Lakeson and ask to be assigned to someone else's desk after explaining the new personal relationship, but we had already put her through so much, and no one else's work met Harrison's expectations.

I didn't know if I was going to be comfortable making this a long-term decision, but in the interim, I would admit it was better to live here in the lap of luxury where it was safe than in the only-sometimes-heated single room that I had been in. The idea of going back there to spend another winter almost freezing to death every single night was just unbearable. Although I would never be able to enjoy the change in my living situation knowing Sabrina was still there.

Tonight I would talk to Harrison about the status of his charges against my landlord or at the very least the possibility of finding new housing for Sabrina. Maybe he would let her stay in the apartment he first gave to me. I could just imagine her face when she saw the city views and luxurious accommodations.

I didn't find any autopsy tools, severed heads, or women's shoes in his closet. So there was no reason for me to tell him no.

There was, however, a limit to the generosity and charity that I was willing to accept from, well, anyone, but especially the man that I was sleeping with.

So I needed to run back to my apartment and grab some clothes, a few personal mementos, and let my best friend know where I was so she didn't try to send out a search party. If she filed a missing person's report and then I was found in the district attorney's home, that would definitely get out, quickly.

I got dressed and then wrote Harrison a note letting him know where I was and that I would be back, just on the off chance he got back before I did. I didn't plan on staying long, though, it was really just a quick in-and-out trip.

I headed downstairs and waved to the doorman on my way out, then put my earbuds into my ears and turned on some music. It had been so long since I just listened to something that made me happy.

Honestly, after last night and this morning, I felt lighter.

Despite the work and workout I had earlier, I felt energized and shamelessly rocked out to some Britney Spears, Christina Aguilera, and a little Pink. I was on cloud nine. This had to be what happiness felt like. I had never let myself truly feel this way before. I was always waiting for the other shoe to drop, but this time, I wanted to feel it. I wanted to bask in this feeling for as long as I could.

It was almost like I was a new person; there was a little dance in my step, and I smiled at people as I walked past them on the sidewalk. Of course, this being New York, they all stared at me like I was on drugs, or a danger to society, or worse, from California.

Since Harrison had taken his car and driver, and it was the middle of the day with the sun still up and people about, I figured it was safe enough to take the subway.

While in the subway, I got this nagging feeling at the back of my neck, the same one I got every time I was being watched. But I was in a good mood, so I decided that it was just all in my head, or people were staring because I was a New Yorker smiling on the subway. That shit was weird. A homeless man naked on a subway was totally normal. A woman smiling and genuinely happy in the New York winter was a sign of the apocalypse. Homeless, you could understand. Crazy was unpredictable.

I ignored the feeling and went about my business, getting off at my stop. Despite the shady neighborhood and the frigid weather, it was still a beautiful day, and I decided I was going to enjoy my walk to my soon-to-be former apartment building.

I still had that same nagging feeling tickling the back of my neck, but I ignored it, thinking it was all in my head. I did at least have the sense to turn off my music and pay a little bit more attention to my surroundings. For the first time I could remember, the guys were not sitting on the stoop, and I wondered if Harrison had made good on his threats to have the building and the landlord investigated.

It didn't matter. I just needed to grab some things, and I'd be out. I ran up the stairs, made it to my door, and closed it behind me. My stuff seemed like it was all still here, like no one had ransacked the place, although I wasn't quite sure how to tell. It wasn't like I had dressers or anything to store things.

I grabbed a trash bag from under the kitchen sink and started throwing in clothes and anything else I wanted to keep.

It took me less than five minutes to get everything I needed. I looked around, seeing if there was anything else, and I realized that there was nothing in this apartment that I even wanted. This was all part of the old Eddie, the one who managed to convince herself that this was what it took to succeed in life. You had to sacrifice until you were miserable, letting people take advantage because of your rental situation. Never again. I was actually thinking about that as I got ready to leave, wondering if maybe that was the area of law I wanted to specialize in. I didn't think it'd make me rich, especially because I had no intention of being on the landlord side of things, but maybe working for Legal Aid or some other legal clinic would make enough to support some kind of life, or who knows, maybe I would end up as Mrs. Harrison Astrid. The notion made me laugh, but something inside of me wanted it to be possible.

"Well, I think that's it," I said to absolutely no one.

I took one last look at the life of the old "Edwina Carmichael" then grabbed the trash bag, slinging it over my shoulder, ready to turn the page to the next chapter of my life. The one where I still worked like a dog but treated myself a little better and let other people, really one person, help me achieve my goals.

"Yeah, I don't even think you're going to be needing that, doll," a deep, heavily accented voice said behind me.

I turned around to see two large men wearing dirty jeans and matching faded black hoodies and knit beanies standing in my doorway.

"Can I help you?" I said, taking a step back.

"We sure hope so, doll," the big one on the left with greasy red curls sticking out from the beanie said. "You see, we were sent to pick up a package."

"A package," I repeated, taking another step back, trying to use my peripheral vision to see if I had anything that could be used as a weapon.

There was an old aluminum bat lying against the bathroom wall. I remembered Sabrina brought it over for something. I thought there was a mouse or a cockroach big enough to be a mouse or something that we'd had to battle.

I moved a little to the left, trying to get a little closer to it.

"Yeah, someone sent us to pick up a secretary, a little girl who's been unable to mind her own business and keep her hands off other people's property. Does that sound familiar to you?" The big red-headed guy said again, taking a large step toward me.

"Sorry to say, but no, it doesn't. I'm not a secretary. I'm a paralegal. And I don't really know my neighbors. I prefer to keep my nose out of other people's business. You understand."

I offered a shy smile, hoping it came off as friendly and they would think they had the wrong person. I tightened my core, trying to stop the shaking that was starting to run through my limbs.

"What's the difference between a paralegal and a secretary?" the smaller man on the right with inky black hair and dark, menacing eyebrows asked.

"Secretaries make more money and do less work," I said, barely keeping the shaking from my voice.

"Yeah, that sounds about right," he snorted.

"Sure wish I could help you, fellas," I said as I shrugged, moving just a little closer to the bat. It was almost within reach. Just another half step or two, and I would be able to grab it. This apartment had never felt so big.

"Yeah, see, here's the thing: I don't think it matters what your job title is because we were given a picture of the package that we were supposed to pick up."

The big guy pulled his cell phone from his back pocket and

turned the screen, showing a picture from the jail cell last night. It was of me, and my arms and legs were wrapped around Harrison. My face was twisted in bliss with my eyes closed, but it was clear enough and easy to tell who the girl in the photo was.

"And you see, I'm pretty sure you're the blonde package that we're supposed to be delivering to our boss."

"I'm afraid you guys have made a mistake," I said, taking another step toward the bat. "There has to be some kind of mistake."

"See, I don't think there is a mistake." The big guy took another step toward me. I threw my bag at him, grabbed the aluminum bat, and swung with all my might, hitting him in the ribs.

He doubled over, and I lifted the bat again, high above my head, and swung it down like an axe, hitting him in the back. He made a pained yelping sound before he landed on the floor with a solid *thunk*.

The little guy came at me next.

"That was almost impressive," he said with a laugh. "Too bad that's the last brave thing you're ever going to do, kitten."

"Oh, I don't know about that," I said. "I'm not the rich bitches you're used to kidnapping."

I took another swing with all my might but the man dodged back, much quicker than his larger counterpart, and then grabbed the bat and yanked it from my hands hard enough that I had to catch myself before I landed on the floor.

"See now, that was just rude," he said before kicking out and hitting me behind the knee, making me fall to the floor on my knees.

The next kick pushed me flat on my stomach, and he pressed his boot in the middle of my back.

"Now, here's what's going to happen. You're going to be a good girl for us. We are going to stand up, all of us. We're going

293

to walk downstairs calmly, and you're going to get in the car that's waiting for us. You're not going to say a word. You're not going to say a thing to anybody cuz, let's be honest, even if you did, what the fuck is anybody in this neighborhood going to do for someone they don't know."

"Please don't," I said. "I can get you whatever you want, like, I have money."

I tried not to cry, but tears were burning behind my eyes, and my hands were shaking. Even my knees felt like they were going to collapse under me at any moment.

The big guy got back on his knees and then finally stood up, still breathing heavily, rubbing the spot on his back where I'd managed to hit him with the bat. A small point of pride grew in my gut. At least I'd fought back.

"No, Seamus. Why don't you lock the door and give me and the girl here a moment alone so I can get some payback and maybe teach her some fucking manners?"

"We don't have time for that," the little guy, Seamus, said.

"Girl, you're screwing a rich-ass motherfucker, a man with a silver spoon so far up his ass he can taste it, and he's allowing you to live in a shithole like this? Shit. Fuck, bitch, we might be doing you a favor."

"You might have a point," Seamus said. "If she stayed here, she wasn't going to survive the winter anyway. Still, we don't have time for any fooling around now. I'm sure you'll get your chance later. Come on, we're running out of time. Pick her up, and let's go."

Seamus and the Big One each grabbed an arm and dragged me to my feet. I tried to fight them, but my back was screaming with every single movement. My head was swimming, and I just wanted to throw up, then curl up into a ball and sleep.

I tried pulling my arms out of their meaty grip, and it was

absolutely useless. There was nothing I could do to get out of this.

Thinking as quickly as I could, I started loosening my shoe, nudging it with my other toe. When we got to Sabrina's door, I used it, kicking it off my foot, trying to hit her door, praying she was home and saw what was happening.

I thought I heard a door open, but I wasn't sure. I was fading in and out of consciousness as I was dragged downstairs and then thrown in the back of a car that reeked of whiskey and cigarettes.

The men argued outside the car for a minute. I thought it was about who was driving, but I couldn't be sure. I was still dizzy, and it seemed like the world was spinning around me. Still, I tried to use the distraction and slide out of the other side of the car. I got about two steps away from it, opening my mouth to scream out for help when a big, meaty hand pressed over my lips and pulled me into a body. The putrid scent of sweat, body odor, and stale cigarettes was nearly enough to choke me. It made my eyes water, and I wanted to vomit.

"What did I say about you being a good girl?"

He pushed me against the car, hitting my head on the door-frame, and everything went dark.

CHAPTER 37

HARRISON

The line went dead in my ear, and I threw my phone across the apartment. It landed somewhere on the thick rug as I let out a wild-sounding roar of frustration.

It wasn't until I flipped over a glass table, shattering the top, that I was able to gain some semblance of control over myself. With a few deep breaths, I tried to center myself and figure out the best course of action.

The first thing I needed was proof. I couldn't believe it was true. Not until I saw it with my own eyes would I believe that Eddie had been taken by the fucking Irish mob.

Until I knew beyond a shadow of a doubt they had her and hadn't just cloned or even stolen her phone, I couldn't tear the city apart looking for her.

If it was true and they had her, then I would break every law, ripping this city apart to get her back. It didn't matter what it took, who I had to pay off, blackmail or even hurt. She would be back in my bed safe and sound by the end of the day, and whoever had dared touch her would be wishing I would only arrest them. They would never see the inside of a cell. Prisoners had rights, and these monsters didn't deserve such consideration.

I would be their judge, jury, and executioner.

I left my apartment, convincing myself that it had to be a joke. It had to be some type of sick prank. My driver was still sitting in front of the building, waiting to pull into traffic to park the car. Instead, I jumped in the back seat and told him to take me to Eddie's apartment.

"The one by the park, sir?" he asked.

"No, the shithole where we found her," I said, running my fingers through my hair and trying to do breathing exercises so I didn't give myself a fucking heart attack on the way to get my girl back.

I closed my eyes and remembered how she was this morning, nearly naked in my bed, reading dissertations and police reports, how she chewed her bottom lip while going through bank and other financial statements, looking for discrepancies. She had even found a few I had missed. She was perfect, and she was mine, and I was not about to let some low-life thug who should rot behind bars fucking take her from me.

Ten minutes later, we were pulling up to the building, and the stoop was surprisingly absent of neighborhood thugs. I didn't have time to think about that. Hopefully, someone else finally reported her slumlord. I hadn't found the time and didn't consider it a priority since she was staying in the safe house.

I ran up the stairs, heading straight toward Eddie's apartment. The door had been replaced but was unlocked, so I pushed my way in. It was empty.

Her stuff was still lying around, and there was a large black garbage bag in the middle of the room. It looked like she had been shoving clothes inside of it. I made a mental note to buy the poor woman some actual luggage when I got her back. And I would be getting her back.

"Who are you?" a feminine voice asked behind me.

I turned around to see a short, pretty woman with dark hair pulled into a high ponytail on top of her head.

"Harrison," I said. "Who are you?"

"Are you the one she was seeing? The Neanderthal who threw her over his shoulder like some kind of caveman and put her up in a swanky apartment by the park?"

I nodded, not really feeling the need to explain my actions to some random girl in the hallway. "Do you know where she went?"

"Some guys came and took her. Two men dressed in dirty clothes with thick accents came and carried her off."

"You saw them? Where did they take her? Why didn't you stop them?" I couldn't sit still. The violent mix of fear and rage flooded my veins, and I had to move.

I paced around the small room, running my fingers through my hair, pulling it at the ends, needing some type of outlet other than yelling at this poor girl.

"I didn't stop them because I'm not stupid." She rolled her eyes before leveling a bored expression at me. "Eddie kicked off one of her shoes, making sure it hit my door so I would see the men who took her. I didn't call the police because I figured you would be here in a matter of minutes and look, just like magic, *poof!* Here you are."

"How did you know I was coming?"

"Because Eddie is my bestie, and she tells me everything. From what she says, I think you are an overbearing asshole, but she likes you a lot. And the one thing you can always count on with overbearing assholes is, they have a protective streak. Who the fuck else would have her arrested for dating another man?"

"Why would she kick off her shoe?" I didn't have time to

address any of the shit she said. I knew Eddie had to consider her a friend, and she'd given me enough information to go on. Still, none of this was making any sense.

"There is this old story about a female reporter who was investigating the mob. She told her brother that if she were ever abducted, she would try to leave a shoe behind so they would know what had happened to her. She was abducted and left a shoe."

"Did they ever find the reporter?" I asked, not sure why the answer felt so important at the moment.

"That reporter didn't have the district attorney personally looking for her." I wasn't sure if the look in her eyes was confidence or a challenge. Either way, it helped keep me focused.

"What more can you tell me about the men that took her?" I asked, staring her down and meeting her glare.

She gave me a single nod like she approved of my determination.

"I can tell you there were two of them. One was a redhead. They both had thick Irish accents, and they got into a new black sedan. No license."

"What do you mean by no license? You didn't get their license plate number? How could you not have gotten their license plate number?" I was yelling and rambling, but it didn't matter. The only thing that mattered was getting Eddie back.

"No, I didn't get their license plate number because they didn't have one. There was no license plate, front or back, and there was nothing posted in the windows."

"Still, you should have called the police. At least they would have been able to chase them down faster."

"I doubt it." She shrugged. "You arrived maybe five minutes after they left. The police don't respond to calls in this neighborhood very quickly."

I nodded, still pacing the small room, trying to figure out

what my next steps would be. There had to be something I wasn't thinking of. I needed help and I needed it immediately.

"You seem awfully calm about this." I looked at Eddie's supposed friend, who was casually leaning against the door.

"The way I figure it, Eddie will be fine as soon as you do whatever it is they want. She doesn't have anything they could want or need. She doesn't even have the power to be a blip on their radar. So this isn't about her. It's about you. They hurt her, they lose leverage over you. Ergo, this is all your fault, and you will get her back unscathed, or the guys who took her will be the least of your problems."

"Are you threatening me? Do you know who I am?"

"I don't give a fuck who you are. You are just some guy who will break down when I butcher you, just like any other pig. Save her, and I won't have to break out my knives, got it?"

"Threats aside, I'm going to find her, and if I have my way, she will never be back in this dump again," I said honestly. "And you should know I will do everything I can to make her safe. If you think of anything else, call me." I handed her a business card after writing my personal cell phone number on the back.

"I did actually manage to grab a picture of them when they were down in front of the car. Maybe it'll help?" She took her phone out of her pocket, an outdated model, but at least it had a camera, and typed away for a moment on the cracked screen before sending me two pictures.

The first one of them showed the car very clearly. The other one was a little grainy, but it showed the men who took her, and Eddie in the car, trying to get out. My heart stopped, and I realized how unbelievably scared she must have been. She probably still was, and I needed to make sure that no one could ever do that to her again.

"When you get her back—and you had better get her back," the girl threatened, "I never want to see her in a place like this again. You take care of her and make sure she takes care of herself, is that understood?

I nodded and honestly felt a little better knowing that Eddie had at least one good friend in her life. I made a mental note that when this was all over, I would find out more about this friend and see if I could help her in any way too. It was the least I could do if she'd looked out for Eddie before I was able to.

With a deep breath, I realized that I wasn't going to be able to do this on my own. I didn't have the resources, and I knew who took her. I knew how little of the police force I could trust.

So instead of calling a police chief or a captain or even the goddamn mayor, I called the two people I knew who were well-versed in dealing with men like this.

I called Luc first to see if he was still at the club.

"Yeah, I'm still here, but I was about ready to head home to the wife," he said.

"Don't leave, I need your help. In fact, I'm on my way back over there now. Get Marksen to the club immediately. I'm going to need both of your help. Someone took Eddie and I think I know who."

"We'll be here waiting for you," he said as I hung up the phone.

I marched down the stairs again, looking for signs of anyone who might have seen her, who might have seen what direction the car went, but the street was surprisingly clear. It was almost like they had intentionally made sure the street was empty at the time they took her.

I got back in the car and in the midst of telling the driver to go to the club, I realized that my hands were shaking and a cold sweat had broken out down my back again. I couldn't be seen like this. It would draw too much attention, and God only knew what would happen if that got back to whoever took Eddie.

CHAPTER 38

HARRISON

"*A*ctually, take me to the penthouse," I told the driver and then sent Luc and Marksen a message.

Change of plan—meet at my place.

Thankfully, there were no accidents, nothing holding me up. This time, I was able to get straight to my home and head upstairs, but I hated it because the apartment didn't feel right.

The entire atmosphere of this penthouse had changed simply from her presence for a single day, and it now felt empty without her here. I took off my coat and threw it on one of the couches, marched over the broken glass from the table still in the middle of the room, and poured myself a drink.

I slammed it down and immediately poured myself another, the burn helping to focus me and take an edge off my anxiety so I could think clearly.

I didn't toss the second one back. I didn't want to overdo it. Eddie needed me to be strong, clear-headed, and focused for her. Instead, I took a sip, set the glass down, and waited.

Thankfully, I didn't have to wait long. Marksen was in my

home within minutes, making calls to friends and friends of friends and seeing if they could figure out who took my girl.

Minutes after that, Luc walked in with a man I didn't recognize. He was tall, not as tall as I was, but far more imposing with his almost-silver eyes and black hair. His nose had clearly been broken at least a few times and his muscles were stacked high, like he never had anything better to do than work out in a gym.

This man wasn't like us. He didn't give off an air of money and prep school. He was a different breed altogether. He was a brawler, but not a dumb one. He looked around the room, cataloging everything in his mind.

I could see just how he took in every single detail, filing the information in case he needed it later. And for once, I thought Luc might have made the right call with who he brought.

Luc introduced the man next to him. "Harrison, this is Sergeant Reid Taylor. He heads my private security team, and he's going to help us find your girlfriend."

The bodyguard nodded.

"Eddie," I said. "Her name is Edwina Carmichael. She goes by Eddie."

"Okay, Mr. Astrid, I'm going to ask you to take a seat," Reid said. "And tell me absolutely everything you know. No details are too small. We need anything you can give us."

I nodded, sitting down on the couch and taking another sip of the whiskey as I told him everything. From my suspicions to the call I got from her number, as well as what her friend saw. I gave him her friend's number when I showed him the picture that she gave me.

"It's not much," he said. "But I've worked with less. I'm sure we can find—"

"Isn't this the same guy who wasn't able to find Olivia when Marksen took her?" I asked, interrupting him and looking at Luc. I didn't have time to deal with a second-rate security force.

"No, he's the guy I hired after I fired my last team because they couldn't find Olivia," Luc said.

"Had he hired me in the first place, I promise you that story would have turned out much differently." Reid crossed his thick arms over his chest and stared me down.

"Not that anyone's asking me," Marksen butted in. "But I think that actually turned out very well, all things considered."

"I don't know how the hell you can say that. Olivia is clearly settling," Luc said, rolling his eyes.

I picked up a crystal glass and threw it across the room, watching as it shattered against the wall, the expensive fifty-year-old Scotch staining the white wallpaper.

"This isn't about Olivia," I yelled. "This is about Eddie. She is in danger, and it is my fault. We need to get her back. You two can bitch about Olivia's bad taste in men later."

The men stared at me in shock for a moment. I stared them each down in turn, my chest rising and lowering with each breath I sucked in through my no-doubt-flaring nostrils. "Help me find her or get the fuck out of my way."

They all nodded, and Marksen got back on his phone, making calls. Luc sent a message to his father to see if he knew if the mob had taken her, and why they would have taken my girl, and where.

Reid took his phone into the other room to call Eddie's friend, and I realized I had never even gotten the girl's name.

I turned back to Luc. "What are the chances this is the O'Murphy clan?"

"I would say pretty high, but something about this doesn't feel like them," Luc said. "After you called me, I called their boss, and they said that they're no longer worried about the work they lost when I decided to break ties. They'd found a bigger whale. I'm still checking with my father and other people, but it seems like they are being funded by someone else."

"What the fuck does that mean?" I asked.

"I have absolutely no idea, but I don't like it," Luc said. "I really don't like it at all. They didn't deny taking her, just denied that you were their target. Is there any other reason they would be after her?"

"No, to them, she is a nobody. I don't understand," I said. "Why her? Why would they go after Eddie? If they know about the case that I'm building against them, why wouldn't they come after me?"

"Because you're too big of a target," Marksen said. "If they go after the district attorney, then the mayor, the governor, the entire state is going to rain holy hellfire on them, but Eddie, as far as they're concerned, is disposable. She's nothing, just your girlfriend."

"But they don't know that. The only thing anybody knows about Eddie is that she's my paralegal. How would they know that she was anything more to me? We just became official last night. As far as the world knew, I was happily engaged to Catherine until about twenty-four hours ago."

"Is there anyone else that knew you and Eddie were a couple?" Marksen said, sitting back on the couch, crossing his ankle over his knee. "They are clearly getting their orders from someone with a bone to pick with the girl."

"No, the only other person I told was Luc, but she was gone by the time I came back from the club."

"Did anyone know you two were sleeping together?" Luc asked.

I shook my head and then thought about it.

"I mean, I'm sure Catherine and my mother suspected, but it's not like it was a problem for Catherine. She didn't care. She was well aware that our arrangement was nothing more than a contract."

"I can't imagine your harpy of a mother was thrilled you were dipping your pen in the company ink." Luc apparently couldn't resist stirring things up.

I gave him a death stare that made him look away.

"Mary Quinn Astrid didn't know that I was serious about Eddie. She thinks I stopped seeing her a little over a week ago." The words tasted like a lie as soon as they passed my lips.

I didn't know what to believe. I didn't know whose fault it was that Eddie was a target. Or whether it was because she was dating me—even though no one was supposed to know—or if she was just the most convenient target close to me, and the mob actually did think that they were just kidnapping my paralegal.

I sat down on the couch, put my head in my hands, and tried to focus. I had no idea what my next move should be. With any other case I worked, I knew what I had to do. Once I had a goal, I could clearly see the path to achieve it, but this time I just didn't know what to do.

Footsteps entered the room. There was a pause, then more footsteps before the wooden coffee table in front of my couch creaked.

"I understand you're a district attorney?" Reid's voice came from directly in front of me. He must have sat down on the coffee table.

I nodded, not willing to look up.

"Does that mean you have connections in the local PD?"

Again I nodded.

"Did you contact any of them?"

"No. I don't know who can be trusted in the police department. This mob has several cousins, brothers, uncles, and friends in the different police precincts," I said, finally looking up into the cold, determined eyes of the bodyguard. "Like most infesting insects, they are best at breeding."

"Good, I'm glad you didn't get in touch with them. I have a few trusted friends on the police force myself. I'm reaching out to them to put an APB out on the car. In the meantime, I have men on the streets checking out the known locations for the O'Murphy clan."

"What do you need me to do?" I asked, needing to do something.

"Keep your phone handy in case I need you to call in police backup, but for the moment, just sit tight." He rose from the coffee table and grabbed his phone again.

"Absolutely not." I straightened and met his gaze. "This is my woman, my responsibility. I need to bring her home safe."

Reid looked at me for a moment and nodded. "Okay, well then, get off your ass, and let's go get your girl."

CHAPTER 39

EDDIE

*P*ain.

It hit me the moment I regained consciousness. A dull ache that radiated through my head, throbbing worse than any migraine I had ever had.

It was so bad my stomach rolled with nausea as I tried to open my eyes, but the blinding light was too much. I then tried to stand up so I could move toward the kitchen and get a glass of water, but that was when I realized I was tied to a chair.

I took long, slow, deep breaths in through my nose and exhaled out of my mouth, trying not to panic as I braced myself to open my eyes again and check my surroundings.

It took a few minutes, but I was finally able to open my eyes and look around.

I was in some dirty room, sitting directly beneath a bright lamp that was pointed at my face. I couldn't see too much around me, only a few feet in every direction.

The only thing I could really make out was the wooden chair with peeling red paint that I was zip-tied to, and the dirty concrete floor. It was cold in here, like I was underground, or maybe in a large warehouse that was too big to be heated. My one bare foot was starting to go numb in the cold.

"Where am I?" I asked, my throat like sandpaper as I tried to speak. My words came out as more of a hoarse croak than anything else.

"Don't worry about that, doll," the big redheaded guy said, stepping into the light. "I doubt you'll be here long."

"What are you going to do with me?" I asked while willing my head to clear so I could think.

"I don't want nothing to do with you," the big guy said, squatting next to me. Then he put his big, meaty paw on my knee and moved it up my thigh. "Well, maybe there's a few things I might want with you. Pretty little thing like you really should know better than to be with a man who can't protect her."

"You're here because of Harrison? Why?" I asked.

I knew why. It didn't take a genius to figure out who this man was and what he wanted. He was part of the O'Murphy clan, and he wanted to punish Harrison for pursuing a case against them.

"It's just a job, it's nothing personal, kitten. Your little boyfriend was looking into our crew, and we don't like that. So when someone offered us a lot of money to force him to stop, well, who would turn down a win-win scenario like that?"

"So you kidnap me? I'm just a paralegal."

"Oh honey, we know you are much more to Mr. Astrid than just a secretary."

"Paralegal," I corrected with a growl.

If Harrison insisted that I never refer to myself as a secretary or anything that could be seen as lower than the station which I had earned, I certainly wasn't about to let some random thug try to demean my hard work either.

"Well, it doesn't really matter. See, we need your boss to drop the case against us. And to stop sticking his nose where it doesn't belong."

"You think kidnapping me and taking me from him is going to make him stop looking? If anything, you're going to set a fire under his ass, and he's going to bring down everyone you've ever even met."

"No, we have the assurances from someone in his inner circle that the second you're out of the picture, she'll make sure he drops the charges and stays out of our business. She has leverage."

"Nobody has that level of control over Harrison," I said. "He doesn't answer to anyone. No one chooses what cases he does or doesn't touch. He is the district attorney. He decides what cases are pursued."

I didn't know why I was trying to explain the basic chain of command in a law office to this guy. I didn't expect him to realize his mistake and let me go. I wasn't that naive. But something told me to get him talking, listening to anything.

Maybe I could buy time. I had to believe that Harrison was looking for me, and if he was looking for me, if he was coming for me at all, I needed to give him as much time as possible to find me.

"Oh, honey, no. This isn't someone who has sway over him professionally. I'm talking about the person who holds the Astrid purse strings. See, they don't like you cozying up to their son. Something about you not having the right pedigree."

"Not a fucking dog," I gritted out.

"Really? You look like a stuck-up bitch to me. Sitting there tied to a fucking chair, and still looking down your prissy little nose at me. You ain't shit. You're just the bitch that thinks she is too good for her own kind and keeps sniffing around men who don't belong to her."

He sucked his teeth in a disapproving way, like he was reprimanding a small child for taking two cookies instead of one.

"If you know what's good for you," I said, glaring at the man, "then you will let me go before Harrison finds you. And he will find you."

The man threw his head back in laughter when he stood back up. The hand that was on my thigh flew through the air, and he backhanded me hard enough that the chair I was in tipped over and I went tumbling to the floor.

My mouth filled with the taste of blood, and my side ached where I had landed. My head was still throbbing, and being struck and then hitting the dirty concrete made it so much worse. The room around me spun as he grabbed the chair and pulled me back up.

"Now, kitten, I don't think you're very long for this world, but you might want to watch that little whore mouth of yours, or your last few hours are going to be very unpleasant."

The man turned and walked out of the light, leaving me alone as far as I could tell. I had no idea who else was in the room, if anyone. I didn't know if people were watching me or if I had any chance of escape.

I let my head hang down as low as I could as I tried to get some semblance of control over the pain radiating through my skull. I wanted to scream, I wanted to run; my entire body was shaking, I was so scared.

Hot tears trailing down my cheeks, I took some slow, deep breaths, controlling the ache in my back, trying to hold back the panic. I needed to stay calm and figure out my next steps.

I knew I needed to buy myself some time. Maybe, if I could humanize myself to these men, they would be less inclined to hurt me. I wasn't some rich woman who lived high above them in the lap of luxury. I was a girl who grew up on the streets, like them. I didn't know if it would make a difference, but I didn't see how I had any better options.

"Can I have some water, please?" I called out into the dark abyss around me, hoping someone could hear me. If I could get someone here talking to me, then I could stall them, hopefully long enough for me to figure a way out of this. And if someone was talking to me, they weren't trying to kill me, or worse.

There was no answer.

"Please, can I get some water? My throat hurts," I said again, letting a sob escape between my words.

I remembered reading somewhere that some men couldn't stand women's tears, that it spoke to something primal in them, and they felt the need to stop them. Of course, on the other side, there were some men who got off on hurting women. I had no idea which kind of men I was dealing with, but I was so scared I wouldn't have been able to stop the tears even if I tried.

"Stop your whining," another, deeper voice said. "I'll get you some fucking water."

A few minutes later, the shorter guy with dark hair and thick eyebrows stepped into the light with a water bottle in his hand. He cracked it open and held it to my lips, then tipped it back, forcing me to take several long gulps before he took the water away and threw it behind him.

I gasped and choked on the little bit of water I wasn't able to swallow fast enough. As soon as I caught my breath, I looked back up at the man who just stared at me, his arms crossed over his chest as he glared.

"Thank you," I said.

"I wouldn't be thanking me if I were you. Why does a nice girl like you have to go and do something so fucking stupid?"

"I don't know what I did," I said.

"You stuck your nose where it didn't belong. You were helping that fucking lawyer bring a case against me and mine. You would think a girl like you, living in the neighborhood we found you in, would have been smarter than that."

"I wasn't," I said. "I was just doing my job. All I was doing was filing papers."

"You going to tell me that rich motherfucker didn't actually have you doing research and investigating?"

"That's not my job." More tears flowed freely down my face. "I'm a paralegal, my job is to file documents, drop things off at the courthouse, or maybe even file a motion or two. I don't do any of the investigative work, I do the busywork. I don't know what Mr. Astrid was working on, he kept it very close to his chest."

It wasn't a complete lie. I was the only one who knew what Harrison was working on. He always kept his cases very close to his chest. Even going as far as sending his secretary to Atlantic City where she would be safe from the blowback.

"Maybe that's true, but you seem like a smart girl, you should know. Sometimes it doesn't matter what you do or how careful you are. People like us often end up under the tires of people like them. You, little girl, are insignificant when it comes to the wheelings and dealings of people like them." The man walked away, his footsteps echoing throughout the space.

After a moment, somewhere in the distance the footsteps paused. Door hinges screeched open, followed by the slamming of the door closing. I was pretty sure this time I was all alone. I couldn't hear anyone breathing. I couldn't sense anyone near me.

With another deep breath, trying to calm my nerves and stop the shaking of my entire body—which was partly from the cold but mostly from fear—I closed my eyes and tried to listen. There had to be something that could tell me where I was.

The silence around me was deafening, so I tried to listen harder and concentrate on the far-away ambient noises. There was something rhythmic, but I couldn't quite tell what it was. Something hitting something wet, maybe? I strained to hear, trying to figure out what it could be. The loud and distinct sound of the air horn of a cargo ship suddenly pierced the air, startling me.

I had to be by the docks. That rhythmic sound I heard had to be waves hitting the dock pilings.

That explained why it was so cold in this room my breath billowed in front of me. Large warehouses were often not heated when they weren't actively in use, due to the cost of heating such large, open spaces.

Unfortunately, knowing that I was by the docks didn't really help me unless I could get out of this chair and find my way out of the warehouse. If I could manage that, there should be tons of people around, including security guards and dockworkers.

Sure, a few probably worked for the mob, but I was willing to bet most were just hard-working people trying to make a living.

I had to believe that.

Otherwise, there was no point in trying to get free.

They would kill me anyway.

CHAPTER 40

EDDIE

I pulled at the zip ties on my wrists, the plastic cutting into my skin.

Thankfully, the cold numbed most of the pain. I pulled with everything I had, but I couldn't make the zip ties budge.

I tried again, pulling as hard as I could, trying not to let out the scream of rage and frustration that pressed against my lips, ignoring the pain biting in my wrists. I closed my eyes, and I thought of everything that I had worked for so far, everything that I was so close to finally achieving.

I thought of the cold, restless nights and the shit apartment I survived, including that fucking landlord who had tried to insinuate that my rent was going to go up unless I performed sexual favors. I thought of every single act of indecency and insult I had suffered in the last twenty-four years of my life, and I refused to let it end like this.

It wasn't uncommon for some women with my background to end up dead before they were twenty-five from overdose, suicide, assault, rape, or other acts of violence, whether random or perpetrated by the ones who were supposed to love and protect us. I refused to end up like those tragic girls. The statistics of impoverished women would not claim me.

Harrison had called me stubborn, and he had no idea how right he was.

Then his face popped into my head. Not the stern look he wore at the office when he was so absorbed in his work that the little line between his brows started to form. Not the proud-looking lift of the corner of his lips—not quite a smile but not a smirk—he had when he put something together that he knew no one else had yet figured out.

No, I thought of the Harrison that I was pretty sure I was one of the only people he showed. The Harrison who looked like the vibrant young man he actually was. When he genuinely smiled, his entire face lit up and his intense, dark blue eyes seemed to glow. When he laughed, truly laughed, it was with his entire body.

Then there was the triumphant smirk he got when he knew that he had made me come harder than I ever had before, when he knew he owned my body and could control everything. That was the Harrison I thought of, and I promised myself I'd make it back to him, redoubling my efforts to force apart the plastic straps binding my wrists together.

Two clicks. I managed to pull the plastic apart two clicks. But thankfully, that was all I needed to wiggle one hand through the loop and free myself. My wrists were bright red, and there were even a few spots of blood that started to smear the white button-down shirt I had stolen from Harrison before I left his apartment. I rubbed the tops of my arms, trying to get the blood flowing and some warmth into my limbs before I bent down and tried to wiggle the tie at my feet. Thankfully, having only one shoe made freeing my feet far easier and less painful than it had been to free my wrists.

As quietly as I could, I stood up and, after shaking my limbs to restore blood flow, stepped out of the bright light that was hanging over my head and waited just long enough to give my eyes a moment to adjust to the darkness. The warehouse looked abandoned. The windows lining the top of the large empty space were mostly broken, and there was more than one bird's nest nestled in the rafters.

With the exception of my chair and the single light that hung from a rafter and plugged into a generator, the warehouse was empty. There were a few piles of fabric in the corners, probably beds for junkies or the homeless. But either way, I didn't see a single soul, and that was more luck than I had counted on.

As quickly as I could, I moved to the closest wall, stepping around broken glass, trying not to cut up the bottom of my foot any more than necessary. I crept along the wall, trying to make it to the closest door, stopping just before I got there and listening.

"No, that's not what we were hired to do. We keep her until we get the word, and then we end her," the first voice said. It was deeper, so I was pretty sure it was the smaller man with dark hair.

"Aye, it just seems like a waste. A perfectly good girl like that, we should get some use out of her before sending her back to her maker." The owner of this voice, with its hint of an accent, seemed upset. It was the larger ginger man who'd hit me.

"We don't have the time. We're under very specific orders."

"What do you mean we don't have the time? We're just fucking sitting here waiting for a phone call. I could be balls-deep in that cunt right now."

I had to swallow down the whimper of fear that rose from my chest, clamping my hands over my mouth in case I couldn't stifle it all.

"I don't understand why we're taking orders from that old bitch anyway," the second voice continued, in a whine that was almost petulant.

"Because not only is that bitch paying us far more than any contract we've ever received, she also assures us that as soon as this is all over and we've taken care of the whore inside, she will make sure her son stops investigating our family. Not only is this one job going to get us through winter, but it's also going to keep everyone out of jail."

"And as I said, I understand that. I just don't understand why we can't take advantage of that girl now. She's here. It's not like they're going to want her back at any point."

I couldn't listen to them anymore. I knew Harrison's mother was an uptight bitch, but sending the mob to kill me seemed a bit extreme even for her. Though Harrison had admitted to me that she may have been behind the kidnapping and blackmail of another girl, to get back at her son-in-law.

What did I know? Maybe this was right up Mary Quinn Astrid's alley. Hell, this might not even have been the first time she'd done this. I'd bet that bitch had a playbook that would be the envy of Al Capone himself.

The only thing that was clear was if I stayed here, I was going to die.

Not today, motherfuckers.

I started backing up slowly, trying to make my way around the perimeter of the room to find another door. There had to be another way out of this warehouse, something that would lead me to safety. I headed back down to the first corner and started moving along the other wall. I was about halfway to the next corner when I was pretty sure I could see another door. It wasn't one of the large metallic doors that would lead outside, but it was something. I didn't know if it led to an office or another room, but there just had to be a way out through that door.

The large metal door behind me opened, creaking on its hinges as the two men stepped inside, one of them on the phone.

"Yeah, I understand, it'll be done immediately, and the photos will be sent from the girl's phone. Did you want her body found or do you want her to just disappear?"

They were silent for a moment. I tried to creep closer to the other door and hopefully my freedom.

"I understand, ma'am. You'll have the photo soon." He hung up the phone and must have looked up to where the chair sat and saw it was empty, because the big one yelled, "She's over there, the little bitch is trying to get away." They both started running in my direction.

As fast as I could, I ran toward the other door, stepping on a shard of glass that buried itself deep in my foot. I couldn't let that stop me. I didn't know if it was the cold temperature or the adrenaline, but I couldn't feel it as I hobbled as quickly as I could to the door. My hands were on the rusted knob and starting to twist when I was grabbed by the back of my borrowed shirt and thrown to the floor.

One of the men grabbed my collar again, yanked me up to my knees, and pressed the barrel of a gun to my temple.

CHAPTER 41

HARRISON

*R*eid came marching back into my living room, where Marksen, Luc, and I were still making calls and trying to find out who would have taken Eddie, and where.

We were pretty sure it was the Irish mob, but the "why" was becoming less and less clear.

I had assumed it was because they found out I had an open investigation on them, but Detective Doyle hadn't been bailed out yet. It wasn't impossible that he'd gotten word to his family, but it wasn't likely. And even then, he just knew of evidence tampering, not that I had connected him to the O'Murphy clan.

"Did you find anything?" I asked, not even trying to hide the emotion in my voice.

"Maybe." He rubbed the back of his neck like he was uncomfortable.

"Spit it out," I said.

"You might want to come into the other room so we can speak privately. This may be a bit delicate," he said.

"Just fucking spit it out!" I had run out of patience the second she was taken. I refused to be delicate or follow any type of ridiculous etiquette when it came to getting her back.

I had already called and threatened two judges that I knew were on the O'Murphy payroll. I was willing to burn down every single bridge and poison every well. I would break every law and ruin my career, taking down every corrupt politician, bribable judge, and dirty cop with me.

So help me God, if there was a single bruise on her delicate skin, I would burn down the motherfucking world.

"Some of my men in the police force overheard others talking. They believe the person who put a hit on Ms. Carmichael may have been your mother."

The entire world stopped for a moment.

There was a distinct ringing in my ears. My heart beat faster and faster as my fingers curled into tight fists. I shouldn't have been surprised, and I wasn't.

There were several emotions swirling in my body, but surprise wasn't one of them.

"I'm sorry," I said quietly, trying to keep a tight leash on my rage. "Did you just say that my mother, Mary Quinn Astrid, was the one who had Eddie taken?"

"It's worse than that," he said, this time losing his look of discomfort. He stood with his feet a little more than shoulder width apart, his hands tucked behind his back.

"How could it possibly be worse?"

"They believe it wasn't a kidnapping. They think it's a hit. They were supposed to hold her until your mother calls and gives the order to execute her. They are thinking they're supposed to hold her for a few days before they kill her, and her body will be found in the Hudson."

My entire body was filled with a cold fire.

Luc stood in front of my face and tried to grab my shoulder, saying something.

I could see his mouth moving, but I couldn't hear the words.

Then suddenly, all of the rage just exploded out of me, and, stepping back from Luc, I sent a right hook straight through the plaster of the closest wall.

A loud howl of rage resounded around the room, and it wasn't until I caught my breath that I realized the sound was coming from me.

Calmly, I pulled my fist from the wall, straightened my shirt sleeves then turned and looked at Luc.

"We need to go. Now."

"Absolutely," Luc said. "Where are we going?"

"We're going to face my bitch mother, and God help her if they've hurt Eddie."

Luc must have seen something in my face because he took two large steps back, his eyes wide and his mouth open before he shook himself out of it and nodded.

"Amelia said she was at a meeting earlier today, but she should be home by now."

"Call Amelia, have her call my mother and verify that she's home. Do not let her know we're on our way," I barked, grabbing my suit jacket and heading out the door, not bothering to look if the men followed me or not.

I didn't really remember the car ride to my family's estate. I didn't remember pulling up or marching into the house. The only thing I remembered was the look of shock on my mother's face when I barged into her sitting room, where she sat surrounded by her friends who were all on some type of committee about saving something completely fucking asinine. Where, as usual, they would spend more money throwing the parties than they actually got in donations for whatever they were raising money for.

"Harrison, darling, what are you doing here?" she asked, a little flustered when she saw my face.

She quickly stood and tried to usher me and the others out of the sitting room to somewhere more private.

The only reason I allowed that to happen was I knew that I was going to lose my shit. And the last thing I needed was the added pressure of being the subject of more societal gossip. If I was going to threaten my mother with death, I didn't need any strangers witnessing it.

I didn't say a word until we were in my father's office.

The only room I knew for certain was soundproofed.

My father was sitting at his desk, typing away on his laptop. He put his glasses on the desk and looked around the room at Luc, Marksen, and Reid.

"What's the meaning of this?" he asked.

"Tell him." I ordered my mother.

"I don't know what you're talking about," she snipped, still trying to put on airs since we had company.

"Tell your husband what you did," I repeated, while taking a few threatening steps toward her.

"I'm sure I have no idea what you mean." She clearly intended to play dumb.

My mother was many things, but dumb, unfortunately, wasn't one of them. It would have been far easier to control her scheming if she was stupid.

"Tell them how you hired the fucking Irish mob to kidnap my girlfriend."

"Harrison, you're acting irrational. Your mother said you and Catherine broke it off." My father rose, standing behind his desk.

"Not Catherine," I growled. "Eddie."

My mother laughed with her hand on her chest. "Calling that girl, a common secretary, his girlfriend."

"Tell him what you did. Admit it," I said again. "Or I swear to God not only will I tell him, but I will also have you arrested and, as I've already promised you, will throw every single thing I can think of at you. I will charge you not only with racketeering and for the kidnapping and attempted murder of my girlfriend, but I will also throw the rest of the book at you. I will make sure that you are charged with Olivia's abduction and kidnapping, as well as for the abuse that Amelia had to deal with, and that no doubt Rose still does."

"You don't know what you're talking about!" She rounded on me, a wild look in her eyes, claws bared.

"I will have you charged with corporate espionage and embezzlement. Every single sin will be brought to light, *Mother*." I spat the last word.

"Everything I've done has been for this family. You and your sister are so ungrateful. You don't understand the things I have done for you. You're going around calling that trollop your girlfriend. She's nothing. She's not good enough for you. She's not good enough for anyone. That is not a woman that you date or marry. That is a woman that you sleep with on the side and hope you don't impregnate, or catch an STD from to bring home to your wife."

"Where is she?" I growled out, hovering over my mother, intimidating her the same way I would opposing counsel if they had tried to play dirty.

"She's where she belongs," my mother said. "I had to do it. After you let the world know your dirty little secret, I had to do something to protect your reputation. You were going to throw it away on some common piece of trash. You need to call Catherine and beg her to take you back."

"If anything happens to Eddie. If a single hair on her head is misplaced—"

"You'll what?" she taunted, facing me. "You can't do anything because anything you do toward me would ruin your career."

"She is more important than my career. I don't understand how you don't get that. Maybe it's because you're a heartless shrew whose only joy in life comes from meddling in the lives of others. But I swear to God, if you do not tell me where she is, I won't bother having you arrested after all. I'll kill you myself with my bare fucking hands. Because if she's not in my life there's no reason not to throw it away."

"Harrison, don't be dramatic." My mother rolled her eyes like she was talking to a petulant child. "I did you a favor. All this girl was going to do was drag you down."

"You don't even know her," I argued.

"I don't need to know her. I know her type. But more importantly, I know what type she isn't. She is not built for the life you need. She would not be the wife to elevate your career. She would drag you down to her level, and I will be damned if I let all the work that I have put into you go to hell for some little gold-digging slut."

"Tell him where the girl is," my father ordered, his voice sterner than I had ever heard.

My father was not a weak man, but he believed that strength was not demonstrated by yelling or showing your hand and letting your enemy see your emotion. The stoicism that I exuded came from him, biological father or not.

"No, I will not let him throw his life away," she screeched.

My father placed both hands flat on his desk and leaned forward, taking a deep breath, his nostrils flaring as he stared my mother down.

"You will tell him where the girl is, and if you don't, I will divorce you. I will leave you absolutely destitute."

"You can't do that," she said, sticking her nose in the air.

"Oh, I absolutely can. Read the prenup. It has a fidelity clause. I'm not the only one that it applies to, dear."

"I can fight that. I can ruin you." She pointed one of her long red claws at my father.

"Let me explain to you exactly how this is going to go down.

You're a bright woman, I'm sure you can follow. I will file for divorce, and then I will persuade every single lawyer worth his salt in the state to shun you."

"You wouldn't dare."

"I would make sure that no lawyer with any talent or ambition would touch your case. You will be left with a public defender who just graduated from a third-tier law school."

"You wouldn't dare," she said again, this time more to herself.

"Try me." The way my father hovered over his desk and the steely calmness of his voice as he spoke sent chills down even my back.

My father was a soft-spoken man who listened more than he spoke. Because of that, many people assumed he was weak. They thought this assumption was confirmed when it came out that I was not his biological son, and that he knew and raised me anyway.

This man was not weak. I hoped that I had spent enough time at his side that his strength and grace rubbed off on me.

This was the man I hoped that I could become, but only with Eddie at my side.

My mother looked at my father for a few moments. I thought this actually had been the first time that he had ever raised his voice to her, and finally, she relented.

"They took her to a warehouse on the docks, but you'll never get there in time." She shrugged like she was talking about missing a movie.

CHAPTER 42

HARRISON

*I*mmediately, Reid was on his phone ordering men down to the docks to start searching.

"This isn't over." I stared my mother down before I turned on my heel and ran out the door, back to my car.

"Get out," I told the driver as I ran down the sidewalk.

I didn't offer another explanation. I just took the key fob and got behind the steering wheel as Reid slid into the passenger side.

I looked back at Marksen and Luc. "Meet us down there."

I stabbed the "ignition" button without bothering to buckle my seat belt and hit the gas, pushing my Mercedes-Benz class to its full potential as I maneuvered through New York City traffic. I raced through downtown New York with a complete disregard for my safety, the safety of the man next to me, and of every single citizen who happened to be in a car or walking through the streets.

The only person I gave a thought to was Eddie.

I needed to get to her before the worst happened. I just knew in my bones that I was racing against the clock because my mother wasn't going to give up that easily. She was going to do something to hurt the only bit of joy that I had ever found in my life.

To his credit, Reid didn't say a word about my driving. He just grabbed the bar on the side door and held on while barking orders into his phone.

He had several men on the streets, all moving toward the warehouses on the docks as quickly as possible, and one man he called his eye in the sky, which I gathered was a guy sitting behind a laptop somewhere.

"The eye in the sky has narrowed down the possibilities to two warehouses. I say I send my men to one, and we go to the other."

"Sounds good," I said. "Tell me where I'm going."

He directed me toward the warehouses. We pulled up in front. And the second I saw the black SUV without license plates sitting in front of one of the warehouses, I knew we were in the right place.

Reid made some type of motion that I assumed indicated he was going to go around on the other side, and I was to go in the closest door.

"Wait," he said. "Are you armed?"

"No," I said, not even realizing until that moment that I should have been.

He grabbed a Glock from his ankle holster and handed it over. "Do you know how to use that?"

I looked at him before turning off the safety, pointing it toward the ground, and moving to the door.

Reid ran over to the other side, and I waited for some type of signal. And then Eddie screamed.

My blood ran cold, and I knew I couldn't wait anymore.

I pushed through the door and immediately saw them. They had Eddie down on her knees, blood leaking from one of her feet and bruises marring her perfect face. Her blonde hair was dirty and matted, and a gun was pressed to her temple.

"I still think it's a waste," said the big red-headed guy I recognized from the pictures her friend sent me.

"She wants the photos now. We're going to do it now," the smaller man next to him insisted, keeping the gun trained on Eddie's head.

"Put down the weapon and back away from the girl," I demanded, pointing my gun at the smaller man.

They both turned to face me, the big guy looking shocked.

The little one looked me up and down and smirked.

"He ain't going to use that," he said. "Prissy little rich boys aren't taught how to shoot. Even if he does, there are two of us and one of him. What is he going to do?"

I aimed a little lower and shot the shorter man in the thigh, dropping him to the ground. He started wailing and screaming while I adjusted my aim toward the big guy who took several steps away from Eddie.

When I looked at Eddie, she was scrambling on the ground, reaching for the smaller guy's gun. He tried to hit her and grab it himself.

She cocked her hand back and punched him right where the bullet had penetrated.

The man screamed bloody murder as Reid came in, guns drawn, from a door behind Eddie.

With his gun trained on the two men, I rushed forward, grabbed Eddie, wrapped her in my arms, and held her to my chest. The relief I felt holding her in my hands was overwhelming.

"Are you okay?" I asked her as I looked her over for any more serious injuries.

The large bump on her head and the cut on her foot told me I needed to get her to an emergency room immediately.

She wrapped her hands around my shoulders, laying her head on my chest as I held her and started to cry.

"Never again," I said. "This will never happen to you again."

"How can you promise that?" she said. "Your mother is the one that arranged this. If we're still together, she's going to keep coming after me."

"No, she isn't," I promised. I cradled her head in my palms and looked deeply into her bloodshot eyes. "I want to make sure that everybody knows you are protected. You cannot be touched, because you are mine."

"And how exactly are you going to do that?" she asked. Even injured and no doubt in shock, she was too smart for her own good.

I did the one thing a lawyer should never do. I asked a question I didn't know the answer to. "Edwina Carmichael, will you marry me?"

CHAPTER 43

HARRISON

*I*t had been three days since I almost lost the most amazing woman to ever step into my life.

And I was making damn sure it never happened again.

Eddie was wearing a simple white sheath dress with a white suit jacket over it. I'd offered her a custom-made ball gown and a big ceremony in a church. I'd offered her the princess wedding of every girl's dreams. The kind that was splashed all over the tabloids, and the mayor attended.

She'd looked me dead in the eye and told me that people like us did not belong in a church making vows in front of God.

People like us answered to a much higher power—the law.

It made me love her so much more. She didn't just understand how I thought. She was the same. I told her that once, and she didn't believe me. Eddie harped on our different backgrounds, education, social status, and everything that I found irrelevant.

It didn't matter.

She was wrong, and I got to spend the rest of my life proving it to her over and over.

Originally, we were going to do this the proper way. Plan a large reception, and make a spectacle even if it was just a judge to marry us, but my mother would not back the fuck off.

After we found out she was not only behind Eddie being taken by the mob, but she was also the mastermind behind Olivia's kidnapping, I wasn't willing to give her any time to plot. I hadn't even told her where or when the ceremony would happen, although I had no doubt she would find it regardless.

We stood in front of Judge Thomas, a close friend of mine since law school. Only my father, Luc, my sister, Marksen, Olivia, and Eddie's best friend, Sabrina—who had only threatened to butcher me a couple of times—were our witnesses as we professed our love to each other.

Judge Thomas was happy to officiate our wedding.

He even paused his murder trial for a fifteen-minute recess to get it taken care of immediately, before Eddie wised up and left me for a man with power and sexy robes. His words, not mine.

About three minutes after Judge Thomas started his speech, a commotion erupted outside the courtroom, filled with feminine screeches and loud banging sounds as things were toppled over. We all stopped and faced the door, waiting for the inevitable.

Sure enough, Mary Quinn Astrid threw open the doors like she was walking into a courtroom drama with the damning evidence that would lead to the real killer being arrested. That woman lived for the drama so intently she had dressed in a white pantsuit and had a net veil pinned onto the ridiculous, tiny hat perched in her hair.

"I object to this marriage. That woman is nothing but a two-bit gold digger, and she has tricked my son into marrying her without even a prenup."

"There is a prenup," my father said, standing up and blocking her path to where Eddie and I stood with our hands clasped.

"Who has looked it over? She is a legal secretary. She could have snuck something in. This entire wedding is a sham and cannot happen."

"I wrote the prenup myself," I called out. "It states if we divorce, *she* gets it all."

There was some sick pleasure in watching my mother's face pale and then turn a deep red in fury.

The whole situation was improved even more when Marksen rolled his eyes, reached into his jacket, pulled out his wallet, and handed Luc a stack of cash.

"She has tricked you into doing that. She has seduced you! She is a con woman and needs to be in jail. She is—"

"Madam, this is a private affair. Get out of my courtroom," Judge Thomas ordered.

"You can't make me. Do you know who I am?" she screamed.

Sabrina stood and walked toward my mother with a creepy smile. She just kept walking toward her with her arm outstretched, her finger dripping something red.

Mary Quinn Astrid backed away for a moment, then knowing her Chanel suit would be ruined, pressed past Sabrina, who left a massive red smear over her stark white jacket.

"You bitch." Mary's hand reached out to slap Sabrina, who just stared her down. I didn't think anyone had ever faced my mother and not flinched.

My father grabbed her wrist to stay her hand.

"I am holding you in contempt of court." The judge banged his gavel, and the bailiff put her in cuffs.

It was the funniest fucking thing I had ever seen and the best damn wedding present I could have gotten.

We watched her be carted off, then Judge Thomas looked at Sabrina and asked what was on her hand.

She held it up, still covered in red gloop, and licked her finger. "Ketchup." She smiled.

I couldn't help it. I started laughing. Genuinely laughing, hard enough I doubled over. It took a second, but soon, everyone joined in laughing at the sheer ridiculousness of the entire situation.

My father and I were still discussing the ramifications of what my mother had done and if it was better to handle it publicly or in-house. Neither of our concerns included my mother's reputation but rather how she would spin the story and use it to slander Eddie.

I'd been a prominent figure even before I took public office, which meant any blood in the water, and the reporters would come swarming. I didn't want Eddie to have to deal with that.

But I wasn't prepared to let my mother get away with her meddling either.

That was a problem for later. Today was about watching my mother get arrested for causing a scene and legally binding myself to my partner.

It may have been wrong for me to enjoy the spectacle as much as I did. But I never claimed to be perfect.

"Now, where were we?" Judge Thomas asked, and I turned my gaze back to the only woman who ever mattered.

"I'm still not signing that bullshit prenup," Eddie said firmly.

"You should. I'm loaded."

She rolled her eyes at me and smiled.

"Can we speed this along?" I asked. "You have a murder trial to finish, and I would really like to get to my honeymoon."

Judge Thomas laughed. And did the abbreviated version of the vows.

"Do you, Harrison Phillip Astrid, take Edwina Morgan Carmichael to be your lawful wedded wife?"

"I do," I said, and a warmth spread through my chest as I smiled down at my Eddie.

"And are you, Edwina Morgan Carmichael, really sure you want to do this?" the judge asked, and I shot him a dirty look. He shot a shit-eating grin back at me. "Seriously, you can still sign that prenup and take everything."

"I am absolutely positive," she said, pulling my attention back to her.

"Well, if you insist. By the power vested in me by the State of New York, I now pronounce you man and wife. You may kiss the bride, then get the fuck out of my courtroom. I have more important shit to do."

I laced my fingers in her hair before pulling her into an earth-shattering kiss. Our friends and family cheered and followed close behind as I picked her up and carried her out of the courtroom.

"What now?" she asked.

"Now, you and the ball and chain are coming with us to celebrate this happy occasion with dinner and a few drinks while we welcome you into the family," my father said.

"What do you say?" I asked Eddie. "You up for a small family dinner with your new ball and chain?"

"That depends. Will your mother be there?"

"Absolutely not," my father answered for me, then turned to Sabrina and asked if she would like to join.

"Sure, where are we going?" she asked, wiping the last of the ketchup from her fingers with a wet wipe before tucking her arm through Eddie's as soon as I set her down.

"I made reservations at The Grid if that is okay."

"That sounds great," Eddie said, lacing the fingers of her free hand with mine.

"That is amazing. I know the chef, and I am going to give him hell," Sabrina said, rubbing her hands together like a scary little gremlin.

I really was going to have to watch my back around her, but she had spent the last four years watching my girl's back, and for that, she was family.

I even had a proposal to fund her own restaurant if she was interested.

All of that would have to wait until after the honeymoon.

* * *

DINNER HAD BEEN AMAZING, full of laughter and embarrassing stories. It was exactly what Eddie and I needed to celebrate the beginning of our new life together.

Once it was over, I was ready to take my bride home and make love to her until the flight preparation was completed for the jet we'd be using to take us to a tropical getaway for a full two weeks of blissful vacation.

Another first for me, but I was looking forward to it. This was why I couldn't for the life of me understand why Eddie insisted we head back to the office, just the two of us, before going home.

"What is this all about?" I asked, sitting behind my desk.

She sat on my lap and opened my laptop. I kissed her shoulder and let my hands wander down her long legs while she typed away, and then I heard the printer warming up.

"You'll see," she said. "We have a little more work to do before we can leave for our trip."

"We really don't," I said. "The O'Murphy clan has all been arrested. They are being charged with everything, and since they kidnapped my wife, I recused myself from the case."

I kissed the back of her neck and moved my hands up her thighs. "The lawyer taking over is competent, and I gave him everything he needs. I hear most of them are trying for a plea deal. They will plead guilty and get a chance at parole in thirty years or so."

"That isn't what we need to take care of," she said rudely, ignoring my wandering hands.

"Then what is it? Did you want to get half naked in my bathroom again for old times' sake?" I teased.

She let out a sexy, throaty laugh and stood to grab the papers off the printer.

"Sign this," she said, handing me the stack of papers.

I took the documents, and the second I saw the words "postnuptial agreement," I threw them down on the desk.

"No. I told you it was my prenup or none."

"This isn't a prenup. It's a postnup. I drew it up myself. Look it over. For me?" She batted her eyes at me.

"One of these days, that isn't going to work," I warned.

"As long as that day isn't today, I can live with that. Now, can you live with this?"

I read over the agreement.

Not only was it well written, but it was fair.

Not solely to me or her, but to both parties, like a proper contract should be.

It stated that if the parties reached a point at which divorce was discussed, then the parties would attend counseling sessions for a time no shorter than six months. Both parties would see individual counselors at least once a week and couples counseling as often as required, no less than once a week.

If children were involved, counseling would include them as well as any recommended by the therapist. It went on to say that assets gained during the marriage were all community property. However, assets obtained prior to the marriage and things such as inheritance were not considered community property.

"What is this?" I asked.

"It's what I believe is fair, and so you know that at no point did I consider marrying you for your money. You should know I drew this up yesterday, and I e-mailed it to your father to approve."

"Did he approve?"

"Not exactly. He felt that it was a ridiculous contract that, while it should be signed and filed, we should forget was there because there is no end to this marriage."

"He is a wise man," I said as I signed the papers and moved them over for her to sign as well.

She signed with her new name, "Mrs. Edwina Astrid."

"Now that that is settled, there is just one more thing."

"What's that, wife?"

"I think this time you should be the one half naked in your bathroom."

EPILOGUE

CHARLOTTE

*A*fter setting my cello case to the side of the study door, I smoothed my hair and took a deep breath before entering.

My father was at his desk, as usual.

No matter how far back I thought, I didn't have a single childhood memory that didn't involve my father hunched over his desk working.

I remembered mistaking him for the mean man, Scrooge, from *A Christmas Carol* when I was eight. In my defense, there were numerous parallels. Take away the hooked nose, gray hair, and English accent but leave the mean-spirited greed and complete disregard for humanity and you'd have a carbon copy of Lucian Manwarring, Sr.

Tucking my hands behind me, since I knew he hated the sight of my short, unladylike nails, I patiently waited in front of his desk for him to acknowledge my presence. My nails were a necessary evil of my *disgraceful hobby,* as my father would put it, of my cello playing.

The only sound in the room was the ticking of the antique mantel clock and the scratch of his pen across a balance sheet.

The minutes stretched by and still I waited.

Twenty-four years old and I waited on my father as if I were still a child.

Every tick of the clock was a damning metronome marking off the time I had wasted.

Time I hadn't spoken up for myself.

Time I hadn't told him to take his money and shove it.

Time I hadn't just turned around and walked away, valuing my time as much as he valued his own.

Tick. Tick. Tick.

It was strange. I never imagined the *tock*. It was a silly game I had played since I was a child. The clock was a ticking bomb, urging me to run. To run out of my father's office for as far and as long as my legs would carry me.

Tick. Tick. Tick.

Each *tick* ratcheted up the suspense.

The trick was never to imagine the *tock*. That was the boom. The end. Time was up. Especially if I imagined it and I was still standing in front of my father's desk.

If that happened, then I lost the game.

Finally, my father looked up. In his usual brusque manner, he announced, "You're getting a bodyguard."

"But—"

"I don't want to hear any back talk. There have been too many shenanigans with the daughters of the wealthy lately. I'm not taking any chances with my investment."

"You mean your daughter," I said under my breath.

"I mean my investment," he corrected. "Now stop wasting my time. My decision is final."

"Do I at least have a say in who you hire?"

Having already dismissed me, he didn't bother to look up as

he scribbled a note with his pen. "No. He's waiting for you out in the hall. Now leave."

There was no point in arguing.

Exiting his office with my head down, I walked straight into a wall of muscle.

Two strong hands grasped my upper arms, my shocked gaze clashing with a pair of dark, arrogant eyes.

"Hello, brat."

Tick ... TOCK.

To be continued...

Reluctantly His
Gilded Decadence Series, Book Four

THE GILDED DECADENCE SERIES

Ruthlessly His

Gilded Decadence Series, Book One

**His family dared to challenge mine, so I am going to ruin them...
starting with stealing his bride.**

Only a cold-hearted villain would destroy an innocent bride's special
day over a business deal gone bad...

Which is why I choose this precise moment to disrupt New York High
Society's most anticipated wedding of the season.

As I am Luc Manwarring, II, billionaire heir to one of the most powerful
families in the country, no one is brave enough to stop me.

My revenge plan is deceptively simple: humiliate the groom, then
blackmail the bride's family into coercing the bride into marrying me
instead.

My ruthless calculations do not anticipate my reluctant bride having so
much fight and fire in her.

At every opportunity, she resists my dominance and control, even going
so far as trying to escape my dark plans for her.

She is only supposed to be a means to an end, an unwilling player in my
game of revenge.

But the more she challenges me, the more I begin to wonder... who is
playing who?

Savagely His

He dared to steal my bride, so it's only fair I respond by kidnapping his innocent sister.

Only a monster with no morals would kidnap a woman from her brother's wedding…

Which was precisely what I've become, a monster bent on revenge.

After all, as the billionaire Marksen DuBois, renowned for being a jilted groom, my reputation and business were in tatters.

There was nothing more dangerous than a man possessing power, boundless resources, and a vendetta.

I would torment him with increasingly degrading photos of his precious sister as I held her captive and under my complete control.

She'd have no option but to yield to my every command if she wished to shield herself and her family from further disgrace.

She was just a captured pawn to be dominated, exploited, and discarded.

Yet the more ensnared we become in my twisted game of revenge, the more my suspicions grow.

As she fiercely counters my every move, I begin to question whether I'm the true pawn… ensnared by my queen.

Brutally His

Gilded Decadence Series, Book Three

From our very first fiery encounter, I was tempted to fire my beautiful new assistant.

Right after I punished her for that defiant slap she delivered in response to my undeniably inappropriate kiss.

As Harrison Astrid, New York's formidable District Attorney, distractions were a luxury I couldn't afford.

Forming a shaky alliance with the Manwarrings and the Dubois, I was ensnared in a dangerous cat-and-mouse game.

As I strive to thwart my mother's cunning manipulations and her deadly alliance with the Irish mob.

Yet, every time I cross paths with my assistant, our mutual animosity surges into a near-savage need to control and dominate her.

I am a man who demands obedience, especially from subordinates.

Her stubbornness fuels my urge to assert my dominance, my need to show her I'm not just her boss—I'm her master.

Unfortunately the fiancé I'm to accept to play high society's charade, complicates things.

So I rein in my desire and resist the attraction between us.

Until the Irish mob targets my pretty little assistant… targets what's mine.

Now there isn't a force on earth that will keep me from tearing the city apart to find her.

Reluctantly His

Gilded Decadence Series, Book Four

First rule of being a bodyguard, don't f*ck the woman you're protecting.

And I want to break that rule so damn bad I can practically taste her.

She's innocent, sheltered, and spoiled.

As Reid Taylor, former Army sergeant and head of security for the Manwarrings, the last thing I should be doing is babysitting my boss's little sister.

I definitely shouldn't be fantasizing about pinning her down, spreading her thighs and…

It should help that she fights my protection at every turn.

Disobeying my rules. Running away from me. Talking back with that sexy, smart mouth of hers.

But it doesn't. It just makes me want her more.

I want to bend her over and claim her, hard and rough, until she begs for mercy.

That is a dangerous line I cannot cross.

She is an heiress, the precious daughter of one of the most powerful, multi-billionaire families in New York.

And I'm just her bodyguard, an employee. It would be the ultimate societal taboo.

But now her family is forcing her into an arranged marriage, and I'm not sure I'll be able to contain my rising rage at the idea of another man touching her.

Unwillingly His

Gilded Decadence Series, Book Five

The moment she slapped me, I knew I'd chosen the right bride.

To be fair, I had just stolen her entire inheritance.

As Lucian Manwarring, billionaire patriarch of the powerful Manwarring family, my word is law.

She's a beautiful and innocent heiress, raised to be the perfect society trophy wife.

Although far too young for me, that won't stop me from claiming her as my new prized possession.

What I hadn't planned on was her open defiance of me.

Far from submissive and obedient; she is stubborn, outspoken and headstrong.

She tries to escape my control and fights my plan to force her down the aisle.

I am not accustomed to being disobeyed.

While finding it mildly amusing at first, it is past time she accepts her fate.

She will be my bride even if I have to ruthlessly dominate and punish her to get what I want.

ABOUT ZOE BLAKE

Zoe Blake is the USA Today Bestselling Author of the romantic suspense saga *The Cavalieri Billionaire Legacy* inspired by her own heritage as well as her obsession with jewelry, travel, and the salacious gossip of history's most infamous families.

She delights in writing Dark Romance books filled with overly possessive billionaires, taboo scenes, and unexpected twists. She usually spends her ill-gotten gains on martinis, travels, and red lipstick. Since she can barely boil water, she's lucky enough to be married to a sexy Chef.

ALSO BY ZOE BLAKE

CAVALIERI BILLIONAIRE LEGACY

A Dark Enemies to Lovers Romance

Scandals of the Father

Cavalieri Billionaire Legacy, Book One

Being attracted to her wasn't wrong... but acting on it would be.

As the patriarch of the powerful and wealthy Cavalieri family, my choices came with consequences for everyone around me.

The roots of my ancestral, billionaire-dollar winery stretch deep into the rich, Italian soil, as does our legacy for ruthlessness and scandal.

It wasn't the fact she was half my age that made her off limits.

Nothing was off limits for me.

A wounded bird, caught in a trap not of her own making, she posed no risk to me.

My obsessive desire to possess her was the real problem.

For both of us.

But now that I've seen her, tasted her lips, I can't let her go.

Whether she likes it or not, she needs my protection.

I'm doing this for her own good, yet, she fights me at every turn.

Refusing the luxury I offer, desperately trying to escape my grasp.

I need to teach her to obey before the dark rumors of my past reach her.

Ruin her.

She cannot find out what I've done, not before I make her mine.

Sins of the Son

Cavalieri Billionaire Legacy, Book Two

She's hated me for years... now it's past time to give her a reason to.

When you are a son, and one of the heirs, to the legacy of the Cavalieri name, you need to be more vicious than your enemies.

And sometimes, the lines get blurred.

Years ago, they tried to use her as a pawn in a revenge scheme against me.

Even though I cared about her, I let them treat her as if she were nothing.

I was too arrogant and self-involved to protect her then.

But I'm here now. Ready to risk my life tracking down every single one of them.

They'll pay for what they've done as surely as I'll pay for my sins against her.

Too bad it won't be enough for her to let go of her hatred of me,

To get her to stop fighting me.

Because whether she likes it or not, I have the power, wealth, and connections to keep her by my side

And every intention of ruthlessly using all three to make her mine.

Secrets of the Brother

Cavalieri Billionaire Legacy, Book Three

We were not meant to be together... then a dark twist of fate stepped in, and we're the ones who will pay for it.

As the eldest son and heir of the Cavalieri name, I inherit a great deal more than a billion dollar empire.

I receive a legacy of secrets, lies, and scandal.

After enduring a childhood filled with malicious rumors about my father, I have fallen prey to his very same sin.

I married a woman I didn't love out of a false sense of family honor.

Now she has died under mysterious circumstances.

And I am left to play the widowed groom.

For no one can know the truth about my wife...

Especially her sister.

The only way to protect her from danger is to keep her close, and yet, her very nearness tortures me.

She is my sister in name only, but I have no right to desire her.

Not after what I have done.

It's too much to hope she would understand that it was all for her.

It's always been about her.

Only her.

I am, after all, my father's son.

And there is nothing on this earth more ruthless than a Cavalieri man in love.

Seduction of the Patriarch

Cavalieri Billionaire Legacy, Book Four

With a single gunshot, she brings the violent secrets of my buried past into the present.

She may not have pulled the trigger, but she still has blood on her hands.

And I know some very creative ways to make her pay for it.

I am as ruthless as my Cavalieri ancestors, who forged our powerful family legacy.

But no fortune is built without spilling blood.

I earn a reputation as a dangerous man to cross... and make enemies along the way.

So to protect those I love, I hand over the mantle of patriarch to my brother and move to northern Italy.

For years, I stay in the shadows…

Then a vengeful mafia syndicate attacks my family.

Now nothing will prevent me from seeking vengeance on those responsible.

And I don't give a damn who I hurt in the process… including her.

Whether it takes seduction, punishment, or both, I intend to manipulate her as a means to an end.

Yet, the more my little kitten shows her claws, the more I want to make her purr.

My plan is to coerce her into helping me topple the mafia syndicate, and then retreat into the shadows.

But if she keeps fighting me… I might just have to take her with me.

Scorn of the Betrothed

Cavalieri Billionaire Legacy, Book Five

A union forged in vengeance, bound by hate... and beneath it all, a twisted game of desire and deception.

In the heart of the Cavalieri family, I am the son destined for a loveless marriage.

The true legacy of my family, my birthright ties me to a woman I despise.

The daughter of the mafia boss who nearly ended my family.

She is my future wife, and I am her unwelcome groom.

The looming wedding is a beacon of hope for our families.

A promise of peace in a world fraught with danger and deception.

We were meant to be the bridge between two powerful legacies.

The only thing we share is a mutual hatred.

She is a prisoner to her families' ambitions, desperate for a way out.

My duty is to guard her, to ensure she doesn't escape her gilded cage.

But every moment spent with her, every spark of anger, adds fuel to the growing fire of desire between us.

We're trapped in a dangerous duel of passion and fury.

The more I try to tame her, the more she ignites me.

Hatred and desire become blurred.

Our impending marriage becomes a twisted game.

But as the wedding draws near, my suspicions grow.

My bride is not who she claims to be.

IVANOV CRIME FAMILY TRILOGY

A Dark Mafia Romance

Savage Vow

Ivanov Crime Family, Book One

Gregor & Samara's story

I took her innocence as payment.

She was far too young and naïve to be betrothed to a monster like me.

I would bring only pain and darkness into her sheltered world.

That's why she ran.

I should've just let her go…

She never asked to marry into a powerful Russian mafia family.

None of this was her choice.

Unfortunately for her, I don't care.

I own her… and after three years of searching… I've found her.

My runaway bride was about to learn disobedience has consequences… punishing ones.

Having her in my arms and under my control had become an obsession.

Nothing was going to keep me from claiming her before the eyes of God and man.

She's finally mine… and I'm never letting her go.

Vicious Oath

Ivanov Crime Family, Book One

Damien & Yelena's story

When I give an order, I expect it to be obeyed.

She's too smart for her own good, and it's going to get her killed.

Against my better judgement, I put her under the protection of my powerful Russian mafia family.

So imagine my anger when the little minx ran.

For three long years I've been on her trail, always one step behind.

Finding and claiming her had become an obsession.

It was getting harder to rein in my driving need to possess her… to own her.

But now the chase is over.

I've found her.

Soon she will be mine.

And I plan to make it official, even if I have to drag her kicking and screaming to the altar.

This time… there will be no escape from me.

Betrayed Honor

Ivanov Crime Family, Book One

Mikhail & Nadia's story

Her innocence was going to get her killed.

That was if I didn't get to her first.

She's the protected little sister of the powerful Ivanov Russian mafia family - the very definition of forbidden.

It's always been my job, as their Head of Security, to watch over her but never to touch.

That ends today.

She disobeyed me and put herself in danger.

It was time to take her in hand.

I'm the only one who can save her and I will fight anyone who tries to stop me, including her brothers.

Honor and loyalty be damned.

She's mine now.

RUTHLESS OBSESSION SERIES

A Dark Mafia Romance

Sweet Cruelty

Ruthless Obsession Series, Book One

Dimitri & Emma's story

It was an innocent mistake.

She knocked on the wrong door.

Mine.

If I were a better man, I would've just let her go.

But I'm not.

I'm a cruel bastard.

I ruthlessly claimed her virtue for my own.

It should have been enough.

But it wasn't.

I needed more.

Craved it.

She became my obsession.

Her sweetness and purity taunted my dark soul.

The need to possess her nearly drove me mad.

A Russian arms dealer had no business pursuing a naive librarian student.

She didn't belong in my world.

I would bring her only pain.

But it was too late…

She was mine and I was keeping her.

Sweet Depravity

Ruthless Obsession Series, Book Two

Vaska & Mary's story

The moment she opened those gorgeous red lips to tell me no, she was mine.

I was a powerful Russian arms dealer and she was an innocent schoolteacher.

If she had a choice, she'd run as far away from me as possible.

Unfortunately for her, I wasn't giving her one.

I wasn't just going to take her; I was going to take over her entire world.

Where she lived.

What she ate.

Where she worked.

All would be under my control.

Call it obsession.

Call it depravity.

I don't give a damn… as long as you call her mine.

Sweet Savagery

Ruthless Obsession Series, Book Three

Ivan & Dylan's Story

I was a savage bent on claiming her as punishment for her family's mistakes.

As a powerful Russian Arms dealer, no one steals from me and gets away with it.

She was an innocent pawn in a dangerous game.

She had no idea the package her uncle sent her from Russia contained my stolen money.

If I were a good man, I would let her return the money and leave.

If I were a gentleman, I might even let her keep some of it just for frightening her.

As I stared down at the beautiful living doll stretched out before me like a virgin sacrifice,

I thanked God for every sin and misdeed that had blackened my cold heart.

I was not a good man.

I sure as hell wasn't a gentleman… and I had no intention of letting her go.

She was mine now.

And no one takes what's mine.

Sweet Brutality

Ruthless Obsession Series, Book Four

Maxim & Carinna's story

The more she fights me, the more I want her.

It's that beautiful, sassy mouth of hers.

It makes me want to push her to her knees and dominate her, like the brutal savage I am.

As a Russian Arms dealer, I should not be ruthlessly pursuing an innocent college student like her, but that would not stop me.

A twist of fate may have brought us together, but it is my twisted obsession that will hold her captive as my own treasured possession.

She is mine now.

I dare you to try and take her from me.

Sweet Ferocity

Ruthless Obsession Series, Book Five

Luka & Katie's Story

I was a mafia mercenary only hired to find her, but now I'm going to keep her.

She is a Russian mafia princess, kidnapped to be used as a pawn in a dangerous territory war.

Saving her was my job. Keeping her safe had become my obsession.

Every move she makes, I am in the shadows, watching.

I was like a feral animal: cruel, violent, and selfishly out for my own needs. Until her.

Now, I will make her mine by any means necessary.

I am her protector, but no one is going to protect her from me.

Sweet Intensity

Ruthless Obsession Series, Book Six

Antonius & Brynn's Story

She couldn't possibly have known the danger she would be in the moment she innocently accepted the job.

She was too young for a man my age, barely in her twenties. Far too pure and untouched.

Too bad that wasn't going to stop me.

The moment I laid eyes on her, I claimed her.

She would be mine… by any means necessary.

I owned the most elite Gambling Club in Chicago, which was a secret front for my true business as a powerful crime boss for the Russian Mafia.

And she was a fragile little bird, who had just flown straight into my open jaws.

Naïve and sweet, she was a tasty morsel I couldn't resist biting.

My intense drive to dominate and control her had become an obsession.

I would ruthlessly use my superior strength and connections to take over her life.

The harder she resisted, the more feral and savage I would become.

She needed to understand… she was mine now.

Mine.

Sweet Severity

Ruthless Obsession Series, Book Seven

Macarius & Phoebe's Story

Had she crashed into any other man's car, she could have walked away—but she hit mine.

Upon seeing the bruises on her wrist, I struggled to contain my rage.

Despite her objections, I refused to allow her to leave.

Whoever hurt this innocent beauty would pay dearly.

As a Russian Mafia crime boss who owns Chicago's most elite gambling club, I have very creative and painful methods of exacting revenge.

She seems too young and naive to be out on her own in such a dangerous world.

Needing a nanny, I decided to claim her for the role.

She might resist my severe, domineering discipline, but I won't give her a choice in the matter.

She needs a protector, and I'd be damned if it were anyone but me.

Resisting the urge to claim her will test all my restraint.

It's a battle I'm bound to lose.

With each day, my obsession and jealousy intensify.

It's only a matter of time before my control snaps…and I make her mine.

Mine.

Sweet Animosity

Ruthless Obsession, Book Eight

Varlaam & Amber's Story

I never asked for an assistant, and if I had, I sure as hell wouldn't have chosen her.

With her sharp tongue and lack of discipline, what she needs is a firm hand, not a job.

The more she tests my limits, the more tempted I am to bend her over my knee.

As a Russian Mafia boss and owner of Chicago's most elite gambling club, I can't afford distractions from her antics.

Or her secrets.

For I suspect, my innocent new assistant is hiding something.

And I know just how to get to the truth.

It's high time she understands who holds the power in our relationship.

To ensure I get what I desire, I'll keep her close, controlling her every move.

Except I am no longer after information—I want her mind, body and soul.

She underestimated the stakes of our dangerous game and now owes a heavy price.

As payment I will take her freedom.

She's mine now.

Mine.

ABOUT ALTA HENSLEY

Alta Hensley is a USA TODAY Bestselling author of hot, dark and dirty romance. She is also an Amazon Top 10 bestselling author. Being a multi-published author in the romance genre, Alta is known for her dark, gritty alpha heroes, captivating love stories, hot eroticism, and engaging tales of the constant struggle between dominance and submission.

She lives in Astoria, Oregon with her husband, two daughters, and an Australian Shepherd. When she isn't walking the coastline, and drinking beer in her favorite breweries, she is writing about villains who always get their love story and happily ever after.

ALSO BY ALTA HENSLEY

HEATHENS HOLLOW SERIES

A Dark Stalker Billionaire Romance

Heathens

She invited the darkness in, so she'll have no one else to blame when I come for her.

The Hunt.

It is a sinister game of submission. She'll run. I'll chase.

And when I catch her, it will be savage. Untamed. Primal.

I will be the beast from her darkest fantasies.

I should be protecting her, but instead I've been watching her. Stalking her.

She's innocent. Forbidden. The daughter of my best friend.

But she chose this.

And even if she made a mistake, even if she wants to run, to escape, it's far too late.

She's mine now.

GODS AMONG MEN SERIES

A Dark Billionaire Romance

Villains Are Made

I know how villains are made.

I've watched their secrets rise from the ashes and emerge from the shadows.

As part of a family tree with roots so twisted, I'm strangled by their vine.

Imprisoned in a world of decadence and sin, I've seen Gods among men.

And he is one of them.

He is the villain.

He is the enemy who demands to be the lover.

He is the monster who has shown me pleasure but gives so much pain.

But something has changed…

He's different.

Darker.

Wildly possessive as his obsession with me grows to an inferno that can't be controlled.

Yes… he is the villain.

And he is the end of my beginning.

Monsters Are Hidden

The problem with secrets is they create powerful monsters.

And even more dangerous enemies.

He's the keeper of all his family's secrets, the watcher of all.

He knows what I've done, what I've risked… the deadly choice I made.

The tangled vines of his mighty family tree are strangling me.

There is no escape.

I am locked away, captive to his twisted obsession and demands.

If I run, my hell will never end.

If I stay, he will devour me.

My only choice is to dare the monster to come out into the light,
before his darkness destroys us both.

Yes... he is the monster in hiding.
And he is the end of my beginning.

Vipers Are Forbidden

It's impossible to enter a pit full of snakes and not get bit.

Until you meet me, that is.

My venom is far more toxic than the four men who have declared me
their enemy.

They seek vengeance and launch a twisted game of give and take.

I'll play in their dark world, because it's where I thrive.

I'll dance with their debauchery, for I surely know the steps.

But then I discover just how wrong I am. Their four, not only matches,
but beats, my one.

With each wicked move they make, they become my obsession.

I crave them until they consume all thought.

The temptation to give them everything they desire becomes too much.

I'm entering their world, and there is no light to guide my way. My
blindness full of lust will be my defeat.

Yes... I am the viper and am forbidden.
But they are the end of my beginning.

SPIKED ROSES BILLIONAIRE'S CLUB SERIES

A Dark Billionaires Romance

Bastards & Whiskey

I sit amongst the Presidents, Royalty, the Captains of Industry, and the wealthiest men in the world.

We own Spiked Roses—an exclusive, membership only establishment in New Orleans where money or lineage is the only way in. It is for the gentlemen who own everything and never hear the word no.

Sipping on whiskey, smoking cigars, and conducting multi-million dollar deals in our own personal playground of indulgence, there isn't anything I can't have… and that includes HER. I can also have HER if I want.

And I want.

Villains & Vodka

My life is one long fevered dream, balancing between being killed or killing.

The name Harley Crow is one to be feared.

I am an assassin.

A killer.

The villain.

I own it. I choose this life. Hell, I crave it. I hunger for it. The smell of fear makes me hard and is the very reason the blood runs through my veins.

Until I meet her…

Marlowe Masters.

Her darkness matches my own.

In my twisted world of dancing along the jagged edge of the blade…

She changes everything.

No weapon can protect me from the kind of death she will ultimately deliver.

Scoundrels & Scotch

I'll stop at nothing to own her.

I'm a collector of dolls.

All kinds of dolls.

So beautiful and sexy, they become my art.

So perfect and flawless, my art galleries are flooded by the wealthy to gaze upon my possessions with envy.

So fragile and delicate, I keep them tucked away for safety.

The dark and torrid tales of Drayton's Dolls run rampant through the rich and famous, and all but a few are true.

Normally I share my dolls for others to play with or watch on display.

But not my special doll.

No, not her.

Ivy is the most precious doll of all.

She's mine. All mine.

Devils & Rye

Forbidden fruit tastes the sweetest.

It had been years since I had seen her.

Years since I last saw those eyes with pure, raw innocence.

So much time had passed since I lusted after what I knew I should resist.

But she was so right.

And I was so wrong.

To claim her as mine was breaking the rules. Boundaries should not be broken. But temptation weakens my resolve.

With the pull of my dark desires…

I know that I can't hide from my sinful thoughts—and actions—forever.

Beasts & Bourbon

My royal blood flows black with twisted secrets.

I am a beast who wears a crown.

Heir to a modern kingdom cloaked in corruption and depravities.

The time has come to claim my princess.

An innocent hidden away from my dark world.

Till now.

Her initiation will require sacrifice and submission.

There is no escaping the chains which bind her to me.

Surrendering to my torment, as well as my protection, is her only path to survival.

In the end…

She will be forever mine.

Sinners & Gin

My power is absolute. My rules are law.

Structure.

Obedience.

Discipline.

I am in charge, and what I say goes. Black and white with no gray.

No one dares break the rules in my dark and twisted world… until her.
Until she makes me cross my own jagged lines.

She's untouched. Perfection. Pure.

Forbidden.

She tests my limits in all ways.

There is only one option left.

I will claim her as mine no matter how many rules are broken.

THANK YOU

Stormy Night Publications would like to thank you for your interest in our books.

If you liked this book (or even if you didn't), we would really appreciate you leaving a review on the site where you purchased it. Reviews provide useful feedback for us and our authors, and this feedback (both positive comments and constructive criticism) allows us to work even harder to make sure we provide the content our customers want to read.